Simon Osmond. A rising young

Malcolm Harley. Osmond's friel

Rose Harley. Malcolm's ambitious wife.

Lady Rosnay. An impish, imperious old lady, once a great beauty.

Alix Lynn. Lady Rosnay's granddaughter, who wants to marry Simon Osmond.

Arthur Darett. Simon Osmond's secretary.

Mrs. Amy Darett. Arthur's mother, who is not aging well.

Molly Marne. A musical comedy actress with a morphine habit.

Sophia Minns. Molly's sister, a domestic servant.

Sir David Kames. A wealthy baronet, buying his way up to the House of Lords.

Bertie Luttrell. A notorious gossip.

Madame Berthe Finck. The owner of Maison Montespan, a very smart shop.

Reginald Fortune. A deceptively amiable country doctor and amateur sleuth.

Lomas. Chief of Scotland Yard's C.I.D. and Reggie's close friend.

Superintendent Bell. Lomas's superior, who never had an idea of his own.

Dr. Anneler. A chemist with whom Reggie frequently consults.

Jenks. Reggie's laboratory assistant.

Herr Stein. A Swiss chemist.

Herr Fora. A Swiss perfumer who supplies Maison Montespan.

Joshua Clunk. A solicitor.

Joan Fortune. Reggie's serene and beautiful wife.

Sam. Reggie's chauffeur.

Plus assorted politicians, servants, theater people, and partygoers.

Shadow on the Wall

A Mr. Fortune novel by

H.C. Bailey

Rue Morgue Press
Lyons / Boulder

978-1-60187-019-3

Rue Morgue Press
87 Lone Tree Lane
Lyons CO 80540

Printed by Johnson Printing
Boulder, Colorado

PRINTED IN THE UNITED STATES OF AMERICA

Meet H. C. Bailey

The first Mr. Fortune stories by H.C. Bailey appeared in book form in the early 1920s at the same time that Arthur Conan Doyle was publishing what would be the final adventures of Sherlock Holmes. Just as Holmes was at his best in the shorter form—with the grand exception of *The Hound of the Baskervilles*—Reggie Fortune was, for the most part, more successful with readers when taken in short doses. Perhaps no other major fictional detective of the Golden Age appeared in as many short stories as the cherubic country doctor turned detective. Starting with *Call Mr. Fortune* in 1920 and ending with *Mr. Fortune Here* in 1940, Bailey published an astonishing twelve collections of Fortune short stories, not counting three omnibus collections of previously published material.

Why Bailey, a successful author of more than thirty adventure and historical novels, whose first novel, *My Lady of Orange*, was published in 1901 during his senior year at Oxford, waited until 1934 to publish his first full-length Fortune book, is a question to which we'll perhaps never know the answer. And, at that, his first two published mystery novels, *The Garston Murder Case* and *The Red Castle Mystery*, released in 1930 and 1932 respectively, didn't even feature Mr. Fortune.

The detective of record in those two books and nine subsequent volumes was Joshua Clunk, a coarse, hymn-quoting attorney who is not above employing extralegal means to clear his own client and suss out the real murderer. Yet, like Fortune (and unlike so many other fictional sleuths of the Golden Age), Clunk is happily married. And, like Fortune, Clunk is extraordinarily fond of children, the protection of whom is a theme that runs through much of Bailey's work, perhaps because children in the Britain of this era did not always enjoy a happy family life. The upper classes shunted them off to boarding schools and the lower classes forced them into jobs at a young age.

While Clunk and Fortune may move in different social circles, the two operate in the same world. They combined their talents to catch a killer in *The Great Game* (1939) while secondary characters appear in both series.

Critics have labeled the Clunk novels whodunits in the deductive style while calling the Fortune stories intuitive crime novels, suggesting that Mr. Fortune relies more on his knowledge of human behavior than on physical evidence in solving his crimes. And while it's true that Mr. Fortune is convinced, as in *Shadow on the Wall*, that murderers leave behind shadows of their deeds, he solves his crimes through careful examination of what evidence he's able to amass and close observation of even seemingly trivial details. The Fortune novels are perfect specimens of the fair-play detective novel of the Golden Age. And, like so many other sleuths of that era (Margery Allingham's Albert Campion and Dorothy L. Sayers' Lord Peter spring immediately to mind), Reggie Fortune is a somewhat mannered sleuth, given to odd turns of phrase and eccentric behavior. But we'll leave it to H.C. Bailey himself to fully describe Mr. Fortune. His 1942 essay "Meet Mr. Fortune" follows this introduction.

While Bailey was considered one of the five most important British mystery writers of the Golden Age (roughly 1913 to 1953), he is perhaps less well-known today than his contemporaries. Born in London on February 1, 1878, Henry Christopher Bailey was the only child of Henry and Jane Bailey. Between 1890 and 1897 he attended City of London School, a highly regarded day school which produced a very large number of nationally known writers, scholars and scientists (it was the first school in England to offer courses in chemistry). The school also enjoyed a unique relationship with journalism and publishing firms. In his last year, Bailey was named Head of School, responsible for out-of-school discipline and representing the school at official events.

Having won a scholarship to Oxford's Corpus Christi College, he was a classics scholar studying Latin and Greek language, literature and history. Small in stature (his pictures make him look a little like the actor Barry Fitzgerald of *Going My Way* fame), he was ideally suited to coxswain his college's eight-man rowing team. In spite of this, his daughter Betty said that he did not make friends easily and was quite lonely while at university, which may explain why he began his solitary work as a novelist as an undergraduate. He took a first-class honors degree and went to work as a correspondent for the *Daily Telegraph*, a leading Tory newspaper of the time, which, as his great-nephew Geoffrey Guest suggests, may tell us something about Bailey's politics. He worked there as a drama critic, a war correspondent and as a leader (editorial) writer.

After he retired from journalism in 1946, Bailey and his wife Lydia (*née* Guest) moved to North Wales and took up residence at Bernina, a house built as a holiday residence by Lydia's father, a Manchester physician. It was at Bernina that the two had first met, in 1905, when Bailey visited as a boarder. The Guests had moved to Wales in 1904, taking in boarders to help make ends meet since it had cost so much to "launch" Lydia's elder brothers, Leslie and Austin, their father having died at 56 in 1897. Eighteen-year-old Lydia was already familiar with the 27-year-old journalist and author from his books and through Austin, who had met Bailey through a mutual friend from Bailey's days at day school. In a letter to her daughter Mary, Lydia remembered that fateful meeting: "Well—then Father came next year, in 1906, and we were engaged—and married in 1908, lucky me." The two took up residence in London where their two daughters were born, Betty in 1910 and Mary in 1913. Betty studied archaeology at London University and excavated Greek temples while Mary took a degree in math from Oxford and worked as an accountant for a London firm. Mary never married and Betty had no children. Like their parents, both girls enjoyed tramping in the Swiss and Austrian Alps where the family often vacationed.

Indeed, part of the reason that Bailey and Lydia moved to Bernina was because that part of Wales reminded them so much of the Alps. Lydia described Bernina as a "lovely house, high on the mountainside facing south to hills across the valley with the sea to the west." The house was quite isolated. The small village of Llanfairfechan was located in the valley below Bernina. Villagers there described their famous neighbor as "a small shy man who continued to dress formally and collected postal cards." His great-nephew suggests that this was an imperfect summation of an accomplished man who probably did not interact with the locals on more than a superficial level.

Geoffrey Guest recalls visiting Bernina as a young boy with his brother. "I was struck by the beauty of the house and its surroundings. On the first floor there was a central hall which was large enough to contain a dining table on which all meals were served. On each side of this hall were two large rooms. One of them was HCB's study. Its large windows gave him views of the encircling mountains and valleys. Two quite large hulls of rowing shells he coxed at Oxford stuck out of one of the study walls. On the other wall was a photograph of a biplane, the first to cross the English channel. HCB had accompanied the pilot on that first flight as a reporter for the *Daily Telegraph*. Across from his study was the living room whose french windows led to the garden." The two boys were shepherded about the house and surrounding area by Lydia and her daughter Betty, "two very gregarious and vivacious women." Bailey himself did not interact much with the two boys

"At night there was the ritual of the lighting of the oil lamps," Guest remembers. "The house had no electricity so twelve or so oil lamps were lit as darkness fell. When we went to bed we took an oil lamp with us. The only source of heat in the living quarters was an open fire in the living room on the first floor. On chilly nights our Aunt Lydia would place a large ceramic bottle full of very hot water at the bottom of each bed."

It was at Bernina that Bailey died on March 24, 1961, at the age of 83, having published his last novel, *Shrouded Death*, eleven years earlier. What was remarkable about his career was not just the sheer number of novels and short stories that he published in his lifetime but that most of his output was produced while he was working full-time as a journalist. Given his prodigious output, it's a bit surprising to note that he produced only three books after his retirement from the *Daily Telegraph* in 1946 at the relatively young age (for a writer) of 68. It just might be that he took retirement seriously. He and Lydia loved hiking the hills of Wales and no doubt this was a fine way for a private, solitary man to fill his final years, content in the knowledge that he would be remembered as one of the finest of the Golden Age mystery writers.

The Pulitzer Prize-winning poet, Stephen Vincent Benet, may have summed up Bailey's career as a mystery writer best when he wrote: "Perhaps Mr. Reginald Fortune comes nearest to the dream of all good detective-story readers—the dream of the lamp lit again in Baker Street, the fog settling down outside and Watson smoking his pipe by the fire when the knock comes at the door. Not that Fortune is in any sense an imitation of Holmes—he is a distinct and admirable creation, with his individual mannerisms and methods. When he says, as he sometimes does, 'not a nice murder, Lomas,' one feels the cold and authentic shiver in the spine."

Tom & Enid Schantz
April 2008
Lyons, Colorado

The editors would like to acknowledge the contributions of Geoffrey Guest and other Guest family members in the writing of this introduction.

Meet Mr. Fortune

An introduction to a character by his creator

by H.C. Bailey

M<small>R. FORTUNE</small> has a modest nature—or that kind of vanity—which avoids personal advertisement.

Continual and growing curiosity about what he is really like, his private life, his training, the early, obscure years of his career, and his way of thought upon crime and the world has, however, produced so many misleading statements that he has been persuaded to allow a brief sketch of a biography.

Reginald Fortune was born less than fifty years ago, the only son—there were several daughters—of a doctor of moderate means in good general practice in one of the wealthier suburbs of London. Reginald was educated at Charterhouse and University College, Oxford. Neither at school nor university had he any particular distinction but a general popularity. Schoolmasters and tutors pronounced him the most ordinary of amiable youths, though one or two remarked that he had an abnormal capacity for being interested in any subject, from prehistoric religion to the new physics. Men who were boys with him report that the only uncommon thing about him was his interest in everybody.

It was always understood that he should become a doctor and succeed to his father's general practice. Reginald accepted this destiny with cordial satisfaction. Yet when he went on from Oxford to a London hospital he found, to his mild annoyance, that he was developing a certain specialized ability, first as a surgeon, then as a pathologist. Rather plaintively and against his will he accepted this call and proceeded to study in the clinics of Vienna.

His own statement is that there were two formative educational influences in his young life, first the professor who had amassed a larger amount of useless knowledge than any man in Oxford, secondly Sir Lawson Hunter whose "European reputation as a surgeon has been won by knowing his own mind."

It was agreed by his contemporaries and his seniors that he might have done very well either in surgery or pathology. He became uncommonly sound in diagnosis and had the poise and the manual dexterity which make a surgeon. The love of investigation, the patience in scientific method, the flair which the pathologist requires were equally well developed in him. Nevertheless he went back to the suburb of his birth and took an assistant's share of his father's placid family practice.

He will always maintain that this is what he was made for, the cure or care of the common ills of life, the children's measles and the parents' rheumatism. It is his opinion that the specialist is inevitably a rather absurd and unhappy person, doomed to narrow thought and incomplete appreciation of the world. In pensive moments he will mourn the fate which made him one. But against specialization he has steadily protected himself, keeping touch with all kinds of knowledge and everything which the natural man enjoys.

What compelled him to specialize was two cases of crime in his suburban practice. The speed and certainty of his apprehension, his insight and power of inference from slight, obscure facts commended him as the ideal expert to the chief of the Criminal Investigation Department, who, as he complains bitterly, would never let him alone afterwards. Yet Reginald cannot have been wholly unwilling. There is no doubt that the real forces which determined his career were his quick and deep interest in the drama of humanity, his consciousness of power to divine and deal with human motives, and his affection for the victim, the "underdog," in the strife of the world. He would smile away the notion that he has any ambition to "ride abroad redressing human wrongs." He dislikes philanthropists. But it is a fact that the suffering of the weak is apt to excite him to his most ruthless efficiency.

Nothing of that is suggested by his looks or his habits of life. He continues, in spite of years which must be called middle age, to look about twenty-five, a rather plump twenty-five, but of a fresh and innocent face which might be younger. An irreverent damsel christened him "Cherub," and the name has stuck. His fair hair is ample and unfaded still. His blue eyes have still a simple candor, or a wistful childlike surprise at this wonderful world. His round cheeks keep a schoolboy complexion.

He lives at his ease. No human pleasure, from the higher poetry or the profounder speculations of science and philosophy to chocolate cream, is alien to him, except the sport which consists in killing creatures and the social ceremonies which draw crowds. He has been accused of an excessive interest in food and drink, and his appetites of this kind are hearty and, apart from an absolute refusal to take any interest in port or whisky, of a catholic extent. But it is believed that, after the presence of his wife, his garden and his laboratory give him his dearest delights.

Concerning the principles and methods of his work in crime, there seems to be some misapprehension. Some of his most studious and appreciative critics have classified him as an "intuitionist detective." This is, for example, the decision pronounced in the introduction to the Oxford University Press selection of detective stories in the "World's Classics" series, where the late E. M. Wrong thus amplified it: "Mr. Fortune feels atmosphere more keenly than any other detective, and is marvelously accurate in his judgment of character."

In accord with this is the Scotland Yard estimate of Superintendent Bell, "wonderful how he knows men," which ascribes to him something like a sixth sense for the perception of the motive and personality behind actions.

Reginald would disclaim with a plaintive protest this abnormal power or any other abnormality. His piercing judgments of character he explains as purely rational inferences from the facts of a case. A slight, apparently insignificant piece of evidence, he is wont to argue, may often be decisive as to the nature of the unknown person who has been active. The accuracy of his inferences, in his interpretation of his mental processes, is due to the fact that he is wholly and intensely the ordinary man, feeling about things and people and reacting to them in the natural way.

He is wont to say that he has an old-fashioned mind. Insofar as this refers to morals it means that he holds by the standard principles of conduct and responsibility, of right and wrong, of sin and punishment. Modern theories that the criminal is the product of a wicked society, that he should be treated as the unfortunate victim of illness, that retribution is unjust and so forth, are for him the perversion of a fraction of the truth into an absurd general rule.

For general rules of any kind he has small respect. The maxim that the only general rule is: There are no general rules—is a favorite of his. He does not always accept the law of a case as justice and has been known to act on his own responsibility in contriving the punishment of those who could not legally be found guilty or the immunity of those who were not legally innocent. In his capacity to judge each case he has the absolute confidence of the surgeon called in to decide how a patient should be treated, when the choice of treatment will determine life or death, happiness or misery. And Reginald's standards of justice and right are those which the common sense of the common man has shaped.

On the conviction of a criminal he has sometimes been heard to repeat the phrase of the old divine "There, but for the grace of God, go I." But this does not proceed from the comfortable philosophy that anybody may be a rascal if circumstances impel him that way. Mr. Fortune's theory is that the original impulse in a great deal of crime is a motive which many or most people feel. The distinction of the criminal is that he indulges it to extravagance. For that extravagance, when it wrongs others, Mr. Fortune finds no excuse in difficult or tempting circumstances. A cruel crime is to him the work of a pestilential creature, and he sees his duty in dealing with such cases as that of a doctor in treating illness. The cause must be discovered and extirpated. There is no more mercy for the cruel criminal than for the germs of disease. Both must be made innocuous. The measures taken against both must be such as to diminish the danger of further infection. That the criminal may be born to commit crime as a bacillus is born to cause suffering and death, Mr. Fortune agrees with his whole mind. For that mystery he has no explanation, but his philosophy is that the business of the human reason is to make the world safe from both. He is pained at the admiration which finds anything mysterious in his success. All his investigations, he will insist, proceed by the tried and proved methods of science, careful and minute and exact observation, interpretation of the facts by scientific knowledge, formation of a hypothesis and the testing of it by further investigation and experiment.

The modern specialization which exalts criminology into a separate science he smiles at as a pedantic and delusive arrangement. All the sciences from astronomical physics to paleobotany, he will maintain, are required in criminal investigation, and in addition every other department of human knowledge, millinery or mountaineering, from the garden of Eden to Russian films. The real specialist in criminology would be omniscient. The effective practitioner, he says modestly, is the ordinary man who knows enough of everything to know his way about in anything and can use his mind in a scientific way.

Not that he has any superstitious faith in science. He takes all its present conclusions as provisional and trusts them only so far as they will do the day's work for him, with a perfect faith that they will be superseded by something more effective tomorrow. On each new theory which comes forward to supersede them he turns an impartial and critical eye. So he will smile at the newer psychologies, as putting the oldest religions into a fresh and inconvenient jargon, and go his hopeful and ruthless way believing heartily in God and the devil and the power of the human mind to know which is which and give an effective hand to either.

H. C. BAILEY

Chapter I

Mr. Fortune Remembers His Philosophy

THE history of this war may most lucidly begin with a certain garden party at Buckingham Palace. That was not the actual beginning, but it contained the moment in which Mr. Fortune first suspected there was a war.

For one reason or another—politics and Parliament were some little excited—the party was earlier in the season than usual. The summer had been kind, and the palace gardens offered their mannered elegance at its best in a flood of sunshine mitigated to the clothes of ceremony by a gentle western wind.

Mr. Fortune lingered out of the social orbit of his wife, extricated himself from the crowd, and sat down in lonely peace where trees gave him shade from which he could contemplate the ripple of light on the lake. After a little while of happiness his eyes opened wide to gaze with plaintive surprise at a dapper man strolling towards him in the studied gait of an actor.

The man arrived, stood over him a moment smiling, and sat down by his side. "Well, Reginald, I asked Mrs. Fortune whether you were here and she said, 'If he still is, he's trying to get away from whoever is with him.' "

"So I am," Reggie mumbled. "Joan's always right."

"She knows you very well," said the chief of the Criminal Investigation Department, arranging himself to pretty effect. "To understand all is to forgive all, what?"

"I shouldn't trust to that if I were you, Lomas," Reggie murmured severely.

"Matter of fact, I hardly expected to find you. You funk these shows, don't you? Not one of those who can 'walk with crowds and keep their virtue'!" Lomas put up his eyeglass and surveyed the ornate crowd marshaled in two dense masses on either side the lane of turf down which the king and queen were walking. "I don't blame you. This is a parade of rabble."

Reggie moaned. "The true official mind. Only happy in a vacuum. Where everybody's somebody, there no one's anybody. But I like that. It suits my simple taste. This crowd is all right: the common people of whom I am the chief. Bein' very human. Makes me feel kind and comfortable."

"At a distance," Lomas smiled.

"You're envying their humble pleasures. Run away and talk to the king—'nor lose the common touch.' "

"No, thank you. He's talking to a future prime minister."

The king in fact was talking with two men, one of them a slim, tall fellow in the extremity of correctitude and much at his ease, whose face was a pleasant mask, the other of a square make and heavy, sullen brow who could not be still.

"Oh, my country!" Reggie sighed. "Which of 'em is our comin' chief of men?"

"They'll probably toss for it," said Lomas. "Don't you know them? Harley and Osmond, the twin young hopes of the opposition. They're bosom friends. It's a standing joke, one can't do without the other. Harley has the wise head, and Osmond has the drive, like Dilke and Joe Chamberlain in the old days."

"Is that so?" Reggie murmured and contemplated the pair dreamily. "Chamberlain and Dilke—neither of them was ever prime minister. It was the wise head who went to smash."

"Harley will never smash," Lomas smiled. "He's a safety-first man."

Reggie gave him a fleeting glance of wonder. "Well, well," he sighed and turned again to watch the twin politicians. The king had passed on, and they were joined by a large exuberant man and an old woman in a wonderful frock. "Who are their fullblown friends?"

"Good Gad, you know Lady Rosnay."

"Oh, ah. I do. No man escapes that fate. But I'm feeling very innocent today. And she wears a new makeup every time. Who is the male?"

"He's Kames—Sir David Kames—very big business—buying his way up to the House of Lords."

"Harmless hobby," Reggie mumbled. "Even useful. Promoting respectability. Looks as if he needed it."

"I daresay." Lomas glanced round and drew nearer. "I didn't hunt you out to make conversation, Reginald."

"No. I thought not. No," Reggie sighed and gazed at him with sad eyes. "What's the matter?"

"What about that Poyntz case?"

"Oh, that!" Reggie's eyes opened wider in surprise. "Nothing in that. Suicide."

"Quite sure?"

"My dear chap!" Reggie reproached him. "Absolutely. Mrs. Poyntz got out of bed after some restless hours of the night. I rather think she said her prayers. Little damp place on the quilt as if she'd knelt and cried. However. She put on a wrapper, drew it close round her, and sat down in a deep chair.

She had that service revolver in her right hand. I should say she shut her eyes. She put her head back, she pressed the barrel of the revolver hard against her right temple—as if she wanted to feel it hurt—and then she fired. That's all."

"No possibility of anyone else assisting?"

"Oh, no. No. She did it all herself. Position of body and limbs quite natural and voluntary. Not any struggle, not any trace on her of use of force. Only possible explanation, deliberate suicide."

"I see," Lomas frowned. "And that's the whole of the medical evidence?"

"Yes, I think so. All that's relevant. What did you want?"

"I wanted to know why she did it."

Reggie shook his head. "No medical answer. Quite healthy young woman. Clean-living woman. Not been eatin' much lately. Probably felt rather run down. Nothing abnormal. Tired. Low spirits. Wished she were dead. And made it so. That's the only inference from the physical facts. Quite a common type of case. Poor girl."

"Yes, it's a sad business," said Lomas cheerfully. "Shall we go and get some tea?"

"One moment. One moment. Happy to relieve your anxieties. But what were they? What was worrying the higher intelligence?"

"Nothing definite. Trifles. She seemed to have kept all her papers. Her love letters were in the bedroom, not meddled with. But some paper had been burnt on the bedroom hearth."

"Yes. I saw that. Yes. Might have been something that annoyed her. Possibly the last straw. But possibly trivial."

"Quite," Lomas nodded. "Hopeless to guess. We asked her husband— he's in the Air Force, you know, down at Condover—if he knew of anything that had happened to upset her, any unpleasant letter. He denied it violently. Very fierce. Another trifle."

"Yes. Natural state of mind. Yes. Whether lying or not. Anything else?"

"There was another thing. They have a small daughter, a child of ten, away at school at Seaford. As soon as the death was splashed in the papers, somebody sent her an anonymous letter. 'Ask your daddy why Mummy killed herself.' "

Reggie lay back and stared across the gardens at the moving crowd. "Well, well," he murmured. "And did she ask Daddy?"

"No, she'd only just heard her mother was dead. She broke down over the letter and cried her heart out. The school sent the thing on to us. We found no trace of origin. When we put it to Poyntz he said it was a piece of filthy spite."

"Yes. That was true, anyway. Did he say who had a spite against his wife and him?"

"He swore he didn't know. Swore rather hard."

"Oh, yes. That might be true also," Reggie mumbled.

"Quite. According to your evidence, probably it is. Anyway, the letter is insignificant."

"My evidence is all right," Reggie murmured. "Speakin' physically, she killed herself. No probable, possible shadow of doubt. Which ends the case of Mrs. Poyntz. Very satisfactory and consoling." The round blue eyes which gazed at the movement of the ornate crowd grew dark and dreamy. "Lomas, old thing," he said plaintively, "do you remember that stuff in Plato? About everybody living in a cave in this life. All we see is only fleetin', cheatin' shadows of what things really are and what's really going on outside ourselves and our hole. And we argue about 'em as if they were the truth. Shadows on the wall of a cave where we're prisoned—distortin' shadows—that's the only stuff we're given to work with. And we believe we make facts out of it. Hopeful creature, the human animal. A sad world, Lomas. Providence expects a lot for its money."

Lomas laughed. "Very profound, Reginald. You often become gloomily profound when you can't make a mystery of a case. Come along. You'll be better after tea."

But they were cut off from it. An old lady was approaching them with so majestic, so definite a purpose that they had to wait for her.

Whether Lady Rosnay was magnificent or a figure of fun is a question much disputed in her later years. She had the form and face of a woman bred to a high dignity of beauty. The chances were always even whether she would carry it as it deserved or with a graceless freedom, adorn it like a queen in a palace or a queen of burlesque.

As she came to them she looked something between the two. Her walk was stately. She wore a dress of orange and silver tissues in dramatic elaboration, a dress which might have shown her a glorious creature when she was thirty years younger, which made sardonic discords with her white hair and a thin, wrinkled face, the older for much bright painting. The recognition she gave them was a mixture of a royal greeting and an impish grin.

"What are you two mystery men about hiding here?" The question came a tone too loud, but the high voice had a pleasant husky quality.

"Talking philosophy," said Reggie. "I was telling him about Plato. He's a much better man now. He isn't going to believe in anything."

"I knew you were devoted to each other." Lady Rosnay made a grimace. "Don't tell me it's turned to a Platonic affection."

"Oh, no. That's all right," Reggie purred. "We hate each other like brothers."

"What's the matter?" Her sunken brown eyes gleamed above their darkened rims. "Have you quarreled over the Poyntz affair?"

Two experienced faces showed her a mild, amused bewilderment. "Poyntz?" Lomas asked. "Oh, the woman who was found shot in her flat. It hasn't come up to me. Nothing in it, is there, Fortune?"

"No, I saw nothing. But I always like to make work for you. What ought I to have seen, Lady Rosnay?"

Lady Rosnay gave out a cackle of laughter. "You do disappoint me. I thought it was just the case for you to show off in. It's dripping possibilities of sentiment. Don't say you have stopped being sentimental, Mr. Fortune. You were the last, lone creature with a tender, domestic heart. There won't be one shoulder left for me to cry on."

"Oh, yes. Here you are. Magnanimous and tender. Come and tell me all."

"I suppose the girl did kill herself," said Lady Rosnay.

"Why shouldn't you?" Reggie purred. "Or alternatively why should you?"

"She was so good she was an utter fool."

"Oh, no. No. Doesn't work," Reggie objected. "To be an utter fool you need some sin."

"Bless you! There's nothing nobler than a man of sentiment," Lady Rosnay laughed.

"Yes. I am rather noble. It baffles the evil mind. But pursuin' your fallacious theory—why should a woman of simple virtue kill herself?"

"Lord, it's just what silly virtue is always doing. Lucy Poyntz"—Lady Rosnay made an inarticulate sound of amusement—"she was born to be afraid of living, an insanely chaste creature. When she had a man look at her, she thought she was being devilish wicked. And of course they did look. She was as pretty as an angel. What oafs men are!"

"Yes, she was pretty," Reggie murmured. "You think some man looked too long?"

"I think some halfwit made love to her, and when the girl found out what he meant she felt she had betrayed her darling husband, so she didn't deserve to live with him any more and must kill herself, and that would be everlasting damnation, which would be just perfect."

"Rather a neurotic explanation," said Lomas.

Lady Rosnay laughed. "Virtue is a neurosis, isn't it?"

"How young you are," Reggie sighed. "Was her husband fond of her?"

"Lord, yes, devoted. A calf, poor devil!"

"Thus sentiment breaks out of the hardest young mind," Reggie murmured. "Thank you so much, Lady Rosnay. You've made it all clear—except who the man was that made love to her."

"The town's full of men louts enough."

"A certain bitterness about that." Reggie contemplated her with dreamy eyes. "Who is it meant for?"

"The whole silly mess," said Lady Rosnay sharply. "It's nauseous for people to flaunt their feelings at you. Now I suppose you creatures will make us talk Lucy Poyntz till the end of the season."

"That's pessimism," Lomas smiled. "There are weeks yet to find another scandal."

Lady Rosnay began to talk of the delights which the season had still to produce. She condemned the new seriousness of society ... she defamed hostesses ... and she wanted to know if Mr. Lomas and Mr. Fortune were coming to the Victorian Ball.

Lomas had not heard of it.

How like Scotland Yard! It was the largest organized tumult of the year—for the benefit of the most angelic charity yet invented—she was lending her intolerable old house for it—as the perfect example of Victorian muddle—they would look hideously uncomfortable and natural—everybody was to dress up in some nineteenth-century fashion—nothing barred from young Queen Victoria to young Oscar Wilde.

She chattered fast, but her eyes were searching the crowd with a hungry anxiety.

"It sounds very amusing," Reggie said sadly. "Which is Lomas to be, Lady Rosnay? The bridal Victoria or the esthetic Oscar?"

"I have too much style for either," Lomas protested.

She spared a moment to look them over. "He should be D'Orsay. The last of the dandies. That face always needed whiskers. And you—you had better be Pickwick, Mr. Fortune—plump and sentimental in silk tights." She turned again to watch the crowd. The glaring color of her thin lips was compressed.

It appeared to Reggie that she was looking at Osmond, the rising politician. Osmond had parted from his indispensable friend Harley. He walked with a girl who was visibly proud of it, a girl of more feminine curvature than the fashion yet allowed, but severely clothed in black and white.

"I must find my infant Alix," said Lady Rosnay. "These affairs bore her so she'll be insufferable. The girl has no notion of playing the fool. She was born unable to grow up. Most of them are now. Goodbye." She kissed her hand to them. "Don't forget, Pickwick and D'Orsay."

"Goodbye," Lomas sped her parting. "There's Miss Lynn—with the suckling prime minister."

"My God!" Lady Rosnay said. "Simon Osmond!" She made a grimace at his square and unkempt shape. "That's what a man of destiny looks like nowadays. Let me rescue the girl before he finds out she is all conscience. What have I done my grandchild should be ridiculous that way?" She swept across the lawn.

"Well, well," Reggie turned vague eyes on Lomas. "What was all that for?"

Lomas laughed. "My dear fellow! Of all futile questions! The Rosnay never has a meaning. A born inconsequent. They say it was delicious fifty years ago."

"You think so?" Reggie sighed. "Rather bitter."

"Oh, she's a cat," Lomas shrugged.

"But I like cats," said Reggie plaintively, and they went to tea, and he found a reproachful wife again.

When he had taken her home, he subsided into an easy chair and the evening papers. Few men read less in newspapers, but he finds them a grateful means to vacuity of mind.

As he turned these pages, he frowned at a splash of headlines about an Air Force disaster. The curt story beneath related that Squadron Leader Roger Poyntz, stationed at Condover, had that morning taken a single seater airplane on a testing flight, been seen to dive from a thousand feet at a hundred and twenty miles an hour with his engine running till he crashed on the bombing range where he was found dead.

Reggie lay back. His round face was white, and he shivered a little. "I wonder," he murmured.

Chapter II

The Dark Staircase

IN THE dressing room of Mr. Fortune were spread out the clothes which his great-grandfather wore when, having been consulted by Queen Victoria over the arduous arrival of King Edward's first back tooth, he was commanded to dine with her majesty.

Mr. Fortune put on the trousers gingerly. They were ample about the body but of a frank tightness below. He had never liked his legs so little. In the swelling frills of the shirt, the high neckcloth and broad bow, the pomp of the coat's high shoulders and velvet collar, he found consolation.

"A presence! A personality!" he murmured to the image in the mirror and called his wife to admire.

She came, she saw, she gurgled. "Baby grandpapa," she said. "Cinderella's doctor in a pantomime. My poor child! Can you move?"

"Give me time. The head will not turn alone. Body action required. The legs must go delicately thus." He slid in short waltz steps. "Yes, very impressive. The perfect physician. A doctor of the days when men believed in medicine. I was born too late, Joan. Goodbye."

He drove away to Lady Rosnay's ball.

Rosnay House was built a hundred years ago, when the ancient, noble, and disreputable family of Rosnay, through the demand of the new civilization for the coal under its barren acres, first acquired money of its own to spend. After entering that blessed state, the Rosnays defied their traditions by a shrewd conduct of affairs. Even until yesterday, while the riches of other old estates were melting in the furnace of the world's swift change and the secluded dignity of their London mansions gave place to Babylonian piles of luxury which should be a commercial proposition, Lady Rosnay's childless age remained wealthy and Rosnay House still stood aloof in its corner grimly palatial without, ostentatiously splendid within.

Its guests came first into a hall of gilding and frescoes from which a marble staircase led, first in one broad flight, then by two branches on either side, to the landing that opened on a corridor of vast rooms furnished with a jumble of the delights of the nineteenth century. At the end of that corridor could be seen another staircase, steep and dowdy, off which the familiar friends of the house knew where to find snug places for moments of intimacy. That staircase climbed at last to the floors which provided the cupboards of rooms wherein the owners of the splendor below were content to lie of nights and live any part of their lives which was private.

When Reggie came into the hall it was already congested with a throng so eager to identify one another in their disguise, to envy and laugh at the figures others made, that only a thin column moved upward.

He made his way through an incongruous medley of all the fashions of the last century which rarely found a twentieth-century body or head to look natural in them. Frocks cut so low that they asked for a white amplitude of shoulders and bosom displayed lean and square boyish rigors, and above the ballooning gowns meant to be crowned by ringlets or chignons, shorn heads became small and mean. The men had no better luck. Mr. Fortune remarked with a qualm that frilled shirt and stock and high-shouldered pomp of coat declined to go with the sleek hair of the modern male, required flowing locks at least, if not wings of whiskers. It was some solace he had not the low comedian touch of a mustache.

In a mild melancholy he ascended to Lady Rosnay. She had done well with herself. Her pile of white hair, indeed, was all wrong for a gown of the Second Empire, and the diamond tiara in it had a grievous jaunty tilt. But below the paint of the wrinkled old face she was admirable. Out of the shimmering gold of her frock rose gracious lines of shoulder and neck still full and smooth and white.

She made eyes at him. "Lord, not Pickwick," she said. "It's the family apothecary." She pressed his hand. "Kind creature," she laughed. Then she winked at him. "Raffish, ain't we? Go and talk to Alix."

Her granddaughter stood a little behind her in the solemnity of a girl whom duty bids assist at the foolish diversions of the old.

She surveyed Reggie with surprise which had no welcome. "I thought you never came to these things, Mr. Fortune," she said.

"That's why I'm here, Miss Lynn."

"Oh, a special honor for us! How kind of you!" A sarcastic emphasis, a glance at the old lady told him that she was not pleased with her grandmother's word of gratitude.

"I wouldn't dare to be kind to you," Reggie murmured, and he contemplated her through closing, dreamy eyes.

She was a comely sight even in the neighborhood of a grandmother who showed what she might hereafter be. Tall enough for a woman and of a graceful generosity of form, she bore it with an erect, alert vigor which declared an eager appetite for life and challenged. She had her grandmother's impertinent nose and chin, but their sharpness was lost in the young charm of her complexion, which had the milk-white color sometimes granted to set off such red-brown hair as she had and her grandmother's once had been. Miss Lynn's hair was long enough to make a glowing mass above her white neck in which any Victorian woman might have gloried.

She had chosen to show herself, not in the denudation and waves of the early fashions, not in the stiff shapelessness of crinoline, but the modesty, the severe waist and stately flowing lines of the earnest eighties. It was wisely and well done.

"I came in thankful curiosity," Reggie smiled.

"What are you curious about?"

"Curiosity," Reggie explained, "to observe the diversions of the great and thankful for the opportunity. It was very kind of Lady Rosnay." He lingered on the word which had annoyed Miss Lynn.

Her golden brown eyes, brighter than her grandmother's, but not more gentle, flashed at him. "Do make the most of it," she said and turned away.

A man was standing before Lady Rosnay. "God bless my soul! Who are you?" she cried and had some excuse. His loose evening coat was of black velvet outside and white satin within. It opened upon a waistcoat embroidered with large flowers in gold. The studs of his soft silk shirt were large cameos. He carried a stick of ivory with a purple tassel. His black hair was luxuriant and in a calculated disorder, but the wave of the forelock which fell over his square brow seemed to be natural.

"The spirit of the English renaissance, Lady Rosnay," he said. The voice was deep, the tone incisive with something of mockery. "Don't you recognize me?"

"Lord, yes, I was only being civil, Mr. Osmond," she cackled.

Osmond received from her granddaughter a greeting of the curt incivility by which youth means nothing or anything and passed on. Lady Rosnay sent a glance at his broad back, which was not amiable.

Mild interest in these demonstrations made Reggie wander after him. Either he had not many friends there or he was being as melodramatic as his clothes. He made short work of claims to acquaintance, he prowled alone, his dark face set in sardonic gloom. His prowling was divided between the mirrored ballroom where the earliest revellers, not numerous, were dancing old waltzes to modern rhythms and the white drawing room, not much smaller and as yet fuller, in which people waited for and talked over, to, or at their friends.

Reggie loitered there. The noise and movement were less staccato. It offered the better chance to see what if anything Osmond's impatience was looking for.

Observation was disturbed by a wheezy, genial voice. "What, Fortune, are you here? A book of revelations, isn't it?"

Reggie found himself cornered by a fat man of purple complexion who meant to talk. He surrendered without a struggle. Through a generation Bertie Luttrell had worked for the fame of knowing all the gossip. He might be instructive.

"Rather like the chorus of a tourin' musical comedy," Reggie murmured.

Breathing huskily, Luttrell nodded approval. He had come in his usual evening clothes. "We're a feeble folk, old man." His bloodshot eyes twinkled at Reggie. "When we try to wear anything that shows us off, it shows us up. Nobody has any individuality nowadays. We're bred as a herd, my boy, a herd of insignificance. Our fashions camouflage us all to the lowest common terms of respectability, which isn't necessary, God knows. We don't dress, we cover ourselves. Here we are putting on clothes that want a bit of wit to wear 'em, and we're touts and boobies. Look at that fellow"—he nodded at Osmond.

"What, the bullnecked romantic?" Reggie enquired. "Very dashin'. Who is he?"

"My dear boy, you're too innocent. It's Osmond, our coming statesman. He's dressed himself as the young Disraeli to tell you so. It's deuced revealing, isn't it? In his daily clothes, he's only a sample of our mass-production forceful politicians, outsize in the head. In that fancy dress, he's the wicked woman hound of the movies."

"Friend of yours?" Reggie murmured.

"I've known him ever since he came up." Luttrell drew nearer. "He's not a bad fellow, you know. Just a prize fighter in politics, but deuced human. He only wants the earth, and he's out to have his little pleasures while he's getting it."

"A man and a brother, what?" Reggie turned from contemplation of Osmond's lonely prowling and drawled incredulity. "Man of many friends? They don't seem to be here."

Luttrell gave a throaty laugh. "Osmond don't make friends of men unless they're going to be useful. He's a thruster and a bit of a bully. In the party, they kowtow to him as a first-class fighting man, and God knows they need one, but they don't love him. It's the women Osmond goes after."

"He wouldn't be the first politician that women pushed up to the top," Reggie mumbled and with the plaintive gaze of the sufferer from a bore looked vaguely round the company.

"Nor the first that has wrecked himself on women," Luttrell was quick to answer. "I'm not a betting man, but I'd lay you evens Osmond ends that way."

"Any particular woman?" Reggie yawned.

"Oh Lord, no. He's run too many," Luttrell chuckled.

"Like that?" Reggie mumbled.

"You never can tell when a scandal will break, my boy." Luttrell gave him a knowing nod.

"As you say," Reggie drawled. "Well, well. Oh, he has found a friend."

Osmond had been taken in hand by a lively youth who made a pretty figure in a green dress coat with gold buttons, who laughed him out of his gloom and bustled him through the crowd.

"That's young Darett. Osmond's just captured him for a secretary. A shrewd move. Arthur Darett's a gentleman. He'll be very useful. It's not so good for Darett."

"The young man's got him into society," Reggie remarked.

Osmond and Darett had joined a little group of two women and a man. "Oh, that's nothing," Luttrell wheezed. "They're Osmond's backers. You know Malcolm Harley, don't you?" The correctitude of Harley was indeed superciliously undisguised in ordinary evening clothes. He made a sarcastic contrast with the flamboyancy of Osmond. "Queer pair to do the David and Jonathan," said Luttrell. "Fellows say they don't know what the devil Harley was at to link up with Osmond. Harley's always been a sound man, clever enough for anything and a worker and all that and devilish sure-footed. He was safe for the next cabinet, and he looked like getting an option on the leadership. This partnership with Osmond means he does the giving and Osmond does the taking. But there it is, he's simply fallen for the fellow. Friend that's closer than a brother, passing the love of women and all that, don't you know? There's a bit of the devil in Osmond. He comes over people when he wants 'em."

"Does he?" Reggie mumbled. "Very disturbin'. Yes. Who are the ladies?" He was contemplating the elder of the two, a thin gray-haired woman wearing a graceful black gown of no period, who somehow, with no likeness in her slight form and sad face, resembled Lady Rosnay.

"What, don't you know the finest woman in London?" Luttrell spluttered. "That's Harley's wife, dear boy."

Reggie blinked and glanced at the other lady. She was in the later-nineteenth-century style, slim but of emphatic femininity, she was of a blonde beauty almost without flaw and without distinction. In her little circle she led the conversation, merrily vivacious, all her body talking.

"Mrs. Harley. Oh, yes," Reggie said. "Who is the old one?"

"Darett's mother." For the first time Luttrell's thick tones were without a sneer. "Poor creature. She's aging damnably."

Reggie's professional eye confirmed that. Mrs. Darett was not in good health. He found more interest in the discovery of the cause of her resemblance to Lady Rosnay. She was more artistically painted, but the color scheme was similar. Her lips showed the same unusual tawny red.

He was surprised by the outbreak of Luttrell's bronchial laugh. But it was not directed at Mrs. Darett or at him. When a plaintive glance asked for explanations he saw that Luttrell was looking another way: looking at movements in the crowd: that was Alix Lynn coming purposeful: Luttrell watched her or someone beyond.

Alix made her way to the group of Osmond and Harley and was taken into it with a welcome of affectionate familiarity.

Luttrell poked a finger at Reggie's ribs. "Oh, yes. Meaning she's another of Mr. Osmond's backers." Reggie contemplated him dreamily. "Thanks very much."

"You watch it, my boy." Luttrell winked, and his congested eyes rolled in a survey of the room.

After a moment of general talk in the group, Alix and Osmond detached themselves, and she went off on his arm towards the ballroom.

"Not much of a dancing partner, eh?" said Luttrell. "There's better fun than dancing, old man. Now look. This is drama."

Another woman was approaching Harley's diminished group, a small woman in frills and furbelows.

"The fallen angel," Luttrell wheezed, and Reggie winced. The phrase was absurd, with enough truth in its absurdity to be unpleasant. She had a pretty doll's face, but she was being a tragic doll. The pouting mouth drooped at the corners, the blue eyes stared wide, her round cheeks were pale, she moved listlessly. "Molly Marne, old man," said Luttrell.

Reggie did not need that. Half the town knew Molly Marne by sight, a darling of musical comedy, risen to new fame in parts of passion. He had a mild, humorous liking for the high colors of her acting. It was to be feared that she would act off the stage—but he had an uncomfortable doubt whether this dull, blind stare was art.

Mrs. Harley made much of her. Harley was graciously gallant, young Darett gay. She was not cheered. She looked away from them, beyond them.

"Poor wench," Luttrell said. "Looking for the faithless one. So that's how she's going to take it. Patient misery—in public. I'd like to see her tête-à-tête with the other girl. One of her big scenes, my boy. You know the story, don't you? Osmond couldn't leave her alone till he began to climb. Then he saw that Alix Lynn had her uses, and Molly was left to cool off. I wonder she came tonight—wanted to be hurt, I suppose—she's just that kind of woman. I daresay the Rosnay took pains to get her here. A regular Rosnay touch, setting a castoff girl on a man, and the Rosnay doesn't want her Alix to go to Simon Osmond. She knows his kind, the old witch. But it's a shallow game. A girl don't break with a man because she meets one he tried before her—not nowadays, if girls ever did—she would rather have a fellow with experience."

Reggie made no answer. He waited for more. But it did not come. Molly

Marne moved away from the Harley group in the sleepwalking manner of her arrival. Luttrell gave a grin and a grunt of leave-taking and sidled his bulk across the room, but not after her. He made for the Harleys.

Reggie watched him a moment. He had an intimate welcome. Reggie followed Molly Marne. It was not difficult to overtake her, and having passed he turned and stood close by her as she passed into the ballroom. A faint aromatic fragrance came to him, familiar and unfamiliar. He saw her eyes and discovered why even at a distance they looked so blue. The pupils were unnaturally small, almost lost in the turquoise of the iris. She went on into the ballroom and stood still, staring at the dancers as if she did not see them. Osmond and Alix Lynn were not to be seen. She was captured by a large and florid man in the pink uniform of a hunt, Lady Rosnay's companion of the garden party, Sir David Kames. He carried her off to dance.

"Well, well," Reggie sighed and drifted away. His round face was childlike with a plaintive wonder. " 'The world is so full of a number of things, I'm sure we should all be as happy as kings.' "

With difficulty he obtained for himself a glass of barley water—he had no affection for champagne, and he knew too well that who drinks any wine in Lady Rosnay's house gambles wildly. He took his chastening fluid to a corner and drank in solitary, pensive meditation and sat long and was not comforted.

From that he rose and wandered away to look bewildered into one room and another. He saw Mrs. Darett talking to a secretary of state, he saw Mrs. Harley dancing, but of all those who exercised his wondering mind, none.

After patient unfruitful endurance of the ballroom he sought cool air and quiet again. He had removed himself as far as might be from the band. He found a small room empty, with its balconied windows open. He was sitting there when he heard a scream and the thud of a fall.

The sounds came from overhead. The staircase which led to the private parts of the house was close by. Reggie went up as fast as the stricture of his 1840 trousers allowed. The upper part of the staircase was in darkness. He stumbled over something. His hands came upon the bare shoulder of a woman. He smelt the scent which had come to him from Molly Marne.

The dark stairs above were creaking beneath swift footsteps. He made haste after them.

Chapter III

The Light in the Corridor

REGGIE came up to the landing and saw through the darkness a glimmer of light which went out as he looked. He groped for switches. On the landing and down the corridor lamps flashed out, but not to the corridor's end. He ran on and found another switch. The light which that made shone white upon the wall of the servants' back stairs. A shadow moved swiftly down the wall and vanished, a man's shadow.

Further pursuit offered no hope. He returned along the corridor swiftly, something short of breath, glancing without hope into nooks and corners which were empty. One of the doors opened, and Alix Lynn came out and looked each way and saw him with a start of surprise that was angry. "Mr. Fortune!" she exclaimed. "What are you doing?"

"Throwing a little light on the matter, Miss Lynn." He walked on past her.

She went after him, calling, "Whatever do you mean?"

"Somebody put all the lights out," said Reggie. "So I put them on."

"Whatever for?"

"To see," said Reggie.

"I mean why were they put out?" she snapped. "What was that noise?"

"Oh, you heard it?" said Reggie.

"I was in my room." She also was out of breath.

They searched the landing. Its light fell on the body of the woman who lay at the turn of the stair. She was Lady Rosnay.

"Well, well," Reggie murmured and looked at Alix.

She did not speak. She started down the stairs, but he slid in front.

The sound of movement and voices came from below. Somebody was sure it was here, somebody else didn't believe it was, somebody stumbled, somebody wondered if they ought to go up.

Reggie knelt by the body. It lay head downwards, the skirts tumbled back from the legs, the bodice pulled off the shoulders, the white hair fallen into a shapeless flood.

"Is she dead?" Alix whispered.

Reggie's hands moved from pulse to bosom and head. "Oh, no. No. Not this time," he told her.

The first of the people below came in sight. "Good God! It's my lady," somebody said. He recognized the choking voice of Luttrell.

"No more, please." He put up his hand against them. "Go down again." He stood up between them and Lady Rosnay, hiding where she lay. He looked at the stairs above and below; he looked at Alix curiously. She frowned surprise.

"Where's her room?" he said. "Go on and show me." Alix did not move, waited to watch him gather the old woman in his arms. "Yes? Anything you want?" he asked.

She turned and ran upstairs. Reggie stood for a moment, scanning the stairs where the body had lain before he followed.

Lady Rosnay's bedroom was small and marvelously full of furniture. Reggie sidled round a gilt Empire table to the big curtained bed and pushed the pink curtains aside with his shoulder to lay her on it. While he stooped over her, there was a splutter of wordless chatter, like a baby's wrath, above his head.

He glanced up. Alix laughed. "Don't be jumpy. It's only Cupid. He hates men, but he won't hurt you."

Reggie arranged Lady Rosnay with deliberate care and drew back to contemplate the curtains. From the point where they met there looked down at him a sorrowful, unachieved likeness to humanity, the face of a small monkey.

"Oh, yes, an American," Reggie murmured. "A capuchin. Well, well. You might get her clothes off. Don't be rough."

"Thank you," Alix said furiously.

Reggie wandered away in the maze of furniture, lingered and sat down by the dressing table. But neither there nor anywhere else did he find what he was looking for, a sign that Lady Rosnay had taken off her tiara of diamonds.

The thing was not in her tumbled hair. It was not upon the staircase. Though Alix had not remarked on its absence. He watched the operations of Alix on the unconscious body with eyes that avoided looking at her.

She was gentle enough. The capuchin monkey came down from the curtains and sat on the pillow by his mistress's head and watched. He did not interfere with Alix, but the white line on his little brown brow twisted, and he stretched out a tiny hand towards his mistress, pushing it shyly nearer till it touched her face. Alix rebuked him. He sat up and prayed.

"I've put her to bed," said Alix.

Reggie came back to the bedside, and the monkey fled up the curtains.

Lady Rosnay made some noise of breathing now; her mouth was open.

Except for that she looked comfortable and not unseemly. Alix had left her hair scanty by the removal of what was not her own, but arranged it in neatness.

Reggie gave her a methodical examination, and the monkey scolded.

"Well?" Alix asked. "Is there anything?"

"Nothing serious, no," Reggie murmured. "Unconscious from slight concussion."

"I suppose she fell."

"Yes, it looked like that."

"Is there anything I ought to do?"

"You'd better not. Her maid will sit by her."

"I shall stay with her," Alix announced.

Reggie crossed the room and rang the bell. "Don't bother," he said. "I'll arrange she isn't left alone. I'll come and see her tomorrow."

"I shall send for her own doctor," said Alix defiantly.

"Alister, isn't it?" Reggie murmured. "You needn't trouble. I'll talk to him."

The monkey had climbed down the curtains and sat on the pillow again. He was stroking Lady Rosnay's face.

She sneezed, she turned her head and whispered sleepily, "Cupid, darling." Her eyes opened wider. Her hands moved under the bedclothes. She looked down at them and made a grimace; she raised herself slowly and stared round the room.

"Mr. Fortune!" she said, and she giggled. "Oh, fie!"

Alix came to her side. "It's all right, dear."

"My angel!" Lady Rosnay was more amused. "Isn't that nice of her, Mr. Fortune? I did have a chaperon. Now I'm happy." But after laughing, her face was distorted with a spasm of pain. "Oh God, I'm all an ache," she gasped and laughed again.

"Mr. Fortune says you're not badly hurt," said Alix. "How—"

"He's mighty kind!" Lady Rosnay muttered.

"How did you fall, dear?" Alix finished her sentence quickly.

"Upside down," Lady Rosnay cackled. "Oh, damn my head. Who found me?"

"Mr. Fortune," said Alix.

"Lord! You dear creature!" she ogled him. "I was standing on my head, wasn't I?" She gave a little scream, she put her hand to her head. "Oh, my hair!"

"Yes, your hair was down," said Reggie slowly.

"Such a gentleman!" she grinned. She beckoned to Alix and, as the girl bent over, whispered hoarsely for him to hear: "Did it all come back?"

"Of course," Alix snapped.

"My life is saved," Lady Rosnay gasped and lay back.

"Yes, I think so," Reggie murmured. "You've talked quite enough. Your maid should be coming. She'll stay with you. Ah, here she is." He moved to the door and conferred with the ancient maid. "Good-night, Lady Rosnay. I'll see you tomorrow."

"But how masterful," Lady Rosnay laughed.

"You called me in," said Reggie.

He went slowly down the steep stairs again.

The sound of the energetic band came to him. A crowd in the ballroom was still jerking earnestly at a waltz. Knowledge of the disaster to the lady of the house seemed not to have spread far. An odd thing, since Luttrell knew it. Luttrell was not playing up to his form.

But, loitering here and there to see if there were any reactions of interest, Reggie was met by Harley. "Mr. Fortune, isn't it? My name's Harley, you know."

"Oh, yes. Yes. How do you do?" Reggie mumbled.

"So glad to meet you. Just let me have a word." Harley was impressively important.

"By all means," Reggie sighed and led the way into the little room at the end of the corridor. The door was shut, but the room was still empty. "What's the matter?"

Harley shut the door again behind them and became confidential. "I wanted to ask if anything ought to be done. Lady Rosnay is a dear friend of ours, and she has only Miss Lynn. I might claim to help in any way. I don't know whether this ball ought to go on—"

"Oh, yes. That's all right. She wouldn't want it stopped."

"I am very glad to hear you say so. But how is the poor lady?" Harley's shrewd face was schooled to sympathy.

"Doin' quite well."

"This is a great relief. It was a dreadful fall for a woman of her age."

"Nasty business, yes," Reggie murmured.

"How did it happen, Mr. Fortune?"

"My dear sir! Oh my dear sir!" Reggie smiled.

"I suppose she doesn't know herself," said Harley.

"Yes. It could be," Reggie murmured.

Harley nodded sage agreement. "Well, I'm so glad you could give us good news," he said and shook Reggie's hand affectionately.

Reggie watched his sprightly back depart. "And that is that," he murmured. He frowned at the little room. Something was strange about it. It was close. The windows had been shut.

He went out. He went home.

Chapter IV

Mr. Fortune is Depressed

THE next morning Mr. Fortune strolled into the room of the chief of the Criminal Investigation Department before ten o'clock. This is unusual.

He found only a secretary in action. "Mr. Lomas not here yet?" he complained. The secretary, as early secretaries should, believed Mr. Lomas was in the building.

"Beautiful faith." Reggie dropped into the largest chair and lit his pipe. "The department's full of faith."

After some time Lomas made a brisk arrival. "Reginald! Good Gad!" He was startled and amused.

"Yes. I've been up some time," Reggie reproached him. "I always feel like that when I see you."

"My dear fellow, that's conceit. Your natural arrogance. You must watch it. I don't want to hurt you, but it's cramping your style." Lomas settled himself at the table and dismissed his secretary.

"Arrogance!" Reggie moaned. "I'm the only humble man I ever met. I always know when I don't know. That preserves me from the grosser blunders. That gives me a start on other fellows. But it's depressing. I am depressed."

"What's the trouble?" Lomas put up his eyeglass and stared quizzical curiosity.

"Want to depress you," Reggie mumbled. "If possible. Desperate effort. However. A duty to society. You didn't go to Lady Rosnay's ball last night—in spite of her pressin' invitation?"

"I did not," said Lomas with emphatic satisfaction, and then he laughed. "You don't mean to say you did, Reginald?"

Reggie sighed. "Oh, yes. Yes. Duty is England's morning star. You didn't know that. Social duty—civic duty—moral duty—all guidin' one—very painful. I went. And queer things happened. Very queer and baffling."

Lomas sat back in his chair and frowned. "Well, let's have all the facts," he said sharply.

"Facts?" Reggie moaned. "Oh, my aunt! What are facts?" But carefully and exactly he told the story of the ball.

"Damn, it is queer stuff," Lomas agreed. "That's the whole of it?"

"Yes. Absolutely. This morning's news—I've talked to Lady Rosnay's doctor—he went round bright and early—she had a good night—he found her very gay."

"The old witch." Lomas gave a short, angry laugh. "She would be. She has the pluck of the devil."

"Oh, yes. Yes. That is indicated. First certain inference. Lady Rosnay is a bold female. The only certain inference—not any particular use."

"Well, what do you make of it?"

"My dear chap. Oh, my dear chap. I don't know." Reggie was plaintive. "That's what I came to rub into you. We don't know anything. And there's a lot we ought to know. A damnable lot. I'm not happy, Lomas. *Je n'ai pas de courage*, same like the lady in the play. I'm afraid. We're only seeing shadows. But there's hell at work."

"Shadows—you mean the shadow on the wall that you saw. Have you any notion who that was?"

"Oh, no. No. Nor am I guessing. Person castin' shadow probably male. Any further opinion merely delusive. Question who made that shadow probably fundamental. Don't fancy you know the answer. You'll only get busy burying the truth. Lots of other shadows dancin' before us."

"Where have you got to now?" said Lomas. "Another edition of your lecture on the delusions of this life?"

"You remember that," Reggie purred. "How gratifying. Yes. I was rather on the spot with that. The mind is not wholly impotent. It did make out we were being carefully shown what was all humbug. Leavin' us in the consciousness of blank and helpless ignorance. Very wholesome and bracing. Are you braced, Lomas?"

"No, dazed," Lomas complained. "Don't be so infernally edifying. What is the practical meaning, if any? You're not trying to work back to the Poyntz case?"

"Yes. That was the simple plan. I like to begin at the beginning. Mrs. Poyntz undoubtedly commits suicide. Person unknown tells the small daughter to ask the bereaved husband why she did. Enter Lady Rosnay to tell us very loud and clear that it was suicide. And the husband also dies: possibly accident, probably suicide. You noticed that? Again it couldn't be murder. All very interestin' and disturbin'."

"I wasn't disturbed," said Lomas with some pugnacity.

"My poor old thing," Reggie pitied him, "I was afraid you weren't. Primitive type of mind. Official mind. Don't notice anything until personally suffering."

"I don't imagine mysteries to amuse myself," Lomas said. "There's nothing in all this if you take it with common sense. The husband and wife had some quarrel. She got hysterical and killed herself. He thought it was all his fault, poor devil, or he didn't want to go on living without her, and he made an end of himself, too. Lord, it's a common case enough. You know that."

"Oh, yes. And the amiable letter to the little girl?"

"Some spiteful mischief maker."

"Yes, I think so," Reggie purred. "A mischief maker, quite expert. I should like to meet that letter writer. It would cheer my humble life. And Lady Rosnay?"

"What about her? She's been chattering scandal all her life. You wouldn't expect her to let Mrs. Poyntz alone."

"Oh, no. No. But it was peculiar scandal. She said some fellow must have been making love to the woman and swore the woman never thought of any fellow but her husband. She swore it was suicide and there wasn't any reason for it. Lady Rosnay could make up a spicier tale than that between one cup of tea and another. Why give us only that? Why the anxiety to impress on the Criminal Investigation Department it needn't bother about Mrs. Poyntz? Several possible answers. She has her reasons for hushing up the Poyntz case, or she was fishing to find out what we thought of it, or she wanted to stir us up to look into it."

Lomas laughed. "Splendid, Reginald. A mystery made out of nothing with three or more contradictory explanations. One of your best efforts."

"Wasn't any explanation," Reggie mumbled. "And I didn't make the mystery. It's all round us. A few things poke out of it and fade away into it."

"Oh, wash out the Poyntz case. We can do nothing with that. Let's come on to last night. You had something actual there. What do you make of it?"

"I don't. Everything dies away into the dark. Very depressin'. Once more Lady Rosnay. Why did she want the great minds of the Criminal Investigation Department at her tiresome ball?"

"Oh, my dear fellow!" Lomas protested. "Don't start making a fuss about nothing again. Why does a woman ask all sorts of men to a charity ball?"

"Very well. No significance. However, she did ask us, and I went, and queer things happened. First queer thing: she was stimulated by my turning up, but Alix Lynn didn't want me. Not so but far otherwise. Strange and sad. Second queer thing: lots of rich people there for Bertie Luttrell to toady, but he loved me best. Very flattering. And from his devotion to me, definite purposes emerged: I was to be instructed that the politician Osmond is a bad man all round and especially a rogue with women. Possible bearing on the Poyntz case."

Lomas made an exclamation of impatience.

"All right, all right. Let's try to have narrow minds. Further purpose of the man Luttrell, to impress on me Osmond is getting hold of Alix Lynn, and Lady Rosnay don't mean to stand it. Some signs he might have been telling the truth in that. However. He also wanted me to believe Osmond has been playing the deuce with Molly Marne. And something has gone wrong with that girl. She came to the ball with morphia in her. General conclusions: Luttrell knows more than he ought to know and—"

"Why do you say that?" Lomas interrupted sharply. "He always did."

"Oh, yes. Yes. He always wants you to think so. But seldom confirmed by outside evidence. Seldom with clear purpose. Either he has his own particular reasons for directin' my attention to Osmond or he was acting on the instructions of somebody behind the scenes."

"Who are you thinking of?" Lomas snapped.

"I'm not thinking," Reggie mumbled. "No material. However. Resumin' consideration of the queer things. Lady Rosnay. Facts about Lady Rosnay's fall complex and confusin'. First and obvious explanation, gentleman who ran away, puttin' out the corridor lights as he fled, knocked her downstairs and stole her tiara. Possibly true explanation, but not coverin' all the facts. No tiara visible when she was found. Kind of absence that hits you in the eye. Yet Alix Lynn didn't notice it—wouldn't notice it when I made her see I was lookin' for something. Lady Rosnay, returned to consciousness, put her hand to her head. Then she asked if we'd collected all her hair. She didn't mention the tiara. Why were they both determined to ignore its absence?"

"Well, what's the answer?" said Lomas.

"I haven't the slightest idea. She might have taken it off before she fell."

"Taken off her diamonds in the middle of a ball?" Lomas exclaimed.

"Not womanly, no. Not likely. However. She may know who stole 'em—Alix may know—or they think they know—and they have their reasons for not telling us who the thief is."

"Quite," Lomas nodded. "That makes sense."

"You think so?" Reggie gazed at him dreamily. "What are their reasons? Shieldin' the thief because he's a dear friend?"

"Women do," said Lomas.

"Yes. It could be. Or because he's a hated enemy. To use the thing against him privately." Reggie's eyelids drooped. "Would you like to be Lady Rosnay's enemy, Lomas? I shouldn't."

"You're thinking of Osmond," Lomas smiled.

"I can't help it. He's a bit of the puzzle. He must fit in somewhere. He might come in here. Alix would hold her tongue for love. Lady Rosnay for hate. To take it out of Alix and Osmond at discretion. If Osmond did the job—or even if he didn't. Yes. I wonder." Reggie's eyes closed. After a moment he spoke again in a small, drawling voice: "If he didn't do it—but the fall wasn't an accident—she was hit—bruise on her chin not made by the stairs—and the fellow who ran away, juggling with the lights, knew his way about the house. Job carefully planned. By someone very intimate with the family of Rosnay. Yes. That might be Osmond—assisted by Alix. Or someone else—assisted by Lady Rosnay."

"Good Gad!" Lomas cried. "You don't suppose she arranged to have herself knocked out?"

"Bold female—as you were saying," Reggie murmured.

"Quite. She's devilish plucky. She's devilish tricky. An imp of a woman. Absolutely incalculable. Your idea is, she arranged a sham assault and robbery—she got you there to testify it was genuine—and her game is to start scandal which will lay it all on Osmond. Well, she's capable of it. I give you that."

"Yes I think so. Some other evidence pointin' the same way. The earnest efforts of the man Luttrell to instruct me that Osmond is a bad egg. The anxiety of Osmond's ally, Harley, to know what I made of it, to suggest that it must have been an accident, to be very sympathetic with poor Lady Rosnay. Indicatin' fear people might put it down to Osmond and a desire to get on record that Osmond's best friend was close friends with Lady Rosnay and knew it was all right. Shrewd fellow, Harley. Not a bad fellow. To look at."

"Harley's sound enough," Lomas agreed. "But I'm not satisfied, Reginald."

"Satisfied!" Reggie moaned. "Oh, my hat! We're tumbling over ourselves jumpin' at shadows. We're being very amusin' to the people who show the shadows. No, I am not satisfied, Lomas. I don't like being funny."

"Well, try to improve," Lomas smiled. "Let's work on your theory—the assault was a put-up job—Lady Rosnay employed a man to make an attack on her and take her tiara. Then who was it?"

"I haven't the slightest idea," Reggie mumbled. "It's not my theory. It's one of the possibilities. With obvious objections—the man hit too hard; also, she didn't mention that she was hit, same like she didn't mention that her tiara had gone. Reticence rather baffling, either way."

"However you take it, she was knocked down," said Lomas. "You say either by Osmond—"

"Or by somebody else. Yes. I got that far. Great effort of the brain."

"And who was the somebody?"

"No. There the great brain failed. You ask too much, Lomas. I'm only human. Not supernatural."

"What about the fellow who was blackguarding Osmond?" Lomas said. "Didn't he occur to you?"

"Oh, yes. He occurred all right. Quite a possible theory. The man Luttrell was probably set on to make me suspect Osmond. He may have been engaged to do the job which was to be put down to Osmond. Neat and economical. Yes. I liked that theory myself. I felt clever over it."

"Take it Luttrell had something against Osmond," Lomas said slowly and watched Reggie with a quizzical smile.

Reggie laughed wearily. "I do. I've only been saying so for half an hour. Sorry it didn't penetrate."

"You've said a lot, Reginald. You noticed a lot last night. Great power of observation. I'm afraid you didn't observe everything. When did you last observe Luttrell?"

"On the stair—callin' people to witness Lady Rosnay lyin' unconscious. Very officious of the man Luttrell. Another little point. I did mention it."

"And then he vanished?"

"I vanished. Carryin' the lady to bed. When I came down—no, I didn't see Luttrell again. He wasn't conspicuous."

"Wasn't he? Last observed calling attention to Lady Rosnay's disaster. I see. Would it surprise you to hear he was found dead this morning in the garden of Rosnay House?"

Reggie sank deeper in his chair. "In the garden," he mumbled. "Whereabouts?"

"Close to the house. A gardener found him soon after nine. Dead and cold. They say he looked as if he'd fallen out of a window. The windows at the back look onto the garden."

"Yes, I know. Yes. Any doctor's report?"

"They called the divisional surgeon. He said there were signs of a heavy fall—not sure about the cause of death, though. He's working on it now."

"Well, well," Reggie sighed. "Another shadow." He rose wearily. "I'd better go and have a look."

Lomas, though he tries to conceal it, is a man of regular life. He was finishing his usual lunch at the usual table of his usual club with his usual companions when Reggie wandered into the solemn room, plaintive and uncertain as a new member whom nobody knows, and drifted into lonely obscurity.

When Lomas came to him, he was mingling sweet pickles with the salad provided for his lobster. He lifted melancholy eyes. "Oh my Lomas!" he sighed. "What I endure for your sake. I needed festive food. This place makes the best things dull."

"You have a debauched taste, Reginald. We live the simple life. There's no better plain meal in London."

"My poor Lomas!" Reggie moaned. "That is the lie in the soul. You really believe it. Plain—it's all too plain, one dead flat of sameness. Nothing has a taste of its own. Except the cheeses. I grant you them. But I am not strong enough for cheese today." He smelt at his white Burgundy and sipped. "A small wine," he sighed. "Anything bigger would have been too big."

Lomas looked at the bottle. "Lord, it's Montrachet. What more do you want at lunch?"

"It's only the minor," Reggie murmured. "I had yearned for something uplifting. I was thinking of a Romanée. If I could have had a lunch to go with it. A vain, vain hope."

"Good Gad! Romanée!" Lomas laughed. "And then an afternoon of sleep, I suppose?"

"Oh, no. No. The brain would have developed full power. But now— now just negative and safe. Well, well. We shall understand each other better." He was brought a duckling and an orange; he squeezed one upon the other and ate.

"What a lunch!" Lomas sneered. "Duck after lobster."

"Yes. Here's richness. Quite barbarous. But it's the only way to get the sensation of food in this place."

"Well, why did you come?" said Lomas impatiently. "What are you going to tell me?"

"Nothing," Reggie mumbled. "That is the humor of it. Nothing to be done with it. Same like the Poyntz case." He finished the best of the duck and looked without gratitude at the remains. He drank a last glass of the Montrachet and rose.

Lomas followed him to a corner in a large and fusty upper room empty but for some ancients quarreling over their whist. He declined coffee with a shudder. "Tastes like this club. Tastes like these cases. A warmed-up muddle. I want something dry, something subtle, yet clear. White curacao. Do they know curacao can be white here?"

"They know and deplore it. But they are patient with showing off. They have seen many irritated experts," Lomas smiled. "So you're going to say it was a natural death?"

Reggie lit a cigar and blew smoke rings. "Oh, yes. Yes. Offensively natural. I was afraid it would be. When the man Luttrell talked to me last night I thought he was pretty far gone. Fatter than ever, bad color, breathed as if he'd got a sponge in his throat. When I saw him today he was green."

"What does all that mean?"

"Myocardial degeneration much advanced. Call it fatty degeneration of the heart. Result of gross living."

"And he would just fall and die from that, would he?"

"He could. Yes. In fact he did. No possible doubt. Actual cause of death, syncope. Heart stopped."

"Why did he fall out of window?"

"I haven't the slightest idea. Might have gone to a window for air—he'd feel the need sometimes—might have been on a balcony—he'd have fits of giddiness. The fall didn't kill him. No grave injury. I should say he was dead when he hit the ground. Bruises look like that."

"Quite a clear case, what?" Lomas frowned.

"Yes. Absolutely. All simple, obvious, and certain."

"Devilish opportune death, though. He blackguards Osmond to you—Lady Rosnay's knocked out and her tiara vanished—some fellow runs away—Luttrell brings people to see what's been done to her—and the next we know about him he's lying dead outside."

Reggie gazed at him dreamily. "Accurate, lucid, and impressive," he murmured. "But you didn't suppose it was any use, did you?"

"You couldn't find any ground for suspicion?"

"I wouldn't say that. No. Not any firm ground. Not any taking-off place. Two little dubious grounds. His shirtfront was crumpled in the abdominal region. That wasn't done by the fall. I should say the shirt had stopped a punch. No correspondin' bruise on the body. However. If he was hit somewhere about the solar plexus, the shock might have been enough to bring on syncope. Hypothesis, not proof, as you notice. Have a little more. Where he was found was underneath the windows of the room I was in just before Lady Rosnay crashed. Windows with a low balcony. They were open when I was in there. It's a little out-of-the-way room. I went there for solitude. After I came down from ministerin' to Lady Rosnay and Harley wanted to be confidential, I took him in there. And then the windows were shut. I noticed that when Harley shut the door. I thought it was rather odd anybody had felt chilly. Not the sort of night for it. If somebody was confidential with Luttrell out on the balcony and made an end of him, adequate reason for closing the windows. Inconvenient to the operator if somebody came out and saw the corpse. There's your grounds for suspicion—a crumpled shirtfront and the shutting of windows—not the sort of stuff to give a jury."

Lomas shook his head. "We couldn't use that. It's not evidence, it's imagination."

"My dear chap. Oh my dear chap," Reggie moaned. "Rational explanation of observed facts. But can't be verified. Baffling case. Elusive, insubstantial case."

"Deuced unsatisfactory," Lomas said. "What we have is, the fellow was in such a state he might have died any moment, and he died. That washes it all out—verdict, natural death, and we can't do anything. But have you any doubt it was murder?"

"Legally murder? I don't know. Nobody ever will know. Morally it was murder all right. However much he deserved it." Reggie finished his cigar. "Not a nice man, the man Luttrell." He contemplated Lomas. "What do you know about that?"

"Lounged round the town all his life. Professional gossip. Purveyor of garbage to clubs and drawing rooms. I shouldn't wonder if he dabbled in dirtier work."

"No. Nor should I," Reggie murmured. "All the more reason for wanting to know who murdered him. We might get near some of his dirtier work."

"Quite. What are the indications? He handed you scandal about Osmond, and then he made a fuss over the Rosnay's crash. That might be faking a case against Osmond or getting ready to blackmail him on a genuine case. Anyway he was busy on Osmond. And he gets murdered."

"Yes. Very suggestive. I thought that. What do you know about Osmond?"

Lomas shrugged. "Public reputation—a thruster, struggle-for-lifer, don't stick at a trifle. He went through the war, starting in the ranks, finished an officer and a gentleman, with a ranker's medal for some sanguinary business. Took his discharge out at Salonika and lost to sight. Came to the surface again with a bit of money from God knows where. He's made it fly, and he's a poor man for politics. That's all."

"Sounds nasty when annoyed," Reggie murmured.

"Just the sort of man to let fly if Luttrell got across him."

"As you say. Yes. It might have been Osmond. Nothing more likely. Nothing so likely." Reggie's voice dwindled. He sat very still a moment, then shivered and grasped the arms of his chair. "But there's more to it than that, Lomas. We're only seeing what's arranged for us and the shadows of the people behind."

"My dear Reginald!" Lomas protested. "Don't be portentous again. You're seeing all that you ever see in clever crime, the bits that couldn't be hidden."

"Yes. It's clever," Reggie said dreamily. "Devilish clever. Remember what you said about the Poyntz case? Some spiteful mischief maker at work. That was the man Luttrell's trade—mischief-making. But he hadn't the brain for big stuff. There's people who strike at life behind him. The mischief makers, unlimited." He gave a queer laugh. "Might be a good business. Goodbye."

"Where are you off to?" Lomas cried.

"Going to call on Lady Rosnay," Reggie mumbled and wandered out.

Chapter V

Lady Rosnay Amuses Herself

WHEN he came to Rosnay House, Reggie was told by a curt footman that Lady Rosnay was not well enough to see anyone. He walked into the hall and held out his hat to unwilling hands. "She'll see me," he said. "Let her know Mr. Fortune is here."

He was put without respect into a small room by the door. But before long the old butler came to him. "I beg your pardon, sir. My lady shall be informed."

"That's all right. Who said she wasn't seeing anyone?"

The butler made the motion of washing hands. "Miss Lynn's instructions, sir. Will you walk upstairs?" Reggie was brought to the white drawing room. "Mr. Fortune," the butler announced.

Two people were there, sitting close together in a conversation which stopped suddenly. Reggie knew Alix Lynn's red head. They both looked round, and he remembered the pleasant face of her companion. It belonged to Osmond's secretary, Arthur Darett.

The two showed no embarrassment. Alix rose to meet him, and Darett stood up smiling. "How kind of you to come," said Alix, with some sarcastic emphasis on the word of thanks, fainter than the night before, but a clear hint to his memory. "Do you know Mr. Darett?"

Reggie exchanged a "How do you do?" and turned to Alix. "Sorry to hear Lady Rosnay isn't doing well."

"I told them to say that to keep people off. We've had half London here."

"Yes, you would have," Reggie murmured.

"I suppose you've heard about poor old Luttrell?" said Darett. "Did you know him, sir?"

"Everybody knew Luttrell." Reggie looked at Alix. "Has Lady Rosnay heard?"

"Oh, yes. That fool Graves told her."

"The butler. I see."

"Well, it doesn't matter," said Alix quickly. "She would have had to know. She had Graves up asking about people here last night, and I couldn't stop him."

"Did she take it badly?"

"Badly? I don't know. She didn't cry." Alix's brown eyes flashed at him.

"Was Luttrell an old friend?"

"I suppose she's known him a long time. Not a friend," said Alix with contempt.

"Poor old chap," Darett smiled. "People didn't think of him that way. He amused them. It's a nasty thing, though. What do you make of it, sir?"

Reggie shook his head. "These things happen. Did you see him last night?"

"Rather. Didn't you? He was talking to my mother and me. I thought he was quite in his usual form, or a bit above. And then this—phut! It's a bit of a facer."

"As you say," Reggie murmured. "Yes. A bad life."

Alix and Darett glanced at each other. Alix began to say something but was stopped by the return of the butler. A meek tinge of triumph colored his professional voice as he asked Mr. Fortune if he would please come upstairs.

Outside the door Reggie lingered a moment and heard an eager conversation begin.

Lady Rosnay was still in bed, but she had arranged herself to defy sympathy with that condition.

She sat up, embanked in many pillows, she wore a coat of orange velvet, and under a lace cap, youthfully coquettish, her white hair was in frozen waves. The sunlight which fell on the pink curtains made a roseate background for the sharp, minute art with which she had decorated her face. A bed table across her knees bore many newspapers which the capuchin monkey, his tiny hands fighting hers, was pulling at and tearing in shreds.

On the sight of Reggie he started back and chattered.

Lady Rosnay held him to her bosom. "You angel!" she laughed and made eyes at Reggie. "You dear creature."

"Which is which?" Reggie asked sadly.

"You are alike." She kissed the monkey's eyes. "But I should always know you apart. Don't be vain. You're only human, Mr. Fortune."

"Yes, so far. Might be promoted to the heavenly sphere at any moment, as things go. However. I'm glad to find you're still down here."

"My dear! Did you come with a wreath? I am flattered. But you can put it on Cupid. He loves to tear up flowers. Don't you, angel?" She tickled the monkey, who squeaked and bit her. "Yes, still alive," she gave a crow of laughter. "That fool Alister told me to stay in bed, just as you did, Mr. Fortune. So here I am. But I feel as fit as a bride."

"Any dizziness, or numb anywhere?" Reggie droned.

"Lord, don't be professional."

"I was thinking about that bruise," Reggie mourned, "the bruise on your chin—rather a wicked blow."

"Bless you, it's nothing. I painted my face and tired my hair, like Jezebel, and now I can't find it myself."

It was indeed effaced by cream and powder. "Not visible, no," Reggie murmured. "Did you see who hit you?"

She rolled her eyes. "Was I hit? How marvelous! I haven't been hit this thirty years—not since poor Nell found me with Randolph." She cackled. "You wouldn't remember, you were a baby, you dear thing. And you believe I can make people hit me still! Sweet of you. Who was the fierce creature?"

"I don't know. I thought you might."

"My dear man, I haven't a notion. I was coming upstairs to—" she stopped, she grinned—"well, to powder my nose, and the lights went out and I felt I was dead, that's all I know. Mighty disappointing—death is just a cluck and everything goes away from you and you're nothing."

"You didn't die," said Reggie grimly.

"Poor dear!" she laughed. "I should have been such a fine case for you. How unkind of me! But what the devil makes you think I was hit?"

"One thing and another. Bruise on your chin, way you fell——"

"Oh, fie! Quite upside down, wasn't I? Thank God my legs are well enough still. Isn't it a stupid world? The fashion is always unfair to a woman who has a decent shape. In my day I could show my body, but I might have been bandy, for all they knew. Now Alix lets you see a pretty pair of legs, but she has to pretend her body is nothing to matter. Well, our men had the best of it, I'll swear. We pretended we were respectable, and thank God we weren't. Now they advertise they haven't any morals, and they are as careful of themselves as invalids and as deadly earnest." She squealed laughter, she pointed a little claw of a hand at him. "Lord, that's hit you off. You're frightened of me."

"Yes. Wondering how long you were going on," said Reggie in a tone plaintive and bewildered as his face.

"Oh, bored! Poor child, you are modern. Why won't the nasty world be serious? So silly, so tiresome, and you're so clever and not feeling at all well."

"Rather tiresome, yes. I was saying—while you wouldn't listen—bruise on your chin, way you fell, and your tiara was gone: also the lights were put out, someone ran away, putting 'em out along the corridor in departure."

"You saw somebody!" she cried. "You brilliant creature. Who was it?"

"I only saw his shadow," Reggie corrected her.

Lady Rosnay made a grimace and quoted poetry in a recitative:

    " 'Some there be that shadows kiss;
    Such have but a shadow's bliss:

There be fools alive, I wis,
Silvered o'er; and so was this.' "

"I wondered what you were going to say about it," Reggie murmured.

"My dear boy, it's sleepwalking. If you're right, somebody was playing the fool—and if you're wrong—well so are you."

"No. I don't think so. Neither me nor the other fellow. Whether he had your tiara or not. By the way, why didn't you tell me last night it had been stolen?"

She laughed. "That's what's puzzling your poor head. Oh, you can be easy. I didn't tell you it had been stolen because it wasn't. It's safe in the bank today. Are you happy now?"

"Not to notice. No. Facts are being so delusive. What about Luttrell? Isn't he dead, after all? He seemed very dead when I examined him. But your tiara had been pulled out of your hair when I found you, and yet it isn't gone."

Lady Rosnay stared at him, and under the paint her wrinkles deepened. "Oh, Luttrell," she said. "I don't know anything about that. Poor devil! He'll be as sorry to die as any man ever I knew."

"Yes, you may be right. I wonder why he died here."

"In his vocation. Chattering at a party. Lord, he's been a rotten life this twenty years."

"Chattering, yes," Reggie murmured. "Whom was he chattering to when he died?"

"Not to me," Lady Rosnay said sharply. "You had me in bed."

"Oh, yes. Yes. Perfect alibi. Did you ask him here last night?"

"My dear man! People weren't asked, they were sold tickets," she laughed. "I don't suppose Bertie Luttrell paid for his."

"You asked me." Reggie was plaintive. "Why did you?"

"To amuse me. You did, my dear. You were sweet as your smug ancestor. A dream of innocence. But you're not amusing today. You're being earnest. It makes me so tired. Go away. Cupid hates you." She pinched the monkey and made him scold. She turned over, reaching for the bell.

"Thanks very much," Reggie stopped the arm. "I can find my way."

She let her arm fall. She lay looking up at him with a queer impish stare, defiant, mocking. "What a clever creature!" she said.

"Oh, no. No. Only careful," Reggie murmured. "Goodbye."

He found his way to the white drawing room. Alix and Darett were still there. "Well, well." He gazed at them dreamily. "She's making a good recovery from this, Miss Lynn. But we'll have to watch her. I thought you'd like to know."

He went out.

Chapter VI

In the Vineyard

MR. FORTUNE has been heard to accuse himself of laxity in the conduct of this case. His argument is that from the moment when he found Lady Rosnay unconscious he had in his possession evidence sufficient to guide him to his final, effective action, which should therefore have been taken much earlier, early enough to save a life or two. He explains that he did not recognize the significant evidence when he observed it, because he had such a confused mass of facts variously relevant thrust upon him by chance and by the enemy, but he will not allow this to be an excuse. A proper energy and rigor of thought, he insists, would have shown him what he must work on, but the mind was slack, content to be careful, to file everything for reference and seek more.

The criticism of the chief of the Criminal Investigation Department on this is not patent: to the effect that it is superfluous of Mr. Fortune to fancy he might have been more diabolical than he was.

By such censure Mr. Fortune is aggrieved. He will protest that his methods were of a clear simplicity and gentleness.

It is true, many people find those qualities in him. The Quintons are convinced that friendship with them and his general kindliness were the origin of his interest in Molly Marne. So they speak of this case with a certain awe, a thrill in their honest and pathetic indignation.

An ability to make people do what he wants in the belief that they arranged it all themselves accounts for some of Mr. Fortune's popularity. There is no more devoted couple in London, of the husbands and wives whose relations are public property, than the Quintons. They have been on the stage as long as anyone remembers. They were each, for incredible years, the first choice for parts of innocent young love. They have become supreme in playing dear old people. Conventional cynicism tells half a truth when it insists that at no time in their lives have they known anything about acting. They have been content to put themselves into any and every play, but it needed art to show themselves so clearly. With a pleasant candor they display what they are just as well off the stage. Generation after

44

generation of gossip has its stories of the Quintons' naive affection and universal tenderness shining in a naughty world.

Quinton is a man of several clubs, for his wife likes him to be manly. He uses them little, but he is in all things methodical. In the hour before dinner on a Tuesday Reggie knew where to find him.

It became clear to Quinton that Mr. Fortune was in need of sympathy. His wife, he let fall like a brave man bearing sorrow, had gone into the country and lingered there, he talked to Quinton as if he had no one else to talk to, he asked wistfully after Mrs. Quinton, as one forgotten by her and all the world. No human condition could more appeal to Quinton. He set himself to comfort Mr. Fortune by telling him all about her and how good she was in her last part.

Sorrowfully, still like a man excluded from the innocent delights his nature craved, Reggie agreed. He also thought she had been delicious—at her perfect best—herself. He discussed the play and her, but chiefly her.

Quinton asked him home to dinner. Alas, he could not. He was cursed with work. But he would walk with Quinton across the park. They walked. He was persuaded into the little Kensington house because Quinton would never be forgiven if Reggie went away without seeing Mrs. Quinton.

She made much of him, and he frankly liked it, though he remained a trifle plaintive. He talked about her in the play and other plays and her. But he would not agree this play had been quite good. She gave him a motherly cross-examination. He labored his answers, he did not know what was the matter, perhaps it was Molly Marne.

The Quintons can be relied on to stand up for anybody who is not known to be cruel. Something of reproach came into Mrs. Quinton's nice voice; there was some vigor in her effort to make him say why Molly Marne did not please him. He was vague. Quite clever, yes, quite strong with her emotions, rather showy, perhaps, rather too much ego about it, matter of taste, people are what they are. His answers dwindled into civil nothings.

Mrs. Quinton told him that Molly was a darling. Of course she had to force a part like that. It was in the character to be violent. A horrid woman, of course, but people would have that sort of story, just hungry passion. Nobody could have done it so well as Molly. Really it was a shame she always had to play that type. People thought she was just the same herself. But she wasn't the least bit. Just a dear child. Anybody could do anything with Molly. She only wanted you to like her. Nothing more, nothing more at all. She didn't care about men the least bit. She was just altogether an artist. She really lived to act.

"Absolute devotion, yes," Mr. Fortune murmured. It appeared that his interest in the subject was only sustained by courtesy. He talked of other things and chiefly himself and with a mild melancholy.

The sympathetic hearts of the Quintons felt that he needed something festive: as a woman Mrs. Quinton desired to educate him. They invited him to lunch at the Vineyard.

It was then the restaurant most in favor with their profession. Reggie arrived before his time and sat patiently in the anteroom. He had some hope that Molly Marne would be visible.

Everybody was in a hurry, everybody was very friendly, he felt the languor of a guest in a large, too happy family before the Quintons came. They at least contrived to maintain their natural placidity through the obligatory manner of being pressed for time. They sat down, and in the intervals of greeting the swift arrivals and departures Mrs. Quinton drank a soft cocktail while Reggie was allowed to take longer over sherry than Quinton. But as soon as he had finished she announced that it was no use waiting for Molly.

"Molly?" Reggie looked puzzled.

"Molly Marne, you know."

"Oh, ah. Yes."

"She said she would come. But she's so vague."

No restaurant makes a greater show of scurrying waiters than the Vineyard. They were bustled through the rush, through kindly noises to a table of honor. The head waiter was voluble—knew just what Mrs. Quinton would like—and fled.

"Jolly place," Reggie murmured.

What she had to like came fast. They had eaten melon, they had eaten fried sole, cold chicken was before them when Mrs. Quinton gave a fluting cry of joy.

Molly Marne stood at the door of the restaurant, looking into its flurry as if she could see no one, came forward a little, giving people who spoke to her little smiles, automatic but pleasant, which for their moments made her pretty face look alive.

The head waiter darted at her and led her on the Quintons. She followed slowly, turning to stare this way and that, wide-eyed as Reggie had seen her at the ball and still as if she could not see anyone. But her blue eyes had become darker. The pupils were of their full size.

Mrs. Quinton was affectionately cross with her. She answered in jerks, fussed at arranging herself. Reggie was introduced to her, was granted a smile and a look from under her eyelashes, and she had no more interest in him. She had no interest in anything. She would not have a cocktail. Melon—she did not know—it came, and she played with it and let the Quintons talk.

She ate little. She drank water. She could not be still. She listened or made a show of listening and had a charming smile to show at most of the right places. When she answered, it seemed that she had to think first and found it hard.

Reggie asked her about her next part, and even that did not make her talk. It was the usual thing—oh, yes, she liked it—she did not know when they would begin. There came a nervous movement of her head, as if she were in pain.

Mrs. Quinton had to be anxiously maternal.

No, that was nothing. She was perfectly well. She always was. Oh, please don't fuss.

Mrs. Quinton was sure she ought to have a rest—go right away and just be a vegetable, darling.

"Perhaps I will," said Molly.

And that was the end of it—of all that mattered.

Mr. Fortune took away with him a memory of a pretty baby's face which had been carelessly made up, which was wan and pinched, of tired, unseeing eyes, of a mind distracted by some struggle.

The memory was to haunt him. When he is inclined to be pleased with himself it comes back still.

A night or two afterwards Lomas rang him up. "Is that you, Reginald? Oh, you are alive. Good. Have you made anything more of that case?"

"What is the case?" Reggie moaned.

"Whatever you like to call it—the Luttrell death, the Rosnay mystery."

"Don't call it anything," Reggie mumbled. "It's shapeless, it's insubstantial. Isn't a case."

"You've got nowhere?"

"Haven't moved. Don't know which way to move."

"My dear fellow," Lomas chuckled. "How correct of you! How admirable! Come and see me in the morning, will you?"

Chapter VII

Behind the Speaker's Chair

LOMAS was in conference with Superintendent Bell. "What it comes to is, you can't find out anything about him," he said sharply.

"Nothing against him, sir," Bell corrected. "It's pretty plain he hasn't got any money to spare, he lives very quiet and decent in that little flat, but he goes everywhere and he makes a good deal of splash. I'd say there's a lot of public men like that, besides Mr. Osmond."

"Quite. 'We ain't got much money but we do see life,' " Lomas quoted. "Not good enough, Bell."

"He's a queer fellow," said Bell slowly. "No doubt about it. What you might call a mystery man. He goes off secret every now and then by what the porter at the flats says. But there, that's in the line of these clever climbers. Kind of advertising stunt to set people asking, 'Wherever is Mr. Osmond?' "

"Yes, that might be." Lomas lit a cigarette. "Better see if you can dig up something about his past."

As Bell went out Reggie came in. "Hullo, Bell!" He nodded at the solemn face. "Are we downhearted? Yes." He collapsed into an easy chair and looked dislike at Lomas. "What's the matter with you?"

"Have you heard what people are saying?" Lomas asked cheerfully.

"My dear chap! Oh my dear chap," Reggie sighed. "Not me, no. I try to be a rational animal. In spite of association with officials. Why do you listen? It's a futile instinct. When somebody's telephonin' near you, you try to overhear, you don't want to, you know what's being said don't matter a hoot to you, but you strain to pick up scraps. Primitive instinct—useless in present stage of human evolution—very strong still. That's what makes gossip flourish. Made the fortune of the late Luttrell. No, thank you. I don't want to hear what people are saying. Not any more. I heard Luttrell, I've heard Lady Rosnay. Result, paralysis of the faculties. 'Thy hand, great Anarch, lets the curtain fall and universal darkness covers all.' "

Lomas laughed. "You're not feeling effective, Reginald? I don't say you're wrong. We haven't been very effective, have we? I'm not bothered about that. There's really nothing to justify any police action. But the case is taking a deuced nasty shape."

"What case?" Reggie moaned. "Isn't a case. Told you that before."

Lomas smiled. "You're devilish precise."

"Precise!" Reggie's voice went up. "My only aunt! Precise! Like a baby definin' a jellyfish."

"Well, I'm talking about the Luttrell-Rosnay affair," said Lomas briskly. "Let's get on. There is some very nasty stuff going round. I've heard it myself in different quarters. The Home Secretary had me over last night asking what I knew about it. The gist of it is that Osmond was the fellow who knocked Lady Rosnay down, that he stole her tiara, and that he did Luttrell in because Luttrell knew too much, accused him or was standing in with him or tried to blackmail him—pay your money and take your choice."

"Yes. It could be," Reggie murmured. "Some of it. Any of it."

"What?" Lomas's mouth remained dumbly open before it began to laugh. "My dear Reginald, you've got into reverse by mistake. You're going backwards violently. A minute ago, you gave me a lecture on the folly of listening to gossip. Now you advise me to believe it. I don't expect the scientific mind to be consistent, but this is too spasmodic."

"Oh, no. No contradiction," Reggie said wearily. "Osmond may be the villain of the piece. Or villain of one act. Quite possible. Fact that gossip says so isn't evidence. But you shouldn't let it put you off. People do sometimes tell the truth. Unintentionally."

"Well, suppose you assume I have some intelligence—" Lomas snapped.

"My dear chap! Oh my dear chap. I do. I'm flatterin' it," Reggie soothed him. "I'm being quite subtle."

"I don't believe what people say," Lomas went on still with some indignation. "What interests me is that this is the sort of thing which is being said—there's a set of feeling against Osmond."

"Yes. The point is well taken," Reggie purred. "That is interesting. Probably significant. Probably fundamental to everything. But we're only seeing shadows, Lomas. As I was saying. Still only shadows." He sighed and contemplated Lomas in a vague and plaintive stare. "However. Never excluding the possibility some of the shadows are veracious—possibility that Osmond did do these little jobs. It exists. You notice that. Luttrell didn't love Osmond. He was handing me scandal about Osmond just before he died. Pleasant thought for him now, if he can think. Who handed you the new edition? You said the Home Secretary. He can't be loving Osmond very dearly. And Osmond's the risin' fighter of the opposition." He raised an enquiring eyebrow. "What about that?"

"You mean the government would like Osmond smashed. Yes, they would. Party feeling will boil up this sort of stuff all right. But I don't believe the whole thing is a trick in the party game. How could it be? Party tactics may spring a scandal on a man at the moment it's going to hurt most. That's a good old dodge. But there has to be something substantial to work on first. Parties don't contrive crime—don't engineer a man into a mess—they only advertise he's in it. Little Sykes"—he referred to the Home Secretary—"was quite correct. He's not a bad fellow for a politician. Brains enough to know what people won't stand and decent, cowardly instincts. The way he put it was, asking if we were doing any work on the rumors about Osmond and insisting that we must be very careful, it wouldn't do for the police to be accused of playing party politics."

"Oh, yes. Very correct," Reggie murmured. "We're all being very correct. And people go on dying by murders which aren't murder."

"People?" Lomas enquired. "Oh, damn, you're going back to that Poyntz case again. You can't link that with Luttrell."

"You think not? It's linked with Lady Rosnay. She linked it."

"Because she talked about it! Lord, all the town talked about it."

"What links Luttrell's death with Osmond? Luttrell talked about him. And all the town goes on talking."

"There's nothing to any of it but talk," said Lomas. "What have you made of it? Mrs. Poyntz killed herself—no possible doubt. Poyntz's death was accident or suicide. Luttrell—death from disease—with a chance that he may have been struck by a blow which may have hastened it."

"As you say," Reggie murmured. "And Lady Rosnay was hit by somebody unknown—and her tiara vanished—and she says she don't know she was hit and her tiara's safe in the bank. And Molly Marne who came to the fatal ball full of morphia isn't using morphia any more—and finding life difficult—either she can't get morphia now or she's trying to do without it. Anyway, she's wretched. Yes. That's all I've made of it. The rest is talk."

"Wait a moment," Lomas protested. "Where are we? What's this stuff about the Rosnay? She wants us to believe she wasn't assaulted and the tiara wasn't stolen? Nothing happened except that she stumbled and fell?"

"Yes. That's what she pretends. And that isn't true. She was hit. And someone ran away. I know that. I don't know her tiara was taken, but I haven't any doubt. You hadn't any doubt. A woman don't put away her diamonds in the middle of a ball."

"Then what on earth is her game?" Lomas frowned.

"I haven't the slightest idea," Reggie murmured. "Talked about that before, didn't we? I told you she took this line on first recovery of consciousness—nothing had happened to bother about, nothing was gone—that was before Luttrell died—say, before she could be sure Luttrell was dead—she now continues on the same line—though Luttrell's death bothers her. She may be protecting the villain of the piece, she may be trying to deal with him some way of her own, the whole thing may be a put-up job. No inference justified. All the rest is talk. But as you say, it has interest. While Lady Rosnay tells us there's nothing to talk about, the talk grows and grows, and it's just the sort of talk against Osmond that Luttrell was giving me before somebody managed that he should die."

"So far as that means anything," said Lomas carefully, "it goes against Osmond. It points to bad feeling between him and Luttrell."

"Feeling—I don't know. Luttrell was working against Osmond, and Luttrell was eliminated. That's the sequence of facts. Looks like cause and effect. Only part of the case that does look like anything definite. The rest— the rest boils down to two unsatisfactory conclusions: somebody knows a lot that we can't get near, and somebody's managing the whole business. The mischief makers, unlimited." He looked at Lomas with melancholy, reproachful eyes. "I said that before," he moaned.

"You did, Reginald," Lomas smiled. "Nice phrase. And so helpful."

"Don't be unkind. I can't bear it. I know I'm not helping. The mind is flaccid. And we've got a devilish case. People bein' done to death for somebody's profit—or pleasure—yes, it might be pleasure—there's more beastly work going on—there must be—and I can't find a way to it. Consciousness of absolute futility. Very depressing. And I have been quite good in my time. The powers are failing."

"Not one idea in your head?" said Lomas cheerfully.

"No useful idea," Reggie moaned. "No. Lots of questions probably crucial. If I knew what was in the letters Mrs. Poyntz burnt—if I knew how Molly Marne took to morphia—my hat, if I only knew why she's gone off it!"

"Where does she come in?" Lomas was suddenly interested.

"I don't know. Luttrell said she came in as Osmond's discarded love. Mrs. Quinton says she never cared for any man. She wandered into the Osmond circle at the ball—Osmond and Alix, Harleys and Daretts, old uncle Tom Cobley and all."

"Rather odd." Lomas lit a cigarette. "Would you be surprised to hear one of the things in the gossip about Osmond is that he uses morphia?"

"Well, well," Reggie murmured. "Surprised? No. Interested, yes. Quite interested."

"You think it's likely?"

"My dear chap! Oh my dear chap. No evidence. I saw nothing to suggest it when I did see him. In the abstract—nothing unusual for a showy kind of man to keep the show going on drugs."

"If he does, it would account for his being rather violent and erratic, wouldn't it?"

"Yes, that is so. Erratic is good."

"Well, he has been, you know. Quite apart from all this business. That's his public form. I'd like you to have a look at him, Reginald. As a matter of fact that has been suggested to me—"

"Oh. The Home Secretary?" said Reggie.

"No. He did ask me if I'd heard anything of Osmond not being well, but no mention of drugs. Some of the fellows on Osmond's own side were saying he seemed rather unstable these days, it looked as if he were on the edge of a nervous breakdown. My idea was, we might look in at the House some night when he was going to let off one of his big bangs."

"Me go to the House of Commons?" Reggie was shrill. "Oh my Lomas!"

"You could tell if he'd wound himself up with a drug, couldn't you?"

Reggie groaned. "I might. Yes. What is life that one should seek it? Well, well. Duty, stern daughter of the voice of God! Thou dost preserve the stars from wrong. Oh Mr. Wordsworth! I don't preserve anybody. However. Faithful unto death. Warn me for the sacrifice, Lomas. Goodbye. I hate you."

A few days passed before the warning came. Lomas rang him up at the hospital laboratory where he was comforting himself with a new investigation of the common cold. Osmond was going to lead a grand attack on the government that night. It was to be sprung as a surprise. It would come on late. The food prices bill was the business on report stage. Nobody liked it, and the government's own people least of all. The scheme was that the opposition would keep up a dull routine debate till ten o'clock or so, as if they were going to let the thing through without trouble. Then Osmond would get up with a slashing speech to taunt all the malcontents on the government side into running amuck. "Sort of thing he does deuced well," Lomas chuckled. "He ought to raise Cain if he's in form. See the idea? The opposition are going to bring down every man. The government people will be taken off their guard, and some of their wild men should go against 'em. Rather good, what?"

"Yes. We are not amused," Reggie moaned. "My only aunt! What have I done that I should have to go into politics? I am a serious mind."

"Quite. This is serious. Just the sort of occasion we wanted. Osmond will have to be doing his damnedest. That should show up the alleged drug habit."

"Very obliging of Mr. Osmond. Yes. Who told you all this?"

Again a chuckle came over the telephone. "Straight from the stable, Reginald. One of the opposition whips. Don't talk about it. It's got to be kept secret or it won't work."

"Oh, yes. I see. That's why they told you. Innocent trade, politics. Well, well."

"What's the matter?"

"I was only wondering why you were told," said Reggie plaintively. "We live by faith, we cannot know—maxims for the Criminal Investigation Department by the Hon. S. Lomas. I suppose you dismissed the vulgar thought that somebody might be managing you—directing you to watch Osmond tonight?"

"Too clever, Reginald. I was told because I asked to be told when Osmond was down for his next big speech. That's all. Come and dine with me at the Academies and we'll go down to the House after."

The lights of Palace Yard were dim behind a steaming rain when their cab drove in, one of a line of cabs and cars. They found the lobby busy. "Several people seem to have been told, Lomas," Reggie murmured, contemplating under the droll statues some women in evening dress. Alix Lynn was among them, and Mrs. Harley. He saw the exuberant bulk of Sir David Kames in vigorous attendance.

"Come along. We don't want to show," Lomas muttered and led the way to the seats behind the speaker's chair, whence officials of importance watch over the antics of their masters.

Two unhappy men in charge of the president of the Board of Trade and his food prices bill looked at them with gloomy wonder. "Fortune wanted to see the show for once in his life," Lomas smiled. "He's very young."

Reggie sat and sighed. The air was of the staleness of a vault, the place dowdy beyond his imagination. He gazed up at the glare of the tawdry glass ceiling, blinked and turned weary eyes to the strangers' gallery. It was already nearly full, and in a front place he saw the red head of Alix beside some blonde comeliness which must be Mrs. Harley.

The front benches on either side still showed the bareness of a night on which nothing would be allowed to happen, but the rest of the green leather was already populous and noisy. A plump man was on his legs, talking fast in a voice of indomitable self-satisfaction. He annoyed nobody, nobody listened. They were absorbed in their own chatter.

"Ever been in the parrot house, Lomas?" Reggie mumbled. "Same standards. Better to look at. Better atmosphere."

Lomas smiled. "They're suffering from excitement. It isn't going according to plan. The government crowd have been warned there's something up. Never mind. All the more of a fight for Osmond. Better test."

Eminent persons came to their places with an accidental manner, put heads together, turned and talked to subordinate heads. A little man bustled round the back of the opposition benches, whispering here and there, came to the front bench and conferred with its leader. From the other side rose a cheer of derision growing louder as he hurried out again. Ministers joined obtrusively in the laugh, and one of them scrawled a note and tossed it across to the opposition front bench. It was read, it was passed from hand to hand with defiant mirth, and an answer flung back.

Harley came into the House, paused a moment at the Bar, talking to some of the little crowd waiting there on events, and stalked deliberately to a commanding corner seat. Its occupant made room for him, more than room, men near leaned over to talk. He answered shortly, he sat back and made himself comfortable.

Lomas stared at him, frowning. The little bustling opposition whip entered again by the door behind the speaker, edged along the front bench, found a place, and whispered something which was passed on to his leader.

"Hallo!" Lomas whispered. "What's up now? Looks like no Osmond."

"Well, well," Reggie murmured and through closing eyes contemplated the high far-off shapes of Alix Lynn and Mrs. Harley. They were both leaning over to scan the House. They talked together.

The plump orator glanced at the clock, glanced at Harley and the empty space beside him, glanced at his front bench, and brought himself to a conclusion of resounding vacuity. He was hilariously cheered. A head bobbed up beside him and wished to withdraw the amendment. Cheers rose louder and merrier.

A still small voice of weary detachment came from the speaker's chair, announcing that the amendment was by leave withdrawn. Then the cheers broke out again and louder still, half jeering, half angry.

Harley was on his feet. He waited for silence with bland composure. His tone, when he could be heard, was quiet and pleasant. He was the man of affairs concerned only to deal with a serious matter reasonably. But soon into his plain arguments came irony, and irony developed into satire, into taunts and jibes which smarted till the weaker, wilder heads on the government benches gave tongue and answered him according to their folly.

He remained bland. He sharpened his attack, and his phrasing was of a more studied, a more contemptuous civility. He was condescending to the wild men. He mocked their moderate leaders. And always he kept up an argument which sounded smooth and fair. He infuriated, he sowed distrust.

When he sat down, the House set up a roar, not so much applause of him as challenge of party to party, outburst of inflamed temper.

"Done deuced well," Lomas muttered.

"Oh, yes. Yes. Just like a fellow teasing dogs," Reggie sighed. "How long do they go on barking?"

They went on for some time. A man who was not Osmond rose behind Harley and raucously seconded him. From a general uprising of the benches opposite the Speaker chose a man of fluent moral fervor. "Oh, no! No!" Reggie moaned and made his way out.

Lomas followed. "You're quite right, Reginald," he agreed. "No use waiting. They'll be at it all night, but Osmond's missed the bus. I wonder what the deuce has happened. Half a minute, old man." He sped away, he buttonholed the hurrying little whip, who did not take it well.

Reggie heard impatience. "What's your trouble? … Quite a good show, wasn't it? … Harley was great, got 'em biting each other's bellies. . . . Osmond? I don't know. He's not in the house. I haven't heard from him. It doesn't matter a damn." The whip escaped.

Lomas came back looking black.

"And that is that," Reggie murmured.

"Yes, rather a flop."

"I wouldn't say that. No. Somebody arranged for you to come and hear Mr. Osmond just when Mr. Osmond didn't find it convenient to talk to you. That's very interesting. We are being managed."

Lomas swore thoughtfully.

"Yes, as you say." Reggie murmured. "Good-night."

Chapter VIII

The Dressing Table

AFTER breakfast next morning Reggie sat on the small of his back smoking a pipe. This is normal. The abnormalities which surprised Mrs. Fortune were that he did not talk, that he was reading, and that he read the papers.

It is not the least of her charms that she never asks for explanations. She pulled his more accessible ear and went out.

Reggie continued to read. The debate had gone on into the small hours and a row. Osmond's name did not appear. Those parliamentary sketch writers who were picturesque made something of his absence: remarking on the strange disappointment of expectation that he would be in the forefront of the battle, and contrasting—not to his advantage—his "Rupert of debate" style with the cool, shrewd tactics of Harley. By Harley they were all impressed. Of the cause of Osmond's absence no word was in any paper. Lobby correspondents left their statement that Mr. Osmond was not in the House to do what work its bald significance could.

Reggie shut his eyes and continued to smoke. He was in that condition when the parlormaid asked if he would see Superintendent Bell. He waggled an acquiescent head.

"Hallo, Bell." His eyes opened to gaze sadly at Bell's square shape. "What are you going to tell me? Found Osmond in the fountains in Trafalgar Square, full confession in the left boot?"

Bell swallowed. "No, sir. I don't know anything about Mr. Osmond. Miss Molly Marne has been found dead."

Reggie squirmed himself upright. His round face was pale. He stared fear. "God help us!" he muttered.

"It's like this, Mr. Fortune: Miss Marne has a little place down at Maidford, what you might call a country cottage, though it's more or less in the town. She's been in the habit of running down there odd times whenever the fancy took her. She didn't keep servants in the place unless she was making a stay. The wife of the man who does the garden used to come in and do for her. She gave out she wanted to be quiet there. I've heard of other actresses using a place like that," Bell frowned dark meaning

"Go on, go on," Reggie mumbled.

"Well, sir, she phoned the woman yesterday she was coming. She got there after tea time, in a taxi—the woman thinks it was a taxi from London. She told the woman not to stay, and when the woman asked about her dinner, she said she'd get that herself and laughed, and the woman just let her know what food there was in the house and went off. As she was going she heard that Miss Marne had turned the bath on. And that's the last thing we know of Miss Marne being alive. Some time after six o'clock last night she had the bathwater running in. This morning the woman went round soon after eight. Everything all in order. But there was no sign of any dinner having been ate. The food wasn't touched. About nine o'clock she took tea up to the bedroom. When she knocked, no answer. Curtains were drawn, Miss Marne lying in bed. The woman spoke to her and she didn't stir, took hold of her and found she was dead and cold. That's what we've got, Mr. Fortune."

Reggie sprang up. "Come on," he said fiercely. "Come on."

"My car's here, sir." Bell followed him out.

The police car shot through needle-eye spaces in clotted traffic. "How did this get to you, Bell?" Reggie murmured.

"The woman ran out for help, and somebody fetched a doctor and somebody fetched the police."

"Oh, yes. Yes. Why did the police of Maidford run out and fetch you?"

Bell cleared his throat. "Well, it's like this: We've been looking up Mr. Osmond's habits, as you might say. Last week I asked the super at Maidford if he happened to know anything of Mr. Osmond going to Miss Marne's place down there. He didn't. He'd never heard of men going to her. But when this happened, he naturally passed it on to me good and quick."

"Quite natural. Yes," Reggie murmured. "Everything is so natural. You start trying to connect Osmond with Molly Marne and the first news you get is she's found dead. I suppose we're going to find it's another of these natural deaths. Who set you working out a connection between Molly Marne and Osmond?"

"That was one of Mr. Lomas's suggestions," said Bell.

Reggie moaned. "Lomas put you onto it. I put Lomas onto it. And then this. We are being useful." His voice went up. "Too damn useful! We're letting ourselves be managed. We're thinkin' what some devil wants us to think—doin' what some devil wants us to do." Bell was shocked. It is not Mr. Fortune's habit to speak profanely. He was also puzzled when the high angry voice fell to a melancholy drone. " 'One, two, buckle my shoe. Three, four, knock at the door—' " and Reggie laughed—" 'Five, six, pickin' up sticks'—I wonder."

"Beg your pardon, sir," said Bell heavily. "I don't quite get you."

"That's the way it goes. Four people dead—three of 'em not bad people—and we make a game of it. How many more yet, Bell? How many more before we think of something to do about it? Feelin' pleased with yourself? I am not."

"There's been nothing we could do in any of these cases," Bell grunted.

"Oh my Bell! Good answer for the day of judgment. We couldn't find anything we could do to interfere with the devil. Nice proud answer. My God! What are we for?"

Bell did not offer any theory.

Molly Marne's cottage was in the shape of a small, suburban villa red and raw. It stood by itself with a conventional garden on every side in a road which served others like it.

A constable met them at the gate and conducted them up the gravel walk to the porch. They had not set foot on the mat which covered the step when the door was opened by a man in plain clothes. "Good-morning, Mr. Bell. You'd like to see her first, eh? She's just as she was except for the doctor examining her, and he didn't move her much."

They went up to the bedroom. It was a pleasant place, full of sunshine. All its color was gentle, pale blue and pale yellow on walls and floor and curtains and bed; it had little furniture, and what it had was silver gray. The only untidiness was a little heap of woman's clothes.

Molly Marne lay on her back. The sheet at her bosom and the pillow were smooth, as if she had never moved from the moment she came to bed. Her eyes were closed. In death her small, pretty face was more than ever like a doll's—a doll of long service. The smooth color of her complexion had gone, blotched by water or sweat; her cheeks were of a livid pallor.

"She looks ill," Bell muttered.

Reggie opened her eyes. In the dull blue stare of them the pupils were no more than points of black. He looked into them a moment, and his face was without expression. He waved Bell away and began to lay bare her body.

When Bell saw him again he was standing away from the bed on which the body and the face, too, lay covered. He contemplated them with the solemn and plaintive curiosity of a puzzled child.

"Well, well," he murmured and turned to the table at the bedside. Beside the lamp on it was a small tube of white metal. "Have they gone over everything for fingerprints?" he asked. "Find out, will you?"

When Bell came back, he was inspecting the dressing table. "No, sir, nothing done yet. Not much time."

"No. Not much good, either. However. Try everything. The fingerprint expert must do that tube. Then I want it." He remained by the dressing table.

His interest in it puzzled Bell. It was orderly, it had nothing but the usual toilet apparatus. Reggie smelt at an atomizer and smelt at a powder puff, smelt at a flagon of scent and smelt again. He lingered over them, sad and curious. Then he opened a drawer of the dressing table, looked into it, shut it, and tried the next one. From that he took out gingerly first a bottle of scent and then a makeup case. The bottle was half empty. He drew the cork and smelt it. The fragrance appeared to give him a certain melancholy satisfaction. But that did not endure. He examined the bottle's label and frowned, he held the bottle up for the light to come through it, turned it at different angles, and set it down with a sigh and gave his attention to the makeup case.

Bell took up the bottle. The label on it was printed with a cubist pattern in which the only words were "*Le Matin d'un Faune.*" Bell read them out in a broad English accent: "Funny names these perfumes have. Means 'morning of a faun,' don't it? A faun—that's a sort of imp?"

"Yes. Immoral child of nature," Reggie mumbled; he was going over the apparatus of the makeup case article by article.

" 'Morning of a faun,' " Bell repeated. "Don't seem to mean much."

"Not musical, are you?" Reggie murmured. "Reference to precious poem and popular musical composition '*L'après-midi d'un faune.*' Languid and sensuous. A faun in the afternoon. '*Le matin d'un faune*'—the faun feelin' full of naughty charm."

"I see. Catchy with some women," Bell disapproved. He pulled out the cork and sniffed. "Oh, sort of hay-making smell—grass just been cut on a hot day—I suppose they get the stuff out of clover."

"That's what you're meant to suppose," Reggie mumbled. "Not likely. No. Amyl salicylate and some of the acetic ethers. Probably made from coal tar."

"Is it a poison, Mr. Fortune?"

"My dear chap! Oh my dear chap!" Reggie moaned. "Shouldn't drink it. Might be depressin'. But not a means to repose."

"You seemed to think it was important," Bell persisted.

"Did I? I don't know what's important," Reggie murmured. He was giving to tubes of lipstick profound consideration. He put them in the case again and stepped back to stand gazing dreamily at the dressing table as if he hoped for visions in its triple mirrors. "Yes. I want all those things," he murmured. "All the cosmetics."

He turned away and wandered about the room, looked in the wardrobe. The dresses inside were few and simple. He took down one after another and turned them over. He came back to the little heap of clothes which someone had flung on a chair in confusion.

By them he stopped, and his solemn eyes questioned Bell. "Anything occur to you?"

"Looks as if she'd been in a hurry to get to bed," said Bell. "But there—I wouldn't say—some of these young women are shocking untidy."

"Yes. That is so. However. The clothes in the wardrobe are tidy. The drawers of the dressing table are very neat. And yet she tumbled this frock off anyhow. Pretty frock, too." He lifted one garment after another and from underneath them a hat. "I think she was in a hurry," he murmured. He picked up her handbag. It contained some money, two handkerchiefs, a tube of lipstick, and a flat gold case to hold powder and mirror. That interested him. It was not quite so thin as most of its kind. He frowned at it. He looked closely at the metal before he opened it. But it showed only the usual mirror on one side, powder on the other. Round the edge of the mirror he moved a fingernail, found a spring, and the mirror opened on a hinge.

"I never saw one like that," said Bell.

"No. Very interestin'," Reggie mumbled.

"I've heard of 'em," said Bell grimly.

"I'm so respectable," Reggie moaned. "That hampers me."

"Made to carry drugs, sir," Bell informed him.

"Fancy that," Reggie sighed. The space behind the mirror was empty, but the inside of the gold case was marked with tiny circles, and round the edge were specks of white dust.

"Look there," Bell grunted triumph.

"I see. Yes. My dear chap, you're marvelous." Reggie gazed at him. "Now we know, don't we?" With delicate care he shut the mirror, he shut the case and put it back in the bag. "Well, well. Turn the fingerprint hounds loose." Bell nodded and strode out.

Reggie moved slowly to the bedside and uncovered the dead face, stood looking down at it.

He heard a hurry of footsteps. He drew a long breath, moved the sheet over her face again, and turned away.

The fingerprint men stood back to let him pass, and when he was gone, "My oath!" one of them winked. "Somebody's for it all right, all right. He's got his hanging face on."

He found Bell in a brisk conference with the local superintendent. They broke it off as he appeared, and their manner was expectant. "Well, well." He dropped into a chair. The determination of his face was lost in languor. "What did your doctor say?"

"He had no doubt she died of poisoning, sir," the superintendent answered. "Morphia, he said."

"Yes. It could be. Provisionally one of the narcotic poisons. Taken by the mouth. That's the present medical evidence. That's all." He looked at them forlornly. "I'll have to do a lot of work," he moaned.

"By the mouth," the superintendent repeated. "No sign of it being given in any food or drink here. Do you think it was administered to her before she came?"

"Not likely, no."

"Would you say she poisoned herself?"

"I shouldn't say. She may have taken the stuff voluntarily. Whether she knew what she was taking, I don't know."

"Ah." The superintendent made a joyful noise. "Now you come and have a look at this, sir."

Reggie was conducted to the front door. The superintendent took up the mat which covered the step outside and pointed to footprints in dried yellow mud on the stone.

"Oh, yes. A man's feet?" Reggie murmured.

"That's right," the superintendent nodded. He brought them back into the house again. "See what it means, Mr. Fortune?" he grinned.

"No. I don't. No. I don't know what anything means."

"Well, it's a bit tricky," said the superintendent complacently. "Now look here. That step was cleaned yesterday morning. They don't have the mat outside like you saw. If you remember, it was fine all day, it didn't begin to rain till seven or so—after Miss Marne got here, after the charwoman went home. When I came round this morning those footprints were on the step and dry. If you think that over you'll see something. The man who made those footprints came after a good drop of rain or he wouldn't have got the gravel of the path on his shoes. So you see there was a man called on Miss Marne last night when she was alone."

"Quite good. Yes. It could be," Reggie murmured.

"It was," the superintendent chuckled. "I've got more than that, Mr. Fortune. You may have heard that Superintendent Bell asked me if I knew anything of a certain gentleman visiting Miss Marne." The superintendent cleared his throat. "It's rather a delicate matter, isn't it? I had a good man on this beat and told him to keep his eyes open. Last night about ten to half-past he was coming along and saw a car by the house here. Misty rain there was, you know. As he got near, a man came along the path from the house in a devil of a hurry and nipped into the car and drove off. Thickset fellow, he says, and that's all he knows, but he got the number of the car. Not bad work. I'm told the car belongs to—well, you know who."

"Our Mr. Osmond," Reggie murmured and looked plaintively at Bell. "Yes. He does get into things, doesn't he? After the passin' of the man Osmond, did your policeman notice if there was any light in the house?"

"He couldn't see any. He went up to the door and rang—no, he didn't stand on the step, I asked him careful—his idea was to ask if the house was all right, just to see what he could fish out. But he couldn't get an answer. So that looks as if Miss Marne was dead or past helping herself when the gentleman went away."

"Yes. That is indicated."

"And you're not sure she knew she was taking poison," said the superintendent triumphantly. "There's your case for you, Mr. Bell."

"Not a nice case, no," Reggie sighed. "Well, well. Have these
fingerprinters done their worst? I want to get on." He gazed pathetically at
the two men. "I have a lot to do," he moaned. He drifted out.

When he came back he had in his hands the white metal tube from the
bed table and the handbag.

"Just finishing," he murmured. "I want the body sent up to me as quick
as you can. I want all the things from the dressing table,"—he sat down and
scribbled a list—"these things."

"The dressing table!" the superintendent exclaimed.

"Oh, yes. Very important," Reggie mumbled. "Probably fundamentally
important." He handed his list to the superintendent. "Just read that over."

While the superintendent read he opened the metal tube and slid from it
into his hand a few white tablets. He frowned at them, peered at them,
dandled them, put one on the tip of his finger and poised it there as if he
were weighing it. "Well, well," he murmured and shut them back in the
tube again.

"Scent and makeup case?" the superintendent read out and stared at him.

"You grasp that?" Reggie smiled. "Good. Come on, Bell. We've got everything now."

Chapter IX

A Politician Explains Himself

MR. FORTUNE stood in a chemical laboratory and condoled with its large, mild chief, Dr. Anneler, over some glass jars.

"Rather a long business. Yes. Rather tedious. Sorry. Life is hard. And then there's these things. Connection not proved. You haven't got to believe in 'em. But we'd better make sure what they are."

He opened the powder case, opened its mirror and put it into Anneler's hands. Anneler brought his thick-lensed spectacles close to the marks of circles on the gold. "Ah, yes. You think these were made by tablets of drugs. That is very likely. And if we are lucky we can get traces." He pointed a plump finger at the white specks round the rim. "I do not think that is talcum powder."

"No. Nor did I. No." Reggie produced the metal tube and slid from it into a watch glass one of the tablets. "What do you make of that?"

Anneler put his head on one side. "The same size as the circles in the case?" He bustled away and came back with a pair of dividers and measured. "Just the same."

"Just the same, yes," Reggie murmured. "That is very interesting." He watched Anneler, and his eyelids drooped over a gleam of amusement.

"We infer that the lady might have carried these as a habit," said Anneler.

"That is indicated," Reggie drawled.

"A two-grain tablet—of something, eh?" said Anneler. He picked up the tablet in forceps and suddenly flashed a glance at Reggie. He strode to the glass case which held a balance and weighed the tablet. "Ah. You see? It is not the two-grain tablet which it ought to be. It is a little more than six grains. That is, it is something very much more compressed than usual."

Reggie smiled. "Yes, I thought it was. Yes. Rather significant."

"I do not know what it signifies," Anneler frowned. He manipulated the balance again. "Aha, it is not in grains. It is compounded in decigrams. Four decigrams, you see."

"Yes. I grasped that. Also significant."

"It was compounded abroad, you mean?" Anneler said. "Well, that is likely. You know what it is, Fortune?"

"I don't know. I guess. Work it out for yourself, will you? Also the specks in the case. Goodbye. I have to see Lomas."

Lomas received him with a display of joy. "Good fellow! I thought you'd manage to get through. Well, what about it?"

"Get through?" Reggie's voice rose. "Oh my hat! Not for many long hours. Hurry no man's chemistry. You'll only get errors. What's the matter with you?"

"I want to talk to Osmond."

"Very zealous of you. Might even be some use. Title of piece: Whom were you with last night? Very proper enquiry."

"Thank you. I have to know how we stand first."

"We stand still," Reggie murmured. "We don't move because we can't. Till Science has concluded her careful operations."

"Damn, can't you tell me anything?" Lomas cried.

"Not for publication. No. Not to tell the man Osmond."

"I wasn't going to tell him anything," said Lomas impatiently. "I want to make him explain why he wasn't in the House and why he went to Maidford before he has any more time to put together a story for us. The point is, what line had I better take? Do you see?"

"Oh, yes. That's all right. Quite sound."

"Then don't be so infernally mysterious. You must have your own ideas about the woman's death by now."

"I'm not bein' mysterious," Reggie complained. "Only careful. I have ideas. Several ideas. Very interestin' ideas. But no proof. Don't you go usin' 'em. Here you are: Molly Marne died of narcotic poisoning. Probably diacetyl morphine hydrochloride. Taken orally. Not less than four decigrams."

"Good Gad! Why be so technical?" Lomas exclaimed. "I suppose all that only means a big dose of morphia."

"No. It doesn't. It means she didn't die of morphia. Very important fact. Probably the key fact. Diacetyl morphine hydrochloride is commonly called heroin. More potent than morphia. It was put up in four-decigram tablets, which is also important. Four decigrams are about six grains. Very large dose."

"How much would it take to kill her?"

Reggie shook his head. "No certainty possible. She had a morphia habit. But two or three grains of heroin might be fatal."

"How did she come to take it?"

"I should say she took it herself."

"Damn, that's suicide." Lomas flung himself back in his chair.

"Yes, it could be. Legally," Reggie drawled. "Same like Mrs. Poyntz." Lomas made an impatient exclamation. "All right, all right. Only takin' a comprehensive view. It looks as if the organizers are gettin' bustled."

"The organizers?" Lomas frowned.

"The mischief makers. The people who've been managin' us, Lomas, old thing. The unknown powers who throw the shadows for us to chase. Not too legal, this little murder. What do you think a jury would make of somebody who provided the heroin for her to take?"

"You put him in the dock," Lomas smiled. "A jury will do the rest. Juries don't like dope merchants."

"No, I don't think they'd like this one. Nasty work. There's no evidence yet, but this is how it was done: That poor girl took to using morphia—probably tempted into it—then supplies were cut off—she was starving for the stuff—somebody prepared heroin for her in the size of the morphia tablets she was used to, but compressed so that there was a good fatal dose in each one—"

"Damn, that's a devilish dodge," Lomas exclaimed. "Are you sure?"

"Not proved yet. It will be. Tablets at her bedside double the weight they ought to be by the size. No analysis yet. Anneler's going to find that her usual dope was little two-grain tablets of morphia and grape sugar. He doesn't know he's going to, but he will. Traces of 'em in a gold case she carried. He will also find that the tablets by the bed were four decigrams of heroin. And we'll get plenty of heroin out of her body, poor girl. See? She came down to that cottage by the river starvin' for a morphia sleep—took what she thought was her usual dose—and what they'd provided for her was twice as much or more in heroin. And that was the end of her. Very clever. But a little too clever. Also some loose ends. Failure to allow for use of scientific method by the police force. Very natural but careless. Possibly mere arrogance. They are arrogant, our mischief makers. But it looks hasty. I should say they're feelin' a bit pressed." He contemplated Lomas dreamily. "Heaven knows it isn't our fault, old thing. However. Study to improve."

Lomas made drawings on his blotting pad. "You're at the top of your form, Reginald. That's most ingenious. It's quite plausible. You work in all your facts, you make a deuced convincing explanation how the thing was done—but you don't show any sort of reason why it was done. Why the devil should anybody want to kill Molly Marne?"

"I don't know. I haven't made up my mind. Two obvious possibilities: She could have given somebody away and showed signs of doin' so—or she wouldn't do something she was wanted to do. Reason for murderin' her might be either, or combination of both. There are other possibilities. She might be in somebody's way."

"You mean Osmond," said Lomas quickly. "In the way of his affair with Alix Lynn. That's really a variation of your first theory—she was likely to give somebody away. And if Luttrell was murdered, it was probably for the same reason, and that points at Osmond, too, so it links the two cases. We do want to hear why he couldn't come to the House last night."

"Yes. Quite a good effort, Lomas. Cases probably linked by similar motive. That would do. But it does not provide a link with the Poyntz affair."

"I don't expect it to," Lomas protested. "Damn, Reginald, the Poyntz case is an obsession with you. There's nothing in that but suicide—you certified that yourself. You can't go on to drag a murder motive out of it."

"My dear chap! Oh my dear chap," Reggie moaned. "The reasonin' faculty is not in action. Suicide can be arranged: product of intent to murder."

"Why should anybody want to murder the Poyntzes?"

"I haven't the slightest idea," Reggie mumbled. "We're only seein' the shadows, Lomas. But not without hope. We do know they're only shadows. And sometimes I fancy I may live to bother the people who make 'em. Observe the interestin' sequence: The Poyntzes—plain suicide and nothing but suicide; Luttrell—natural death, but not quite natural; poor Molly Marne—looking like suicide or misadventure, but certainly murder. And the next thing, please?"

Lomas stared at him. His round face had the innocence of enquiring youth. "You're a trifle weird sometimes, Reginald," said Lomas and seemed to make a mental effort. "Well, the next thing for me is to put the fear of God into Osmond."

"That might do good," Reggie purred. Lomas rang a bell. "Oh, is he here?"

"He's been here some time," Lomas smiled. "I thought it would stir him up to be kept waiting."

Osmond was stirred. He came in with a stride that made a noise. His dark face had a flush and a look of fury. "Do you know how long I've been in your anteroom?" he said in a voice to make windows rattle.

Lomas was moving papers. "Good-evening. Sit down," he said. "What was that?" Osmond flung himself at a chair and thundered the question again.

Lomas had a trained gift for insolence. He looked up, he put in his eyeglass and surveyed Osmond's wrath. "I don't know how long you've had to wait," he drawled. "I am investigating a death."

"That's no reason for a muddle of inefficiency," Osmond thundered.

Lomas settled back comfortably in his chair. "You're not doing yourself any good," he smiled. "Get your temper back. People expect you to know that it's your duty to assist the police."

"People expect the police not to play the fool," said Osmond, his deep voice under more control. He pushed back the lock of black hair which fell over his brow and watched Lomas with steady, measuring eyes. "If you want my assistance you've wasted a lot of time."

"You think so? You know all the facts, then?" Lomas asked smoothly.

Osmond laughed. " 'Flat burglary as ever was committed': the Dogberry method. The perfect Dogberry. Is there anybody here to write you down an ass? I hope so."

"You ask for a note to be taken of your answers?" Lomas snapped.

"Of your questions, please," said Osmond.

"You'd better stop fencing." Lomas became magisterial. "I want to know why you didn't come to the House of Commons last night."

Osmond also moved to sit at his ease. "This is comparatively rational," he said in a tone of civil condescension. "But you'll have to satisfy me that the police have any right to question a member of Parliament on the way he performs his duties."

"The way he doesn't perform his duties," Lomas corrected. "Are you claiming parliamentary privilege to refuse any account of how you spent your time when the police require it for the investigation of a mysterious death? I advise you to think again, Mr. Osmond."

Osmond was not disturbed. "I made no claim to privilege, as you know very well," he answered placidly. "I take the ordinary right of every man to refuse answers to police questions unless their significance is made plain. You're creating your own difficulties."

"Very well. As you think it in your interest to show suspicion of any enquiries, I'll make a note of it." Lomas wrote, and Osmond watched him, smiling.

"And now add that was all an invention of yours which I denied," said Osmond. "It's better to have a record complete."

Lomas put down the pen and looked up at him and spoke incisively: "Then I am to take it you understand you're in an ambiguous position and you're not prepared to offer any explanation."

"Not at all. That's invention again. My position is in no way ambiguous. Nothing has been put to me to explain, except the fact that I was not in the House last night, and to that my reply is that the police have no authority to question my political conduct."

"You're prevaricating now. My question had nothing to do with politics. The point is, you had promised to speak, you were absent for the whole debate without giving any excuse or reason, and during your absence a mysterious death occurred. What I ask is, where were you at that time?"

"Who has died?" Osmond asked.

"You want me to believe you didn't know that Miss Molly Marne died last night?"

"I didn't know," Osmond said fiercely. His heavy brow contracted, and his eyes were shadowed. "How did she die? Where did she die?"

"You suggest you're surprised she's dead. You're not surprised I ask you for information about her. You admit you knew her well."

"I have met Miss Marne." Osmond watched him.

"Have you seen much of her lately?"

"Not very much. Miss Marne was good enough to treat me as a friend. But her profession occupied her time, and I have not much leisure."

"Merely friends, you say. You knew her so well that you called on her late last night at her cottage at Maidford where she was alone."

Osmond gave no sign of agitation but a still, steady, watchful gaze. "That is not accurate," he said quietly. "I went to her cottage at Maidford, but I did not see her. I could get no answer when I rang. I concluded that she was not there and came back to town."

"Strange," said Lomas drily. "You broke your engagement for a big debate at the House, without a word to your own people, to go off to Miss Marne at Maidford—and yet you didn't see her."

"It is very strange." Osmond's tone was equally dry and contemptuous. "The only explanation is that a trick was played on me."

"Who by?" Lomas snapped.

"By someone on the government side to prevent my speaking last night."

"Oh. That's a serious charge. Do you put a name to it?"

"No, I charge no one with what I can't prove. But that's the only possible motive for sending me off on a wild-goose chase."

"On your own story, you lent yourself to the wild-goose chase. Why on earth should you run off to Miss Marne when you were down to make a big speech?"

"That is a fair question," said Osmond. "I wondered when you were going to see it was the one thing of importance I could tell you. Just as I was getting ready to go down to the House I was rung up by a woman who said she was Miss Marne's sister speaking from Maidford. She—"

"Wait," Lomas interrupted. "Did you know Miss Marne had a sister?"

"Yes, there is a sister. I've heard Miss Marne speak of her—I may have met her. Miss Marne was born of poor parents. Her real name was Minns. The sister is in domestic service, a cook or housekeeper somewhere. But Miss Marne kept in close touch with her. I think she had warm affections. Well—the woman who rang me up said she was Miss Marne's sister, Miss Marne was at Maidford lying ill and in great distress and asking to see me, I must come. It was an incoherent emotional message, but I was fool enough to think it sincere. I took it to mean that the poor girl had got into some grave trouble. I drove down to Maidford—and then, as I told you, I found the cottage empty. I was unlucky on the way back—I had two punctures, so that I didn't get to London till after midnight. It was of no use to go to the House then, the opportunities of the debate were over. I went to bed. That is the whole history of my movements."

"Two punctures," Reggie murmured. "You were unlucky. Only carry one spare wheel, I suppose?"

"Exactly. I had the first puncture a mile or two outside Maidford. I changed the wheel, which took some time; it was a dark, unpleasant night, as you know. I had not gone much farther when I found the other back tire was gone. I could do nothing but drive on the rim into Westlow, and there it took some time to find a garage and get a man to make the repair."

"Your tires seem to have been in poor condition," said Lomas. "What's the address of this garage?"

"I didn't ask—I had no reason. You will have no difficulty in finding it if you want the man to confirm my statement. There are not many garages in Westlow, I can assure you." Osmond gave a sardonic smile. "As to my tires—their condition is good enough. The punctures surprised me as much as they surprise you. I found nothing suspicious in the tires, but there is no doubt in my mind they had been tampered with."

"Oh, yes," Reggie murmured. "The suggestion is that while you were ringing Miss Marne's bell somebody gave your tires stabs so you shouldn't get back to the House of Commons in time to make your speech."

"Just so. It is obvious that the purpose of the false message was to get me away from the House, but I should have been back in time to speak if the tires had not failed, so that also was arranged."

"Thus confirmin' your theory that the whole thing was a trick of the government to stop your dangerous tongue." Reggie contemplated him dreamily. "Yes, it could be."

Lomas made an impatient noise. "Have you any other explanation, then?" said Osmond with cold civility. "I shall be interested to hear it."

"Oh, I don't explain your statements," Lomas shrugged. "When you were at Miss Marne's door I should have thought you'd have noticed anybody touching your car. You're quite sure you didn't go inside the house?"

A flush came over Osmond's dark face. "I did not," he said fiercely. "As for noticing anybody—the night was pitch dark, misty and raining. Weren't you out last night?"

"I know all about the weather. Very convenient," Lomas sneered. "I suppose it hasn't occurred to you, it was rather odd for a leading politician, when he was down to make a big speech, to go running off to a woman in the country because he had a vague telephone message about her. Emotional and incoherent, you said it was. Weren't you rather incoherent and emotional, throwing everything up to get to her at once? If you've told the truth about that, there must have been something more than acquaintance between you and Miss Marne. Are you going to tell me what it was?"

Osmond took his time. "I said there was friendship," he answered gravely and paused again. "From time to time she talked to me about her affairs. I didn't intend to mention this. I was reluctant to say anything of what she told me as a secret. But now that she is dead"—he paused and drew breath— "if there is some mystery about her death, you may be right to press me." Again he stopped.

"What was the matter with her affairs?" said Lomas sharply.

"When she spoke of them, it used to be about some question in her profession, whether she should accept an engagement or not, what she should do next, and so forth—"

"Money matters," Lomas snapped.

"Not at all. The arrangement of her career, of her future. But that is not the point. Quite recently she has spoken vaguely of being worried. There seemed to be no definite cause, or she wouldn't put it into words. She talked as if something were hanging over her that she was afraid of, or as if people who had some hold upon her were being unpleasant."

Lomas made sounds of incredulity.

"Oh, yes," Reggie murmured. "As if— But what did she actually say? Don't you remember?"

"I remember one afternoon when I called and she had a headache, she said she was worried to death, and when I tried to find out what was the matter she was almost hysterical and cried out that she couldn't tell me, I was to go away."

"So you went," said Lomas.

"And when was that?" Reggie purred.

"Only a few days ago. Now you may understand why I took a message that she was in great distress and wanted to see me as something I had to attend to."

"Quite. Does you credit," said Lomas.

"A few days ago," Reggie murmured. "After the affair at Lady Rosnay's?"

"What affair?" Osmond asked. "Oh, you mean the ball. Yes, certainly after that."

"I meant Luttrell's death," Reggie mumbled. "However. About this mysterious distress of Miss Marne. Any ideas?"

"I have never understood it."

"Oh. Didn't occur to you it sounded something like blackmail?"

"I can't imagine Miss Marne ever gave any opportunity to blackmail her," said Osmond fiercely.

"Can't imagine any cause for her death, what?" Lomas yawned.

"No, none. It amazes me to hear she's dead. I wish you would tell me how she came to die."

"Yes, I wish I could," Reggie murmured. "She died last night. In that cottage at Maidford."

"She was there!" Osmond exclaimed.

"She was there when you went to the door. Alive or dead. She was there when you went away. Probably dead."

"She was there all the while—alone and dying!" Osmond's deep voice went low. "What a damnable thing!"

"Not a nice case, no," said Reggie.

"How did she die—what caused her death?" Osmond asked.

"Investigation proceedin'," Reggie mumbled.

"And you haven't helped us much, Mr. Osmond," said Lomas cheerfully. "So I won't keep you any longer now."

"I've given you all the help I can. I wish it were more," said Osmond and took a careful formal leave.

"Clever, isn't he?" Lomas cocked an eyebrow at Reggie. "That's the fellow they call thunder and lightning. And he kept himself as cold as a fish."

"You think so? I thought he was going to kill you once or twice. Lots of fire in our Mr. Osmond's belly."

"All humbug, the ice and the fire," Lomas shrugged. "Good Gad, he is a politician. Well, he's made a nasty tangle, but I see some ends sticking out."

"Oh, yes. Yes. We want the domestic sister."

"That's all right. Bell was looking for her already. Damn, it is late. Come and have a chop at the club."

"A chop!" Reggie moaned. "Oh my Lomas. Not me. No."

Chapter X

After Dinner

IN A corner of a little restaurant of his affections Mr. Fortune filled his plate again with strawberries Romanoff.

"Good Gad," said Lomas and watched him with admiration. "You're fearfully and wonderfully made, Reginald. How do you retain any activity of mind?"

"The simple life," Reggie murmured. "You're so unscientific. A little fish, a little omelet, a little fruit. And wilderness were paradise enow." He smiled benignly. "You are rather a wilderness, Lomas."

"I want to get back," said Lomas. "Come along."

"Do not fuss." Reggie caught the waiter's eye and asked for Armagnac with the coffee. "Thought is what we need. Sessions of sweet, silent thought."

The coffee came, he sipped, he lit a long cigar and sighed and sank back and smoked with closing eyes.

At last he was persuaded slow and plaintive into a cab.

"I hope Bell has that sister waiting for us by now." Lomas's tongue was loosed as they drove away. "They may have been able to check Osmond's alleged telephone call. Then we shall see what we shall see."

"You think so!" Reggie sighed. "Hopeful fellow. Osmond had a telephone call all right. And if the exchange knows where it came from, that won't tell you anything."

"What, do you mean you believe Osmond's tale?" Lomas was startled.

"I wouldn't say that, no. But he must have had a sudden call that shook him up, or he wouldn't have cut that big debate without a word to his party. The call may have been what he said. Then the people who played the trick are too clever to telephone from where they could be traced. It may have been something quite different. Then he's far too clever to put us onto checking his phone messages if there was a chance we could get a clue. Take it another way: If the sister's honest, she knows nothing about the message. If she isn't, she won't tell what she does know."

"You don't think she's going to be any use."

"Oh, yes. Yes. I think she may be a lot of use." Reggie murmured. "Do you remember—when we were speculatin' why Molly was murdered—I said she might have been in somebody's way, might have refused to do what somebody wanted—and then the man Osmond told us she used to talk as if something were hanging over her and said she was worried to death. Curious agreement."

"Quite. Don't flatter yourself, Reginald. He wanted us to believe she was being blackmailed."

"Yes. It could be. He said he couldn't imagine it himself. Havin' clearly pointed to it. Yes. Interestin' man, the man Osmond."

Lomas laughed angrily. "Damn clever. Too damn clever. His tone about the girl was nauseating. The noble gentleman who was only her friend, who couldn't say a word about her—till he found he had to protect him-self—and then handed us a nasty yarn hinting she had a devil of a scandal in her life—and finished up by swearing it couldn't be. Good Gad! I don't mind a rogue, but I bar the chivalry."

"As you say," Reggie sighed. "However. Truth will out, even in a politi-cian."

They came back to Lomas's room. Superintendent Bell, being rung up, said with subdued reproach that he was there, he had been there some time, and Miss Marne's sister was waiting if Mr. Lomas still wanted to see her. Mr. Lomas did.

Bell brought her in. She was a woman of middle age, like Molly Marne in blue eyes and yellow hair but not otherwise. She had a flat, shrewd face. Her shape was that of a plump man.

Lomas received her with ceremony. He understood that Miss Minns was Miss Marne's sister. No doubt the matter had been explained to her. He was very sorry …

"Sophia Minns is the name." She sat squarely in front of him. "Cook to Sir George Todhunter. Elder sister of Molly Marne, she being born Minns. And her only relation that's left." Miss Minns sniffed.

Lomas understood, of course, this was a great blow to her. He was dis-tressed to ask her questions about it.

"You 'ave to, don't you?" said Miss Minns, and he came to business.

No. Miss Minns wasn't what you'd call surprised to hear Molly was dead. She'd thought a long time the girl was in a bad way, told her so often. Oh, no, she didn't know of anything particular the matter, she was just using herself up, sort of burning the candle at both ends all the time. They mustn't get that wrong. She didn't mean anything nasty. Molly was a good girl. Miss Minns would take her dying oath of that. A good girl!

What she meant to say was, Molly would be acting regular and then traipsing round with these society people all the rest of the night and all the day. Flesh and blood couldn't stand it.

How did she keep going? Ah, that was asking something. Just a bundle of nerves, Molly was. Fair lived on her nerves. Didn't live on her food, anyway. She never ate like a Christian, not this long time.

Lomas sympathized. Lomas asked if she ever took anything for it.

"What do you mean, take anything?" Miss Minns flamed. "She never drank no more than a baby."

Of course not. Lomas was sympathetically shocked. He never thought of such a thing. He meant doctor's stuff.

"She wouldn't never have a doctor." Miss Minns was still annoyed. "I was always at her about it. It's my belief she doctored herself. She used to carry little tablets, I know. That sort of thing never does you no good. What I say is, you must have a doctor to tell you what you want. Often and often I said it. But Molly wouldn't listen, she was that sure of herself—that's how she got on in her business. Always sure of herself, till lately, poor dear."

"Been a change?" Reggie murmured. "Oh, yes. Do you know how that began? Had there been any trouble with anybody?"

Miss Minns stared blankly. "I don't know what you mean. Oh, was you thinking she was crossed in love or something like that? Don't you believe it. Molly wasn't that kind. Has somebody been talking nasty to you? I tell you she was a good girl. There was a gentleman as she liked, I seen him myself, there's no harm in saying so, a member of Parliament, Mr. Osmond his name is, used to come and see her, and I did fancy it might have meant something. I said so to her, chaffing like, but she laughed at me, he'd just stood her friend in some theater business, sort o' big brother to her. Well, he is like a big boy. That sort of man. And Molly, she was just a kid all her life, poor dear. As clever as clever with her acting. Wonderful she was. But only a kid really."

"I see. Yes," Reggie murmured. "I'm sorry." His round face showed hard lines.

"I'm afraid we must say it's a strange case, Miss Minns," Lomas frowned. "Mr. Osmond has been here. He tells me that last night someone telephoned to him who said she was Miss Marne's sister—"

"Me? I never did!" Miss Minns screamed. "That's a lie, that is, I never telephoned 'im in my life. Why ever should I?"

"Well, he says this person said she was you and asked him to come down to Maidford at once because Miss Marne was in trouble and wanted to speak to him."

"Don't you believe it." Miss Minns was furious. "He's lying. I never did hear such a tale." She could be seen thinking about it. "It ain't like 'im, neither," she said more calmly. "Not what I took 'im for. There, you never know, do you?"

"Not always. No." Reggie watched her mental struggles.

"Stands to reason 'e couldn't be certain who it was phoning," she argued. "'E wouldn't reco'nize my voice on the phone, 'e ain't talked to me often enough. But there, what's the sense of it anyway? Why should anyone want 'im to go down to 'er at Maidford? And then to put it onto me!"

"Very unpleasant," Reggie purred. "Raising very important questions, as you see."

"Did 'e go?" said Miss Minns sharply. "Did 'e see 'er? That's the question, I reckon."

"Two questions," Reggie murmured. "He did go. But he didn't see her. So he says. He couldn't get into the house."

"Couldn't get in, while she was lying there dying," Miss Minns snorted. "I say! That's nasty—that's cruel, that is."

"Yes. It's a cruel case," said Reggie. "Does it seem to you unlike her that she should have been there alone at night?"

Miss Minns took time to answer. "I couldn't rightly say that," she decided. "She did go off to Maidford sudden now and then, and she wouldn't 'ave the women that did for 'er sleep in. When she was staying she took the servants. But she used to say she kep' the place mostly to 'ave somewhere for to be right away from things. No, she would have been all alone, poor dear." Miss Minns dabbed at her eyes.

Reggie waited respectfully for the end of that operation. Then he said, "About the tablets she used to take—do you know where she got them?"

Miss Minns stared at him with blue eyes bright and alert again. "From the chemist's, I suppose. I don't know what chemist she went to."

"And you don't know what they were?"

"No, I don't remember ever 'earing. Some patent muck, I expect. I don't 'old with them things. I told 'er so. She only laughed—it was like telling a kid something's bad for her inside—she said they was splendid stuff. Why?" she frowned. "Do you think it was them that killed her?"

"I wouldn't say that. No," Reggie murmured. "I couldn't. Nobody can tell me what they were."

"I don't believe it," Miss Minns announced. "She'd been taking them a long time."

"Since when?" Reggie snapped.

"Ah, I couldn't tell you that."

"You don't know of anybody recommending them to her?"

"'Ow should I?" she complained. "Anybody might 'ave. She knew crowds and crowds of people."

"Yes, she would. Yes. By the way, you haven't mentioned anybody she knew, except Mr. Osmond."

"Oh, lor, I could tell you lots if that's what you want." She reeled off names of actors and actresses.

"Thanks very much. Thanks." Reggie stopped the flood. "And what about people not on the stage?"

"Molly knew lots of grand folks. They 'ad 'er to their 'ouses, since she got on. You know she was a dear. She was just the same to me as what she was as a kid, bless 'er. But I didn't reely know who they were, most of 'em. She wasn't one to make talk of being in society."

"No. Nice girl," Reggie sighed. "Any of them come to her house?"

"I don't know so much. She lived quiet. There was an old lady, I've 'eard speak of, Lady Rosnay, she came sometimes. Oh, and some of Mr. Osmond's friends. Mr. and Mrs. 'Arley—and what was the other?—a Mrs. Dabble—something like that. Very kind people. I 'appened in on 'em once and they be'aved so civil. Mr. 'Arley, 'e's in Parliament like Mr. Osmond. Well, there you are—but what's the good of talking all this sort of thing? Seems to me what you reely want to know is about this 'ere telephone message, if there was one. Taking my name like that!" Miss Minns snorted. "I never sent no message. And Mr. Osmond going down there when she was dying and not seeing her. Ah, it's wicked, that's what it is." She frowned at them and nodded vehemently.

Lomas glanced at Reggie, but Reggie had nothing to say. "Very natural you should feel it," Lomas said. "It's a sad, disturbing case. You can take it we quite appreciate that, Miss Minns. Everything proper will be done." He went on with grave official sympathizing, and Miss Minns was visibly soothed.

As she took her leave, "One moment," Reggie murmured. "Could you tell me where she bought her frocks?"

"Lor," Miss Minns exclaimed, "there's a thing to ask. Just everywhere. The frocks'll have the names on."

"I suppose they will, yes," Reggie sighed. "And who was her hairdresser?"

Miss Minns gaped at him, "Montmorency's she went to, if you want to know," she said fiercely.

"I did. Yes. Thank you. Goodbye," Reggie murmured.

He watched her broad back depart, he settled down in his chair and lit a pipe.

"Why annoy the lady, Reginald?" Lomas smiled.

"These little troubles will occur." Reggie blew a smoke ring.

"You don't believe in her?"

"Believe? Strong word. Not feelin' prone to believe anybody. Don't actively disbelieve. Sophia may have told the truth and all the truth she knew. Assumin' she did, Sophia was quite natural and human. But her mind was in confusion. She wasn't sure whether she thinks the man Osmond is a simple soul or a cunning brute."

"She was prepared to give him full marks till she saw he'd brought suspicion on her," said Lomas. "Suggestive, what?"

"Oh, yes. Yes. But suggestin' different things—first that she knew he was a rogue, secondly that she didn't. However, I incline to like Sophia myself. Takin' her for a devil, she's devilish clever. I may be vain, but I think I know when people are bein' clever with me. Osmond was clever."

"You accept her at face value—good, plain face. I agree." Lomas lit a cigarette. "But then why annoy her?"

"What? My little questions about the dressmaker and the hairdresser?" Reggie smiled. "Oh my Lomas! Don't you see?"

"I do not. It seemed quite futile. If you really want to know that sort of thing, we can find out in half an hour—as she told you."

"Oh, yes. Matter of fact I did know," Reggie murmured.

"And what use is it?"

"I haven't the slightest idea," Reggie mumbled. "My dear old thing, the time has come for tactics. Essence of tactics is surprise. Strategy is forethought. We've had a lot of strategy. On the other side. Not by us, owin' to the sad fact we didn't know we were at war. That hampered me. However. We will study to improve. Strategy of the enemy still obscure, but it has become clear they're fighting. Fighting does reveal presence of an enemy. Have you noticed that? We are now in a position to give 'em a little tactics. Hence my simple futile questions to the man Osmond and sister Sophia."

"To Osmond?" Lomas repeated. "What do you mean?"

"My dear chap, you should listen," Reggie moaned. "He did. He was keenly interested. I asked him whether the time when he found Molly in great distress was after Luttrell's death. I rubbed it in."

"Quite. I remember. He said it was."

"Yes. Rather shaken up, wasn't he? Didn't quite know what to say. It hadn't occurred to him the active and intelligent police force would connect her death with Luttrell's death and Luttrell's death with her doped nerves. Quite a surprise, and more painfully surprisin' because he don't know yet what I mean. Nor do I. Inadequate knowledge more disturbin' to him than to me. Should produce interestin' reactions."

"That's not bad," Lomas admitted. "But what about the dressmaker and the hairdresser and Miss Minns—what's the bearing of that?"

"I just thought it would bother her. Stick in her mind. Safe calculation Osmond will get into touch with her. He must, whether he and she have been playing tricks or not. He'll want to know what she told us about the phone message. She'll remember the hairdresser and the dressmaker. She may tell him—and that'll worry him. And I hope it'll worry some other people. Did you notice?—accordin' to Sophia, the man Osmond's particular friends were intimate with Molly, too—Harley, Mrs. Harley, and Mrs.

Dabble—who is Mrs. Darett, I take it—to say nothing of our bafflin' Lady Rosnay. I should say some of them will be makin' kind enquiries. More reactions possible." Reggie smiled. "By the way—just to give an air of earnest purpose—Bell might look up the dressmakers—tabs are on Molly's frocks, of course—and Montmorency, the hairdresser. He'd better ask if they can tell him anything about her and her friends. He might ask if any of 'em sell a scent called '*Matin d'un Faune.*' By way of making conversation."

"What is the matter with the scent?" said Lomas quickly.

"Nothing. Basis amyl salicylate. Smell rather excitin' to the senses. Quite harmless—if you like that sort of thing. Well, well. Teach me to live that I may dread the grave as little as my bed. You do. Goodbye."

Chapter XI

Lady Rosnay Rings Up

IT IS one of the deepest convictions of Mr. Fortune that he was born to live in the country. Settled as a general practitioner in a countryside of good hills, some water and far prospect, he would have attained, so he will pathetically argue, the perfect happiness which comes only from exact adaptation of ability and duty—given a partner to do the surgery. He has never made any effort to test this forecast.

An affection for the country, when it is spring or summer, does, however, influence the arrangement of his life. Three or four modest country houses he has acquired in succession. From the bank of the Thames and from a riverside in Kent he was driven by the tendency of other people to live there. He requires his country to show a rural emptiness. He went away to make another garden in a still undiscovered valley of the Cotswolds.

There after some long, secluded toil in laboratories, his own and Dr. Anneler's, his wife persuaded him to go for the long weekend which can begin on Thursday night. He was not reluctant. The roses had outshone their first beauty, which he loves best, but the lilies were only just past their dawn.

A small house of mellow stone in quiet and gracious Elizabethan elegance is built in a dimple of the swell of the olive-green hills to take the sunlit air of south and west. Below its rose garden there are a hedge and arches and arbors of sweetbrier. From that an array of diverse lilies spreads to the stream, which winds between a bank golden with St. John's wort and a bank swaying fragrant feathers of meadowsweet under a hazel copse. In the midst sunlight and shadow break upon clear amber water to play with the lilies that float there, white and red.

It was Friday and the beneficent hour after lunch. In the shade of the sweetbrier hedge Mrs. Fortune reclined, a delectable shape. Reggie wandered towards her, stopping to consider one lily and another with the critical joy of an artist in what he has made, stood over her at last and contemplated her.

"Joan," he murmured. "That's you." He kissed her eyes and her hair and stayed in it a moment. A little smile came to her lips.

He lowered a deck chair to its utmost and sat beside her.

There was no sound but the murmur of the stream and a wren's tiny song … till he took a letter from his pocket.

The rustle of paper disturbed Mrs. Fortune. She opened her eyes and saw him reading sheets of typescript: notes by Superintendent Bell on the dressmaker of Molly Marne. "Must you?" she sighed. "This is our time."

"Darlin'," he murmured. "Nothing distractin'. Do you know anything about Maison Montespan?"

"Very smart," said Mrs. Fortune. It is not a word of praise from her. "Nobody smarter."

"Oh, yes. A new shop?"

"No. Not very. It must have been going some years now."

"Do you know anybody who uses it?"

"I'm not sure," she reflected. "I think Alix Lynn does."

"Well, well." Reggie put his letter away. "Did you ever meet a scent called 'Le Matin d'un Faune'?"

"Heavens! No, not by that name. I've met things as bad as it sounds." She wrinkled her excellent nose.

Reggie asked no more questions. He sank back and gazed at her and the lilies.

A patter of feet came near. The parlormaid stood at his elbow. "If you please, sir—"

Reggie lifted himself and stared plaintive horror.

"If you please, sir," the maid swallowed. "Lady Rosnay has rung up. I told her I thought you were out. But she seems very excited. She said I must find you at once, she's in great trouble."

"Oh my aunt!" Reggie moaned. "Sure it was Lady Rosnay?"

"I couldn't tell that, sir. She said so. She said she'd tried Wimpole Street and they said you were here."

"All right. Tell her I am out. Ask her where she's speaking from. So that Mr. Fortune can ring her up when he comes in. See? Run away." He sank down in his chair again.

The moment is memorable in their married life. Mrs. Fortune asked for explanations. "Reggie," she said, "don't you believe it was Lady Rosnay?"

"Faculty of belief switched off," Reggie murmured. "Neither believe nor disbelieve. I'm only bein' careful, Joan."

"My dear," she touched his hand, "you will be? I hate this case. It's ghostly."

"Chasin' shadows. Yes. Shadows gettin' rather jumpy. Don't worry. Takin' great care of Reginald. He's a necessary man."

"Yes," said Mrs. Fortune.

After a little while Reggie stood up. "Well, well. We will now test the alleged Lady Rosnay." He smiled at his wife and wandered away to the house.

The parlormaid met him in the hall. "She was rather annoyed, sir. She said to find you quick, she was speaking from Langton."

Langton is the great house on the Thameshire downs which the family of Rosnay bought from a ruined king of the early railway mania.

"All right," Reggie smiled. "Now ring up Langton and ask for Lady Rosnay." He listened to that tedious process, and when it was completed took the telephone and waved her away. "Mr. Fortune speaking. Is that Lady Rosnay?"

"Oh you dear soul!" a high voice crackled. "At last! It's been maddening. I'm prickly all over."

"Sorry about that," Reggie drawled. "They were just verifyin' the call, Lady Rosnay. There's been some queer work with the telephone lately. However. You bein' you—what can I do for you?"

"Oh my dear! Come here at once. I am in the most dreadful trouble. I can't tell you. You must come."

"Like that? Well, well. If you say so. I shan't be there for some time. It's fifty miles."

"Bless you! You dear creature!" a crow of a laugh came piercing. "Drive like Jehu."

"My chauffeur's so careful. Like me. All right. I'll come along. I'll just have to tell Scotland Yard." The telephone crackled inarticulately. "I said Scotland Yard," Reggie repeated. "Goodbye."

He meditated for a moment and then did ring up the Criminal Investigation Department. "Mr. Fortune speaking. Is Mr. Lomas there? … Never mind. Let him have a message Mr. Fortune is gone to Lady Rosnay at Langton, Thameshire, on her request. Got that? … Good. That's all."

When he had ordered his car, he went back into the garden, but Mrs. Fortune met him and spoke first. "Was it Lady Rosnay, Reggie?"

"Oh, yes. No deception. The authentic old lady. She wants to speak to me. So I'm goin' over. Sorry, Joan."

"What does she want you for?"

"I haven't the slightest idea. I may find out. Doubtful but possible. However. Quite all right." He took her hand and kissed it.

At a steady, stately pace his car made for the Thameshire downs, passed through a region of great cornfields, and climbed the bare whaleback ridge of chalk till they looked southward over rolling miles of green almost as lonely as the sea, farmsteads were so few and villages fewer.

Half an hour of this desert of pale grassland brought them to a line of oak palings stretching away along the road beyond sight. Within the fence there were clumps of beech and here and there an oak, small but aged, and in the waves of turf they saw deer feeding.

"That'll be Langton Park," said Sam the chauffeur. "Sightly place."

"Yes. Pleasant to see a tree again," Reggie mumbled.

They came to a vast entry of wrought-iron gates between stone pillars supporting bogey animals which held the coat of arms of the Rosnays. From a lodge which looked like a beehive a woman came out, opened half a gate, and bobbed curtseys.

Not for the first time in his affairs with Lady Rosnay, Reggie felt that he was being taken back to another century. Before him opened an eighteenth-century vista, sham Gothic ruins of nothing in particular and an artfully artificial lake spanned by a bridge from nowhere to nowhere. The chalk stream which provided the water was made into cascades beside the road, then passed away into obscurity behind unkempt willows.

The waves of the turf beyond it were steeper and broken, the road turned from them to find a more amiable way, but in the rough ground were labors of this century's civilization, hollows filled with sand, green flats and posts with little flags. A woman swung there at her ball, a man watched her.

"Speed limit, Sam," Reggie murmured. As the car slid on slowly he studied these golfers. The man showed in the sunlight the pleasant face of Arthur Darett; the woman—that fair hair, that slim, handsome shape might be Mrs. Harley's. They were left behind. The progress of the car discovered two other people in a hollow under a copse. They also carried clubs, but if they were looking for a ball, the search was not earnest. They moved slowly, they kept very close. There was no mistaking Alix Lynn's red head or the square shoulders and bull neck of Osmond.

"Well, well. Interestin' place," Reggie mumbled. "Get on."

The car shot forward. The house rose into sight above terraced gardens, an Italian palace in bleak, gray stone.

Reggie had a glimpse of someone passing out of sight in the garden as they swung round the last curve to the door. He had hardly crossed the threshold when a scream of joy came down the stairs and Lady Rosnay ran at him. Her pile of gray hair was awry, she fluttered in a frock of girlish pink.

"You dear creature!" she cried and clutched at both his hands. "Bless you! Come, my dear, come up to my room."

He went—not as fast as she.

She stood waiting for him in the doorway of a bedroom, she drew him in and shut the door behind him. "There!" she whispered it huskily. "Look! Look!"

On the pink quilt, very still, lay the tiny body of her monkey.

"The angel's dead," Lady Rosnay wailed.

Chapter XII

The Case of Cupid

REGGIE contemplated the monkey with respectful solemnity, and Lady Rosnay contemplated him. "You nice person," she said in a tone between laughing and crying.

"Is this the scene of death?" Reggie asked.

"No, he died in my boudoir. I brought him here—to be quiet, to be alone, you know. Precious child." She stroked the little brow with a hand that quivered. "My own Cupid."

Reggie waited till the caresses were finished and then moved the body to the side of the bed. It was not yet cold. He examined it inch by inch. It bore no sign of injury. He looked close into the eyes. . . .

"Well, well." He stood erect again and turned to Lady Rosnay. "That's all you wanted me for?"

"My dear!" she clasped his arm. "I want to know what he died of."

"Yes. Natural question of affection." Reggie looked at her dreamily. "No definite answer possible. How did he die?"

"I'll show you just how it happened." She hurried out of the bedroom. "Oh, shut the door for him, poor angel—come in here."

Reggie was brought to a sitting room with pink silk walls and heavy Victorian furniture. A gilt chair stood beside an easy chair at a table in the window, and on the table was a plate which bore a silver knife and fork, a banana skin, and some slices of banana.

Lady Rosnay sank down into the easy chair. Reggie sat on the other. She gave a little choking laugh. "Yes, it was just like this. He always sat where you are. Darling Cupid. And I sat here. For his little lunch, you know. There it is."

"Yes. I see. Yes." Reggie considered the banana coldly. "It was a regular ceremony you and the monkey should lunch here together?"

"I always gave it him," said Lady Rosnay. "He didn't like it if there was anybody but me—even Alix. He was so beautifully jealous."

"And lunch was always a banana?"

"Yes, practically always. Sometimes he had something else with it, but bananas suited him best. They would put it ready, you know, and I would come up here with him to have it."

"Oh. You ate some of it?"

"Quite often. That's what's so awful, you see." She made large eyes at him.

"Is it?" Reggie said stolidly. "Why is that?"

"Precious child!" she wailed. "Darling, darling Cupid, he saved my life, I'm sure he did."

"You think so?" Reggie murmured.

"My dear, that's why I'm so shattered. That's why I asked you to come and help me. It's too dreadful. My poor angel."

"What did he do? And what did you do?"

"The angel always had his little lunch after we had had ours, you know. He was perfectly well downstairs, so merry and wicked, his very best. Then I brought him up here and we sat down, he was so pretty and scolding me to be quick, and I peeled his banana and cut it up. Then I pretended to eat it—oh my dear! I did eat one piece—he loved me to tease him—and sometimes he would come and take a bit out of my mouth. My poor love—he pulled at me when I was going to have another piece, he ate that, he ate some more, and then he stopped—he fumbled with it and dropped it and looked after it as if he didn't see and stretched out for a fresh bit and his little hand didn't reach and he fell over sideways on his chair as if he were going to sleep. Then I picked him up and talked to him, but he didn't take any notice—and I couldn't wake him up at all—and then, my dear!—I knew he was dead, dead in my arms."

"Very distressin'," Reggie mumbled. "About the time—how soon did you begin the banana lunch? About two o'clock? ... Oh, as early as that."

"They were going to golf," said Lady Rosnay.

"Oh, yes. I saw them. About three o'clock you rang me up. And you thought the monkey was dead then. Rather quick."

"My dear boy, it was terrible. He seemed to be gone all in a moment." Reggie gazed at her from under drooping eyelids. "What are you thinking?" she cried.

"Thinkin' it wasn't quite as quick as that," Reggie murmured.

"But it was!" her voice rose shrill. "I tell you it was. After I took him in my arms, he was just limp and helpless, nothing I could do would rouse him, his dear little life just faded away." She paused, she stared at Reggie's impassive, expressionless face. "My dear boy, I'm telling you everything just as it happened. Don't you believe me?"

"Not suggestin' it didn't happen," Reggie mumbled. "The monkey is now dead. I should say it didn't happen quite like that. Probably he was only in a state of coma when you rang me up. Death arrived later. Not very long before I did."

"You mean he was actually alive when I thought he was dead! But that's terrible. I might have saved the darling. I ought to have done something. Oh my dear! I'm a horrid, futile creature."

"I shouldn't say that, no." Reggie's tone was coldly judicial. "I don't know whether anything could have saved him. What was your idea about the cause of death?"

"But of course he was poisoned. Wasn't he? He was poisoned in the banana. He must have been."

"That is indicated. Yes. And what was the poison?"

"Why, something to send him to sleep. Oh my dear, he didn't suffer, did he?"

"Probably not. No. Some comfort in your sorrow. However. Why should a narcotic poison be administered to the monkey?"

"Wasn't it meant for me?" Lady Rosnay whispered. "It must have been."

"You think so? Somebody usin' indirect methods. And who is the somebody, Lady Rosnay?" Reggie sat up. "Who's in your mind?"

"My dear boy!" She giggled embarrassment. "You are so erratic. I never know what you'll say next."

"Oh, yes. Often," Reggie mumbled. "That was what you meant me to say now. Well. Who is it?"

"No," she said sharply. "You're quite wrong. I'm not going to accuse anybody." She seemed to have put off her affectations. Her manner was downright and shrewd. "Here's a horrid thing, and I don't understand it. I asked you here to find out what it means. I can treat you as a friend, can't I?"

"Here I am. Because you asked me. If you want to know what it means, you should help me. But when I'm investigatin' a crime I'm nobody's friend. Well?"

She stared at him, and her eyes were defeated. "Lord, aren't you grim?" she giggled. "What do you think I can tell you?"

"Inference from your story is, the monkey was killed by a narcotic poison introduced into the banana. Rather a powerful poison. His appearance suggests narcotic poisoning. The first question is, therefore, who could have got at the banana? Your servants—that's obvious—what about them?"

"It's absurd. I've had them all for ages. And Graves"—she made a grimace of reverence at the name of her devoted butler—"Graves is wonderful with servants. You know him, don't you? He never makes a mistake."

"Servants acquitted. Yes. Remains you—and Miss Lynn"—he paused, and Lady Rosnay rolled her eyes—"and any visitors present. What visitors have you?"

"There are half a dozen people. Sir Bingham Wilton and his wife and the Hamnets and Simon Osmond."

"Oh. Osmond," Reggie murmured. "That isn't all, though. I saw some others playin' golf."

"Did you? The Harleys and the Daretts, I suppose."

"A Harley—female—and a Darett—male. Golfin' with Osmond and Miss Lynn."

"Yes. I daresay. But they don't count, you see. They're not staying here. They were coming over after lunch to golf—I remember, Alix said so. The Harleys have a place down here, and I believe the Daretts are staying with them this weekend. I haven't seen any of them."

"Harleys and Daretts not present till after catastrophe. Thus eliminated. Leavin' you and Miss Lynn, Wiltons and Hamnets and the man Osmond as potential murderers of monkey. Well?"

"Don't be so ghastly," Lady Rosnay shuddered.

"You feel it like that?" Reggie's half-shut eyes examined her.

"Oh, you're horrible. Poor Cupid, my angel! And it might have been me!"

"As aforesaid. Yes. We eliminate the blameless Wiltons and the insignificant Hamnets. Leavin' the man Osmond and Miss Lynn—and you. One of you three, Lady Rosnay."

"How can you?" She was shrill.

"Curious case," Reggie mumbled. "Takin' one thing with another. I wonder why you had the man Osmond here."

"What do you mean?"

"We don't get on, do we?" Reggie smiled. "The main reason is, you don't tell me the truth."

"Mr. Fortune!" She was for a moment the great lady and then decided to be flippant. "My dear boy, how superior—and how silly!"

"Neither," said Reggie. "Only advisin' common sense. There's more than the monkey's death you have to explain. I don't make a joke of it myself—but that's a matter of taste—"

"You're being hateful!" she cried.

"I'm thinking of the deaths of men and women. You asked me to that ball at Rosnay House, and something queer happened to you and you didn't tell me the truth about it and Luttrell died and a girl who was at that ball died the other day. Now your monkey's died, and you asked me here to see him. You want me to believe you might have been killed with him. Are you telling the truth now? I don't know."

"Luttrell?" she said, and her tone was contemptuous and bitter. "Luttrell has nothing to do with it." Reggie did not answer. "And Molly Marne!" She laughed. "Why do you talk about Molly Marne? Everybody knew she took drugs."

"Did they? Well, well. I suppose the monkey took drugs. And everybody knew it. That's why I was brought to have a look at him."

"But you're brutal," Lady Rosnay wailed. "I asked you to come because I was afraid."

"Yes. I believe that," said Reggie with satisfaction, with relish. "Quite natural. Quite justified."

"Why are you so fierce with me?" she complained. "Why are you so angry?"

"No anger," said Reggie placidly. "Absolute lack of sympathy, that's all. You're bein' quite heartless. Playin' for your own hand. As you please. I can play it out like that."

"I don't know what you want," she wailed.

"I want the truth," Reggie murmured. "That's all. I'm goin' to get it. The monkey has his uses, poor beggar. Ingenious but cruel. Like other episodes. Cruelty attracts my attention. I don't like it."

Lady Rosnay stared at him, and beneath the rouge the wrinkles of her thin face were strained. "Darling Cupid," she whined. "It was horribly cruel. He was the sweetest thing. But I don't know why you're so cross with me. It might have been me as well as him. And I've told you everything, my dear."

"Oh, no. No. At the ball somebody knocked you down, and you said you didn't know it. Somebody took your tiara, and you said it wasn't gone. You mustn't expect me to believe you now."

"Well, I did tell you the truth." She giggled, she gave him an impish look. "I don't know the least how I fell. If somebody hit me, I haven't an idea who it was, it was all in the dark. And the tiara—that was so silly—I never wear my diamonds in that kind of mob, only a copy in paste. I've done that for years. Ever since Kitty Clare's were stolen at the Albert Hall. The paste tiara was taken, of course," she cackled. "Oh my dear, what a moment for the poor wretch when he found what he had got! Two penn'orth of glass. The diamonds were safe in the bank all the time, just as I told you."

"I see. Yes. You told me half the truth. And the same with intent to deceive. Why? Why weren't the police to know that somebody stole your tiara—even if it was only paste? Because you knew who the thief was and wanted to cover him?"

"Don't be absurd. I haven't a notion who he was. I didn't want a fuss about my wearing paste, that's all."

"It didn't occur to you the thief ought to be caught—even if it was the man Osmond?"

"How silly! Of course it wasn't Osmond. You can be sure he knew that tiara was paste without stealing it to find out. Alix knew."

"Oh. Tells him everything, does she?"

"My dear! Haven't you seen them together?" Lady Rosnay made a wicked grimace.

"That's your view. Yes. So you have to acquit Osmond and Miss Lynn of stealing the tiara. The gossip goin' about that he did must bother you."

"Bother me?" she echoed. "My dear soul, if I let scandal bother me, I should have committed suicide before you were born."

"Same like Mrs. Poyntz," Reggie drawled.

Lady Rosnay jerked forward. "I never believed a word about Lucy Poyntz," she said fiercely. "I told you so."

"You did. Yes. You said probably some halfwit made love to her and she thought she'd sinned a deadly sin."

"I said she was absurdly good," Lady Rosnay cried.

" 'Insanely chaste,' " Reggie corrected. "I remember. Yes. It was a defense. Nobody havin' accused her."

"Lord, what nonsense! Everybody is saying she must have had a lover and Poyntz heard of it, and that smashed them both."

"They're sayin' that now. Yes. Kind world. You got in first."

"To say she never cared a straw for any man but her good calf of a husband. And that's true."

"Yes. It could be. Now you're defendin' the man Osmond."

"What a goose you are!" Lady Rosnay gave a crow of a laugh. "My dear, I hate him. I didn't love Lucy Poyntz. These desperate earnest people bore me to death. But Lord, I'm always against fools."

"Includin' me?" Reggie murmured.

She gave him a queer impish look. "If you will be a fool," she said. "I know Osmond didn't steal the tiara. I know fools are saying he did. Don't you see?—that's why I asked him here, to show people it's all nonsense."

"Very noble of you. Other scandal about Osmond goin' round. Concerning Molly Marne. Any views about that?"

"He knew the girl, of course. Women fell for him. God knows why. I'm not young enough to blame the man for that. I wish him at the bottom of the sea. My poor Alix! She might as well be in love with a thunderstorm. But Lord, that's no reason for me to join with fools throwing muck at the man."

"Miss Lynn wouldn't be pleased. No. However. You had Osmond here to tell the world he had your confidence. Magnanimous. And the sequel is, your monkey is poisoned and you might have been."

"You're telling me Osmond did it." Lady Rosnay lowered her voice, and her eyes were intent and tried to be piercing.

"Oh, no. No. Your story, not mine."

"I never said that."

"Meaning of what you said is, three people might have poisoned the monkey: Osmond—or Miss Lynn—or you—or some combination of the same. That bein' thus, what do you want me to do?"

"Find out who it was," she cried.

"Whoever it was?"

"Lord, do you think I want to get anyone off?"

"No. I don't. No. However. You've asked me to take it up. I will. Whether I give you what you want or not."

Her eyes flashed. "Oh, a terrible fellow!" She gave a crow of laughter. "On with you. I shan't whine."

"Let's get on, then. Have you told anybody of the monkey dying?"

"Not a soul. I haven't seen anybody since. I didn't want to."

"Very discreet. Then don't tell anyone. The monkey is quite well—do you understand? I'll take the body away with me, and I'll come back to-night and stay the weekend. Don't tell anybody I'm coming—except Graves—he'll have to sit up for me. I shall be late. Nobody else. What about these Harley and Darett people? Will they be over some time?"

"They're dining on Sunday."

"That'll do," Reggie smiled. "Thank you. Now then. I shall want a suit-case and a couple of towels. Please." Her mouth came open. "To pack up the evidence," he explained.

"Oh, that's ghastly! My poor Cupid." She fluttered away. . . .

Reggie carried into the bedroom the plate and the relics of the banana. He found her on her knees by the bed embracing the monkey and talking to it. She was crying.

He turned his back. He wandered to the dressing table. He smelt the flagon of scent there and recognized the clover perfume of Molly Marne.

"Yes. I'm sorry," he interrupted the farewell. "This isn't any good." He took the monkey from her and packed it into the suitcase. "Thank you. By the way, where do you get your scent?"

"Oh my God," Lady Rosnay gulped a sobbing laugh. "What a weird person you are. The scent! Alix gave it to me. Why do you want to know that?"

"I wondered," said Reggie. "Goodbye."

Chapter XIII

Saturday

FRIDAY night had passed into Saturday morning when Reggie's car came again to the door of Langton House.

The door was opened before he reached it, and silently, "If you please, sir," the butler showed him through the dim-lit hall into a room where the lights were on and an electric fire glowed red. "I thought you might perhaps be cold after your drive." He directed Reggie's eyes to the table on which there was a vacuum jug, plates of sandwiches, whisky and soda. "A little soup, sir?"

Reggie smiled. "Oh, no. No, thanks. Think of everything, don't you, Graves?"

"Thank you, sir."

Reggie stretched out before the fire. "Did anybody notice this little spread?"

"No, sir, that would be quite impossible. I didn't prepare it till the house was quiet. My lady instructed me that you would be late and did not wish your arrival noticed."

"You're very good," Reggie murmured. "You know everything, what?"

"Thank you, sir."

Reggie gazed at the table wistfully. "Soda water, please," he sighed. "Only soda." He tasted it, he sipped. "Yes. By the way, did anybody call this morning?"

"I'm not aware of it, sir."

"And you would be, eh?"

"I should be, sir," said the butler. "Probably I would be." Reggie looked at him over the top of the glass. "Oh. Not quite sure?"

"I mean to say, if one of the ladies or gentlemen met a friend close by— or if it was a friend of the house—someone might call without me being informed."

"Yes. Oh, yes. Anybody asked you this before?"

"No, sir. Not at all."

"All right. Well, show my man where to put the car, will you? Then you can take me upstairs."

A soft-footed procession went up, the butler preserving admirably his dignity between two suitcases which did not balance him, Sam with a suit-case and a wooden box held gingerly.

The butler did not speak till they were all in a bedroom and the door closed. "Splendid," Reggie smiled.

"Now in the morning—when does Lady Rosnay get up?"

"Her ladyship is early in the country, sir. I think she could see you about half-past nine."

"All right. Tell her I should like to see her then. Now put Sam to bed, will you? You know what you've got to do, Sam?"

"I do, sir," said Sam lugubriously.

"Thank you, sir. Good-night, sir," said the butler.

With the wooden box which bothered him and his suitcase Sam was taken away.

When he came back in the morning Reggie was half dressed before the looking-glass and therein observed him with a smile. "Had a good night?"

"Not too bad," said Sam. "Friendly little devil. 'E got into bed with me to finish. Then we was all right."

"Good. Run away." Reggie went on dressing at his leisure till a tap at the door and Graves's discreet voice informed him that Lady Rosnay would like to see him.

He took the box. She was still in her bedroom, reposing in a blazing Chinese wrapper of red and gold on a couch. "My dear creature! I've had such a night! All dreams, a lifetime of dreams. Poor darling Cupid! What are you going to tell me? Have you found out what it was?"

"Not yet. No. One of the narcotics. I think I know which. However. In-vestigation proceedin'. Anneler's very sound. Meanwhile, I want you to have this." He opened the box and took from it another capuchin monkey.

She gave a shriek. "Oh, you are uncanny!" Reggie held the little creature out to her. "Don't, don't." She shrank into her wrapper. "He's so terribly like. How can you? Whatever did you bring him for?"

"Yes. Rather like. That was the idea—I want you to keep him for a bit."

"I couldn't!" she shuddered. "How could I? You heartless thing. Poor Cupid only just gone!"

"That's why he's here. So that the gentle murderer of Cupid should be startled. Might be interestin' reactions." Reggie gazed at her dreamily. "You must be rational. Take it he's one of Cupid's kind, a monkey and a brother, comin' to look about for Cupid's murderer. Same like a human man. A little policeman. Same like me." He put the monkey down on the head of the couch, and it sat crouching, its little wizened face turning from side to side, wistful and bewildered.

"Oh, the poor mite." Lady Rosnay reached up a lean claw of a hand to it:

it drew away, it submitted to a caress. "You're horrible," she said to Reggie. "I can't bear him, and I have to be nice to him."

"That's all right. Usual social conduct," Reggie murmured. "No more required. He needn't be gushed over. I don't want him to go into company just yet. Wait and see if anybody shows curiosity about existence of your monkey. Just be kind to him and keep him in your own rooms."

"I hate you," said Lady Rosnay.

"Oh, no. Not yet," Reggie smiled. "We don't know each other well enough. May I go and have some breakfast?"

"I shan't come down," said Lady Rosnay.

Reggie found the breakfast table well attended. Two men and three women were being conscientiously bright. The red head of Alix Lynn was back to the door. When she heard Reggie shut it, the first sound he made, she turned with a smile which changed its nature as she saw him. What had been gay welcome became conventional, but a certain amusement lingered with a bitter flavor.

She rose and came to meet him. "Mr. Fortune! This is delightful."

"For me. Yes." Reggie shook hands. "I'm afraid I'm taking you by surprise."

"You're always surprising, aren't you?" she laughed. "Did you get in late last night?"

"Quite late. Yes. So sorry."

"You did miss a perfect day. We must make that up to you. Do you know everybody?"

He was introduced to the negligible Hamnets, he greeted the commonplace Wiltons and sat down by them to make a good breakfast and indifferent small talk. Alix took a hearty share of both.

They were, however, near the end of their possibilities before Osmond came.

This time Alix was not so quick to hear the door. She did not turn till he had surveyed the party and announced himself with a careless "Good-morning, everybody."

Then she sent a laugh at him. "What, are you up? This is sleepwalking."

"No, I'm in training—for the domestic handicap—learning to meet the female face at breakfast." Osmond came to the table, a lump of a man made more truculent than his urban clothes revealed by ruddy plus-fours. "Hallo, Fortune!" He displayed surprise, a little late, and some amusement. "How are you? When did you get here?"

"When you were sleepin' the sleep of the just," Reggie murmured.

"Not for me, thanks. Give me the sleep of the winner. We had it last night, didn't we, Alix?"

"Don't brag," she laughed intimacy. "There'll be a vengeance."

"What has been, has been, and I have had my hour. Three up. Three up."

"Three?" Reggie drawled. "Three up—did you say? Oh. The game of golf."

Osmond stopped looking at Alix to look at him, but his pink, round face was without visible meaning. "Yes, we took on Mrs. Harley and young Darett. A pair of tigers. The first time we've beaten them. Do you play?"

"Golf? No. No. The body is desultory, the mind flippant."

"What do you do, Mr. Fortune?" Alix asked.

"I do nothing more thoroughly than anybody I know. I have a happy nature, Miss Lynn."

And Sir Bingham Wilton began a lecture on the art of idleness, and the others talked golf. It was arranged that the blameless Hamnets should play with Osmond and Alix, and Osmond said he would ring up Harley and find out if any of them were coming over.

Filling a pipe in the hall, Reggie saw him shut himself up with the receiver. Sir Bingham, who was a veteran politician, had still some phrases to let off, and Reggie was buttonholed to be an audience. He bore it benignly. Osmond's telephoning took some time.

When he emerged, Sir Bingham was facetious upon the telephone service, with anecdotes, and Osmond growled at him that there was nothing the matter with the telephones if people weren't fools. Sir Bingham remained invincibly civil. "And shall we see our friends again today?"

"Harley's not coming. His missus is a bit off color. Arthur'll be over to lunch."

Sir Bingham was sorry to hear Mrs. Harley was not well. "The effects of your desperate struggle, Osmond." And Osmond grunted that it was nothing and made off.

Sir Bingham, whose face, in spite of his venerable white hair, has a resemblance to that of a young and cheerful pig, without the humor, took Reggie by the arm into the garden.

"A vigorous personality, our friend," he said more in sorrow than anger.

"Forceful fellow, yes," Reggie murmured. "Going strong in politics, isn't he?"

Sir Bingham thought they must say that Osmond had come rapidly to the front. "But perhaps not quite, eh? Not quite. There's a phrase, 'senatorial timber,' you know. Perhaps people don't feel sure our friend is senatorial. There's a something, Fortune."

"You think so?" Reggie said respectfully.

"Well, well, let us say he doesn't influence, he doesn't impress. You know it's an axiom of mine, weight is in inverse proportion to force. Osmond is a valuable man in opposition. He is the attack, the offensive. Audacity, audacity, and again audacity. But really I can't prophesy what we shall make of him."

"Lots of friends, what?" Reggie mumbled.

Sir Bingham's little eyes blinked. Speaking for himself, he had the greatest admiration for Osmond's talents, but he did hear men complain of a lack of stability. He was sorry for it. He was afraid that strange affair the other night would do Osmond a good deal of harm.

"What was that?" Reggie yawned. "Oh, ah. Somebody did tell me. Osmond was down to say his piece, and he didn't turn up. Makin' a bit of noise, is it? What was the matter with him?"

"Ah, that is the question which makes the noise," said Sir Bingham in a confidential manner. "You see, there's no answer. Osmond has not offered any explanation."

"Well, well. Didn't really matter, did it? By what I heard, Harley took his place all right."

Sir Bingham was sure there could be only one opinion about that. Malcolm Harley did admirably. A very, very sound man, Harley. Promised to be one of the best judgments in politics. Undoubtedly that debate had much advanced his reputation. It had long been recognized that he had foresight and sagacity, but people thought he was not fond of hard fighting, he left it to Osmond, he made the schemes for Osmond to carry out. Sir Bingham considered they would hear no more of that. Harley had shown that he could use the iron hand as effectively as the velvet glove. Oh, very good at need. A most punishing fighter. He had delighted everybody. He had taken the lead among the young men. Oh, definitely. If Sir Bingham was any judge.

"Everybody happy," Reggie mumbled. "Well, well. Very kind of Osmond not to turn up. Gave Harley his chance. Friendly action. Great friends, aren't they?"

Sir Bingham pursed his large mouth. He did not think it could be taken quite like that. Certainly Harley and Osmond had been intimate, had acted together. Speaking broadly, Osmond owed his position in politics to Harley. He would never have gone down with the party but for Malcolm Harley's backing. Sir Bingham shook his head. No, one had to admit frankly, men didn't feel safe with Osmond. And this last affair—well, what could they think?

"I don't know," said Reggie. "What do they think?"

Sir Bingham chuckled discreetly. "I could tell you what they said, Fortune. When they found Osmond wasn't in the House, they said, 'Who is she?' "

"Oh, yes. Common form, isn't it? Find the woman—explanation of everything any man ever did."

"Human nature, human nature," said Sir Bingham with an air of wisdom. "There is no use in ignoring it—people are remarking that the night of Osmond's absence was the night of the mysterious death of that actress, Molly Marne."

"Oh. Was it?" Reggie asked. "Did things coincide?"

Sir Bingham gave him a knowing smile. "The evidence at the inquest was that she was alive in the evening and dead in the morning."

"Oh, ah. Does sound like dying in the night," Reggie agreed.

"The inquest was adjourned, of course. But there—you know more about it than I do, Fortune."

"No, no," Reggie moaned. "I never go into these things unless I have to. I don't know anything."

Sir Bingham said that it had made a great sensation, and Reggie agreed that things did sometimes, and on these lines their conversation dwindled till Sir Bingham gave it up and went to find his wife.

Reggie made for some chairs in the shade of the house—the showy gardens of Langton are not planned for repose—sank down with a sigh and filled another pipe.

His somnolence was impeded by vague meditations on the reasons for the existence of Sir Bingham.

From that he was tempted into curiosity over the presence of the baronet at Langton and his conversational maneuvers. Reggie had supposed the Wiltons and the Hamnets a blameless background of respectability for Osmond. If—which was an even chance—Lady Rosnay told the truth when she said she invited Osmond to declare her confidence in him, it might have been reasonable that she should make Sir Bingham come and give the fellow the endorsement of an old cabinet minister of immaculate, dull repute. But she ought to have known he hated Osmond—she must have known. Just in her impish way to bring the two together and hope the sparks would fly. Quite like her to prime the old man and set him onto Mr. Reginald Fortune.

No certainty possible. But the blameless Sir Bingham with his suspicions and his hints had a queer resemblance to the disreputable Luttrell. Rather a nuisance if he finished the same way.

However. It did look as if the old man were being managed—as if Mr. Fortune were there to be managed again.

Reggie finished his pipe and put it away. A small smile came to his face and stayed. "Oh, no. No. Not any more," he murmured and shut his eyes.

Lunchtime was near before he opened them. Voices and footsteps came up through the garden. He beheld Alix and Osmond. They looked as jovial as they sounded. They were a stimulating sight to anyone who felt strong enough for it. They displayed so much energy. All this Reggie's equable mind admitted sadly and was constrained to add more. They went well together, excellently well, beyond any expectations. The woman was altogether womanly, the man very much a man, but he had grown younger and a finer fellow, he went lightly, his truculence and his affectations were gone.

Reggie allowed himself to admire. Alix in a jumper showed him a natural perfection of that nineteenth-century shape to which his taste awards the second prize. She carried it with grace, she was in a quick rhythm of happiness, delighting in herself and in Osmond and a world that was good. Osmond kept step with her, waiting on her, worshipping and in command, servant and god.

Reggie sighed. It was unfortunate that they had to see him and arrive. They stood over him. "One of the world's workers," said Osmond.

"Title of picture—great men and their hobbies," said Alix.

"Yes. As you say. Admirin' the ideal," Reggie murmured.

"Thinking about yourself," Alix laughed and dropped. "Get me a drink, Peter, a long drink."

"Peter?" Reggie raised an eyebrow as Osmond departed.

"Don't you read the Bible, Mr. Fortune? Simon called Peter."

"Oh, yes. Fierce fellow. Cut off some fellow's ear."

Alix looked the way Osmond had gone and laughed affectionately. "If he drew a sword he'd cut more than ears."

"You think so?" Reggie murmured. "Well, well. Proper thing for a woman to think. However. You may be right. Your Simon Peter's lookin' very capable today. Bein' inspired by you."

Osmond came back with long glasses which fizzed. "That's yours, Alix, that's the soft one," he directed her choice; he sat down beside her, and they looked in each other's eyes and drank.

Then she discovered Reggie again and laughed at him. "Oh, so benign! Isn't he a saintly person?"

"Watching us drink with nothing to drink himself and looking like an angel," Osmond chuckled. "Yes, you're more than human, Fortune. And we are being civil, Alix. I say, Fortune, won't you—"

"No, thanks, no," Reggie interrupted. "I only like fizzy drinks to watch."

"We are two brutes, Peter," said Alix happily. "I always was. And now I'm making you."

"You're putting on side. I shall do all the making there is. And all the brute, too."

"Poor Mr. Fortune! What revelations," said Alix. "And he was paying you such compliments."

"Not me. No," Reggie murmured. "She was."

"She only does that behind my back," Osmond laughed at her.

"I don't have a chance to say anything to your face," said Alix, and her own face displayed an agreeable blush.

"You wait, I can be as glum as sin when I like."

"Yes, you do sham, don't you?"

"It's my trade," said Osmond.

"The terrible person." She made a face at him which had something serious in its mockery. "Oh, you are—Peter—Peter." She turned on Reggie. "Not Simon Peter, but the boy who wouldn't grow up."

"Be respectful," said Osmond. "Here's my young man. You're bad for discipline. He's got to believe in me."

Arthur Darett was coming towards them. She hailed him. "Folderol, Arthur. Are you out for your revenge?"

"No, I'm magnanimous. I always recognize the rabbits must win sometimes or the game wouldn't be a game. Also my partner is out of action. When she dies, 'three up' will be found written on her heart." Darett turned to Osmond. "I have some letters you ought to see, sir." He put his hand in his pocket.

"Go to the devil," said Osmond. " 'Ought' is a beastly word at week-ends."

"Arthur's the virtuous apprentice and you're Jack Idle," said Alix.

Darett shook his head at her and pleasantly recognized Reggie. "Good-morning, sir. I'm sorry, this is a demoralizing place. I hope you're keeping serious."

"Oh, yes. Yes. I had some good sleep. With the aid of Wilton," Reggie murmured.

"Peter woke him, poor thing. You'll never do anything in politics, Peter, you're too disturbing."

"He plays a very disturbing game, doesn't he?" said Darett, with a young man's admiring eye on his chief, and then grinned. "Especially at golf."

"You're safety-first people," Osmond grunted.

And they went on amusing themselves, and Reggie, mildly bored, admitted that it was pleasant stuff. They were so sure of each other, they were genial. They had no reserves and needed none. Darett was taken as free of all the secrets of the pair, and he, cheerily impudent, kept within the decencies of affection and respect, like a young brother with a heart of simple admiration.

Lunch called them, and they found Lady Rosnay downstairs. She was in splendor, a frock of alarming yellows, she was in spirits. She chattered inconsequently and without a pause. No one would have concealed bereavement more audaciously. And nobody showed a sign of noticing anything unexpected. That indeed would have been a challenge or a confession of guilty knowledge. She was merely herself raised to the highest power.

But after lunch she faded away, and Reggie went upstairs after her.

"You dear creature. I was sure you'd come," she turned to whisper, with her hand on the boudoir door. "Oh, it feels so funny. Yesterday—my Cupid!—and now you and this strange little waif. Look at him."

As the door opened, the monkey climbed fast up a cabinet to sit on the top and inspect them.

"Cupid would have jumped at me," she wailed. "And then he would have run to his little chair and told me to be quick and get his lunch. Oh, but see!"

The monkey climbed down the cabinet again and hung looking at the glass doors and looking back over his shoulder.

"He is a clever child," said Lady Rosnay. She fluttered to the cabinet, opened it, and took out a plate with a banana and knife and fork. The monkey sprang on her shoulder and reached for the banana, which he could not reach, and squeaked and patted her, his tiny face working with pathetic anxiety that she should understand. "Doesn't he make you cry!" said Lady Rosnay tragically, but produced no tears.

"Monkey's lunch normally shut up in the cabinet?" Reggie murmured.

"Oh, yes, always. Why?"

"Whoever poisoned the banana knew the rules of the house very well."

"Of course. He must have done."

"He?" Reggie drawled.

She stared at him over her shoulder. "Oh, you are creepy. The person, then—the person must have."

"No idea as to personality of person," Reggie mumbled. "However. Possibilities limited." He took the plate from her, and the monkey scolded. "One moment." He examined the banana carefully. "No sign of introduction of extraneous matter in this one. All right. Feed little Methuselah."

She cried out horror. "Ah, what a shame! He isn't, he's just a baby. Don't babies always look a hundred? That's why I love these darlings. My baby!" She drew the sad puckered face against her own. "Yes, I do love you." She sat down in the easy chair by the window and put him on the smaller chair. "There! Sweet! I'm going to call him Baby, Mr. Fortune," she said defiantly. "Ah, my dear, the new one always is Baby, isn't he? Bless you!" She kissed the monkey, who squeaked anger and reached for the banana. "Baby wait one minute, Mother will be so quick." She peeled the banana and cut it up and fed him.

"When you ate a bit of the other, did it taste all right?" Reggie asked.

"Of course it did, or I should never, never have given it him." She snatched at a piece and put it in her mouth. "Yes. It wasn't so sweet—I remember thinking it wasn't very ripe."

"Oh, yes. Yes," Reggie nodded.

"Do you know what it was?"

"Analysis proceedin'," Reggie mumbled. "Well, well. You're doin' quite nicely. Don't bring him into public life yet."

"I shouldn't dream of it. He's far too new. Mother and Baby going to sleep now, aren't they, darling?"

Reggie left her lying down with the monkey on her bosom. He surveyed the silent corridor. He went down by the back stairs and found himself in a hall from which swing doors led to what must be the kitchen region and another door opened onto a gravel square with shrubs about it. He went out that way, and in a few yards found himself on the main drive through the park.

He returned to the house and in the calm between lunch and tea made a loitering exploration of it. The stairs took a good deal of time.

Osmond and Alix and Darett, with the male Hamnet, came to tea late and talked golf without mercy to a conclusion of scoffing challenges on Darett's departure.

"Tell Mrs. Harley to get fit for battle tomorrow."

"Give her my love, Arthur, and tell her she's heartless not to come and be beaten again."

"Cockadoodledo," said Darett. "She can't be giving you lessons all day and every day. Yesterday was enough. We're all dining tomorrow, you know. Goodbye, Alix. Do you want me to do any letters for you, sir?"

"Oh, damn letters," Osmond growled.

"Amen. Goodbye."

When he was gone Osmond sat down in the library and dealt with letters himself, and to Reggie, smoking a dreamy pipe, it appeared that he found composition difficult.

At the first dinner bell he got up with a growl of some profanity, put papers in his pocket, and thudded out.

Reggie took his seat at the writing table. Some epistle had been torn into small pieces, of which a few remained. The purport seemed to be a rebuke from a person in authority. Reggie turned the pages of the blotting book. On one appeared the imprint of an address. He took that sheet away with him.

When he showed it to the looking-glass in his bedroom he read in a backward sloping script the name of Miss Sophia Minns.

Chapter XIV

Sunday

SUNDAY morning saw Reggie go to church.

It is his habit, but on this occasion he would allow that his motives were not wholly spiritual. He had a curiosity to know who would feel a duty to attend. The church of Langton Canonicorum serves both Lady Rosnay's house and the house which the Harleys rented.

When he came out of church his round face was dreamy and sad. The ladies of the two houses, on whom the obligation of attendance was strongest, had stayed away, yet everyone else was devoutly present. Irrational to infer any motive from an action of Lady Rosnay. Mrs. Harley had been announced unwell. The presence of all the others was more against his expectation. Arthur Darett—nothing very strange that he should go to church, only the usual probability that a young fellow would not trouble, but he was a correct youth. Who could expect correctitude from the unconventional Alix and the erratic Osmond? There they were, subdued to earnest solemnity, more attentive than the respectable Hamnets and Wiltons or the smug and condescending Harley or the languid Mrs. Darett.

A baffling couple.

They lingered on leaving the church. They had not reached the gate when Harley was handing Mrs. Darett into his car and Wilton was announcing with an accent of reproof his hopes that Mrs. Harley was feeling better.

Harley assured him she was only rather tired.

Alix and Osmond arrived to hear that. "Sorry, Mac," Osmond said, and "Oh, Mr. Harley, she'll be able to come to dinner, won't she?" said Alix.

Harley trusted so and drove his party away.

On the walk back across the park, the conversation was Wilton's. Of ritual he talked and sermons. Osmond and Alix fell behind but even to each other had nothing to say.

After they came to the house Reggie took the first moment when the corridor was empty to go to Lady Rosnay's boudoir. He found her there and playing with the monkey. "Oh. Kept by the uninvited guest," he murmured.

Lady Rosnay rolled her eyes at him. "Where have you been?"

"I've been to church," said Reggie.

"Oh dear thing," she giggled. "Of course you would. You are so whole-some. But I've been making my soul, too. Works of mercy and charity, you know. Poor Baby, he is so sad and forlorn. I couldn't leave him."

"Seems to be feelin' comforted," said Reggie. The monkey had jumped from her arms and was showing off.

"He's a love." Lady Rosnay made the sound of a kiss at him, and he scolded.

"Education progressin'," Reggie murmured. "Anybody seen him yet?"

"Only the servants, and they think he's my poor Cupid. Geese!"

"Good. I should like him to come down to dinner, please."

"Lord! My dear boy, I couldn't trust him."

"He needn't dine. Just meet the company in the drawing room. Like the small child of a very domestic family."

She laughed. "Oh, I'm the domestic female, I'll bring him, poor Baby. But why, my dear?"

"You never know, you know," Reggie murmured and went out.

Mrs. Harley did come to dinner. She and her husband and the Daretts, arriving with an admirable punctuality, found the Wiltons and Hamnets and Reggie in the drawing room but no hostess.

Wilton took charge and began an oration of small talk. Harley helped him out with cues. Reggie made himself obscure and observed life. He decided that Mrs. Harley's indisposition had been real or was being well acted. She listened gracefully, she smiled brightly, but with some effort of attention, she was languid, and her beautiful face had in repose a look of dullness which he did not remember.

Alix arrived in a gay hurry, and the party had at once more life. Osmond strode in, went straight to Mrs. Harley, was brusque, kindly, rallying. Harley joined in for a while, his hand on Osmond's shoulder, before he turned again to Wilton and drew Osmond into talk with that monument of respectability.

There was movement over cocktails and sherry, and on that Lady Rosnay entered. She stood in the doorway like a sunset cloud, tawny pink to the dead white of her neck and the irregular mass of silver hair.

"My poor people!" She gave a crow of laughter. "We have no morals, have we, Baby?"

On her shoulder sat the monkey. She tickled him, and he chattered and fought at her.

As they turned to look and the men rose, a glass tinkled to the ground. Harley was quick to dive for it, and in his movement another went down.

"I'm sorry, Rose," Reggie heard his smooth voice. "I beg your pardon,

Mrs. Darett." And Mrs. Harley and Mrs. Darett were asking after each other's frocks and saying it was nothing.

Only one person continued to be interested in the monkey. That was Alix.

Reggie wandered across the room and met Lady Rosnay. "Interestin' people, these little people," he murmured. "Had him a long time, what? Does he know everybody?"

"He's very reserved," Lady Rosnay said, and the monkey, being tempted by Reggie's hands, came to him, climbed to his shoulder, and sat up there. "Oh, don't you adore him?" Reggie turned and exhibited himself and the monkey to the company. He was rewarded by condescending smiles or polite distaste.

"Makes you look quite paternal, Fortune," Osmond laughed.

"We're not popular," said Reggie to the monkey and moved with him across the room past eyes which regarded the monkey's unsteady poise with some apprehension or were averted. He lingered by the scene of the catastrophe of the fallen glasses.

"Pray be careful," said Mrs. Harley, shrinking. "He might jump at any-one."

"You think so?" Reggie murmured and moved away.

Alix met him so that he had to stop. "Well, Cupid," she said, and the monkey blinked at her direct gaze and looked away. She put a finger under what would have been his chin if a monkey had one and tilted up the tiny head. Still he would not look at her; he jerked his head away and cowered.

"Lady not bein' respectful, no," Reggie sympathized.

Alix gave him a queer searching stare.

The voice of Lady Rosnay was uplifted. Mr. Fortune must give the angel to Graves. Baby was far too young to come to dinner. She arranged how they should go in.

Reggie found himself taking the negligible Mrs. Hamnet and sitting between her and Mrs. Darett.

It was not the arrangement which he would have chosen for pleasure, but he had no ground of complaint. Lady Rosnay's grading of the party was by the eternal principles—a thing not to be expected, yet very like her.

Mrs. Hamnet was plain and fluent, Mrs. Darett had been handsome but would not take the trouble to talk. It seemed to Reggie that she had changed since he saw her at the ball. She was made up just as much or more: the same unusual tawny shade of lipstick—he glanced at Lady Rosnay—no, not quite the same, or Lady Rosnay's was different. They did not match. And now there was no likeness between the women. Lady Rosnay, who must be years the older, was out of comparison livelier, working hard to be sprightly and please, Mrs. Darett stiffly careless whether she pleased or not, an old woman interested in her dinner, eating and drinking not much but with critical relish.

Reggie said something sagacious about the sweetbread, and that won her heart, and she gave him treasures of thought on gourmandise.

The other people were doing well enough. Neither Wilton nor Hamnet could make much of Mrs. Harley, but even as a languid, silent woman she was good company for a man to look at, and they looked. Osmond found Lady Wilton icy, and he was a bear till Harley's adroit suavity led them both into a comfortable conversation, and Osmond was amusing and she grew kind. Then Harley turned away to Lady Rosnay, who was making merry with an embarrassed Wilton. And on the other side of the table Alix and Arthur Darett enjoyed themselves without responsibility.

Yes. An ordinary, tolerable party. And a useful friend, Harley. Very useful for an awkward man.

The ladies departed, the men closed up, and the useful Harley took Reggie in hand. His talk was of the house with something of the garden. He flattered. Fortune was a connoisseur of both.

Reggie didn't know—had hardly seen anything of Langton—hadn't been there twenty-four hours—chiefly asleep. Fine place. Rather overwhelmin'. He sketched vaguely an old farmhouse in Shropshire and its view—sort of place to retire to—time he slowed down—very amiable to the aged mind.

Harley made fun of him.

"Mind not old in years, no," Reggie murmured. " 'World's so madly jangled, human things so fast entangled.' Lot of work, disentanglin'."

"Your work must be exacting." Harley rose eagerly to the fly.

"Not exactin'. Laborious. Routine. See the way—lot of effort to get through to the end. However." He drank up his claret.

"I suppose most crimes are very confused?" said Harley.

"I wouldn't say that. No. Definite crime—not often. What happened—why it happened—generally simple. Investigation goes all right when the people have gone in for direct action. May be tiresome while they keep off that. As in——" He stopped, he laughed. "Oh my dear fellow! Sorry. Talkin' shop. Let's go to the ladies."

When Harley had pronounced that it was most interesting and drunk another glass of port to assert his authority, they went.

The drawing room at Langton which Lady Rosnay prefers is upstairs, and the stairs have not the processional magnificence of the first flight in her town house. They are nearer the scale of the upper staircase there, though not so steep and with only one turn, they were designed to take, in ease and dignity, no more than a man and a woman abreast. They start at the back of the hall, a large space not brightly lit.

The six men spread out upon them a straggling line of ones and twos.

They were nearly all past the turn when the light there went out. Reggie, who came modestly last, beside, but a step behind, Arthur Darett, stopped and drew back against the wall and looked up at the lamp. "Well, well. That's odd," he murmured. "Only this one, though. See your way, can't you?"

"It's all right," Darett laughed and went on.

They passed on into gloom and, emerging from it into the light from the corridor above, threw their shadows on the wall.

Reggie fell farther behind as he watched. Wilton and Harley—a dumpy shadow and a tall shadow; Hamnet—a shadow comically like Wilton's; Osmond—a lump of a shadow; and Arthur Darett—a slight, slow, waving shadow.

Reggie took the stairs two at a time and reached the top with the others. "Quaint, wasn't it?" he said. "The light that failed. Same like the ball. Not lucky stairs, Lady Rosnay's stairs."

"I don't follow?" Harley frowned at him.

"He means the lights had conked out when Lady Rosnay took her toss," Darett laughed. "That's the joke, isn't it, Fortune?"

"Really?" Harley rebuked him. "Yes, I remember hearing something of the sort."

"Not a joke, no," Reggie moaned. "Curious and interestin'."

What interested him was not the evidence that the shadow which he saw on the night of the ball was such a shadow as Harley made or Arthur Darett. He had decided before this experiment that it could not have been the shadow of Osmond, that it was too tall for him. The subject of his curiosity was the inferences which any of them might draw from his second edition of a darkened stair.

He recognized that as matter for the future. The present was dark with the threat that he would have to play bridge. He followed them into the drawing room, resigned but placid.

His sufferings and his partner's—poor Mrs. Hamnet's correct play was much disconcerted—did not last long. Mrs. Harley decided as soon as could be to make an end of the evening, and Lady Rosnay, at first shrill in protest, then making a gush of fuss over darling Rose's tired eyes, ended by ordering Harley to take his wife home at once.

In this speeding of the parting guests Reggie removed himself. He foresaw more bridge.

It was much later, he was in his bedroom, undressed beneath a dressing gown extended upon a couch, reading Heine and drinking seltzer water, when the door was tapped and the head of Lady Rosnay came round it.

"Not in bed? How horrid of you." She fluttered into the room and sat down on his legs. "My dear, I should love to see you in bed."

"I want a nurse, yes," Reggie moaned.

"Poor boy!" She stroked his cheek. "Well, what are you going to tell me?"

"Nothing. Nothing to tell."

"Oh, how flat! But didn't you make anything of the monkey after all?"

"Did you?" Reggie mumbled.

"I thought it was thrilling. They all looked scared to death. And poor dear Rose! She nearly jumped out of her clothes."

"You think so? Yes, there were reactions. Very obscure reactions."

"I never thought of her, she's so sweet and cowlike. Reggie"—Lady Rosnay cried and clutched him—"do you believe she—"

"No. Don't believe anything. Can't hurry the investigation. Shan't get anything reliable."

"What were you doing on the stairs?"

"Me?"

"Osmond said somebody played the fool with the lights on the stairs."

"Did he? Well, well. Very indiscreet of Osmond. There was a light went out—same like the lights went out on your other stairs."

"Oh, that was it!" She gave a crow of laughter. "And what did you get by it?"

"I haven't the slightest idea," Reggie murmured. He looked at her with closing eyes. "Just assertin' myself. Something may come of it some day. But not tonight. You'd better go to bed." He squirmed to his feet.

"You're a most unsatisfactory person," Lady Rosnay cried.

"Yes, I hope so," Reggie mumbled. "Good-night."

Chapter XV

Monday

ON THE next morning Reggie came down to breakfast at an hour which he considers early. He found a table at which Alix presided over undiluted Wiltons and Hamnets, and the conversation was an infinite deal of nothing. Something nevertheless he learned: the Wiltons and the Hamnets were going at once. Something he contributed: he also would have to go. They condoled with one another on the world's need of their services. The regrets which Alix offered did not suggest any desire to rob the world. She made no mention of the absent Osmond till Wilton asked if they would see him. Then she laughed. "Heaven knows when he'll get up. The only certainty is, he'll be in a hurry then."

Reggie took himself out before anyone was ready to delay him. In the hall he intercepted the butler. "Morning, Graves. I'm off before lunch. By the way—don't know if anybody told you—light on the stairs went wrong last night."

"Thank you, sir. Miss Lynn has mentioned it." Graves's tone and face were respectfully without meaning. "It appears to be in order this morning."

"Probably somebody bumped into the switch," said Reggie.

"That was Miss Lynn's opinion, sir. Thank you, sir."

In benign meditation Reggie went out, walked away through the garden. The opinion of Miss Lynn pleased him. His mind conducted a one-sided dialogue: "My dear girl—taking a proper interest in things—yes, I like people to be interested—you're not getting bothered, are you?—well, well—anybody else feeling bothered?—our Mr. Osmond lies sleeping it off—the night brings counsel—and the next thing, please?—I wonder—I should say things have got to happen—now."

He passed through the garden into the park. He desired to find somebody, woodman, gamekeeper, laborer, any man with an eye in his head, who had been there on Friday morning before the hour of Cupid's last lunch upon earth. A small chance, a faint chance to hunt for, but it is his rule to try everything.

The park lay before him desperately empty. He avoided the broken ground in which the golf course was laid out. " 'Not here, O Apollo, are haunts meet for thee,' " he droned. If anybody had desired to come from the Harley's house to Langton unobserved, the golf links would not be the chosen way.

He scanned the broad levels and saw no creature but Jersey cows and, more remotely, deer.

He made for the region of covert and copse, disturbed young pheasants there without bringing a keeper to attend to him, and wandered on, patient of disappointment, keeping the direction of the drive which led to the far side of the park, the region of Harley's house.

This brought him close to the stream where, before it was manipulated by a landscape gardener, it ran wild. Willows whitened, aspens quivered, little breezes danced and shivered on its pools.

He heard a twig crack on which his own foot had not trodden. He looked aside and stepped behind a willow, and as he moved the crack of a shot came to him—a ping, a thud. He dropped prone behind the tree in bushes which scratched him, put his fingers in his mouth and whistled with all the breath that was in him—gasped and whistled again.

Then he raised himself enough to look round the trunk of the willow. He could see no one, but he heard what might have been someone running away.

"Well, well. Safety first," he muttered and, keeping low, removed himself to another tree to whistle a third time. Then he watched keenly but in vain and heard no more, till a sturdy man in velveteens and leggings came stealthily through the bushes.

Reggie stood up and strolled away. "Here—begging your pardon," said a slow voice of authority. "Half a minute."

Reggie turned smiling. "Yes, rather. What's the matter?"

"Was you staying at the house, sir?"

"Oh, yes. My name's Fortune. Just strolling back."

"I see. Did you happen to hear a shot just now?"

"A shot? Was it? Yes, you may be right. I wasn't noticing."

"Ah. Seemed like I heard someone whistling, too, not so far away, neither."

"Yes. There was somebody whistling. Quite a lot of whistling. I thought that. Rather odd, what?"

"Odd!" the keeper snorted. "Owdacious, I call it. Did you see anybody, sir?"

"No, I haven't seen a soul since I left the house. Funny. What's it all about?"

"Some louts having a lark with me, that's what it is," the keeper growled. "After rabbits, you know. Scaring my birds like that! It's the owdaciousness of it."

"Too bad," Reggie murmured. "Hope you catch the beggar. Have you seen anybody poking about lately?"

"No, I can't call to mind." The keeper scratched his head.

"Any stranger where you wouldn't expect, I mean?"

The keeper gave a wry grin. "What, like as you might be, sir? No, I have not. I'd have known the reason why. By your leave, I'll just push on." He strode away.

Reggie loitered, came to the original willow, and used his penknife on it till a bullet dropped into his hand. He gazed at it. "Third of an inch or so," he meditated. "Not English, I think. Say millimeters. Eight or nine millimeters. Well, well. French army revolver, German pistol, Mauser or Luger. However. Foreign origin, flavor military. General suggestion, somebody who did business in the war. And the man Osmond went through the war. Well, well." He glanced again at the hole in the willow and wandered away along the line which the bullet had taken.

Beyond the stream, he went very slowly and carefully scanning the ground. Some fifty yards away from the willow there was a tall clump of dogwood. He approached that with intensive study but found nothing till just beyond it he came on some flattening of the grass. There he bent low and parted the tufts and the dogwood and was at last rewarded by a small cartridge case caught in the spring of the branches at the roots. "Oh, yes. Probably pistol," he murmured and made for the open and the house.

The keeper, moving briskly round the coverts, kept him in sight. "Thanks very much," Reggie smiled. "Pity you weren't about earlier. No. Perhaps not. No!"

The keeper maintained discreet observation of him till his entry into the garden, his approach to the front of the house proved that he must be, as he pretended, a visitor, then turned sharp and strode away.

"Another disappointment," Reggie chuckled. "I am disappointin' this morning."

When he reached the door his car was already there. "One moment, Sam," he said to the chauffeur. "I haven't said good-bye."

Lady Rosnay, the butler told him, was down, she had gone out into the garden. He found her in a hammock in the sunshine turning over the most trivial of the morning papers.

"Oh, you evasive person," she made eyes at him. "Where have you been? Poor Alix couldn't find you to say good-bye to. She was heartbroken."

"Too bad. So am I. Nearly. I didn't know she was going."

"My dear!" Lady Rosnay giggled. "Of course she's gone up with Osmond. The wretch has a fiend of a car."

"I see. Yes. Been gone long?"

"Lord, I can't tell. Half an hour. She left you her love."

"Did she? Magnanimous girl. Give her mine—with apologies."

"That isn't love," said Lady Rosnay.

"You're so absolute. Well, well. Thank you for a delightful time."

"My dear boy, it's been thrilling. I'm sorry the others were such fogies. David Kames ought to have been here, but the wretch cried off at the last moment."

"Kames? Do I know him?" Reggie mumbled, well aware that he did not and that Kames was the exuberant, wealthy animal with whom she had been talking at the garden party, before she lectured on Mrs. Poyntz; who had been hovering about Mrs. Harley and Alix in the lobby of the House on the night when Osmond deserted it for Molly Marne.

"Of course you do," said Lady Rosnay. "Everybody has to. There's two things you can't escape, death and Kames."

"I have so far." Reggie contemplated her dreamily. "By the way, which minute did the deadly Kames cry off? Before the monkey expired or how?"

"Oh, before. He rang up on Thursday."

"Like that," Reggie murmured. "Well, well. Goodbye."

"But, my dear"—she rose in the hammock, legs, which were still pretty, waving—she became confidential—"you haven't done with it, have you? You'll tell me if you find out anything?"

"Yes. You'll hear when I'm ready. You can be sure you will. Goodbye."

He broke away. He exhorted his chauffeur to drive furiously.

Chapter XVI

Chemical Industry

THAT journey ended at the hospital in which is Reggie's laboratory. The first thing he did there was to ring up his wife. "Yes. This is me. Speakin' from the lab. Finished with Langton. ... Darling. ... Quite all right. ... You're rather bad—and rather dear. Weekend weird but useful. I'm seeing Lomas. I may be going away tonight. Few days. Rather think of calling on Stein. But we'll say I'm going to Glasgow. Nobody can think of a reason why I should go there. You are dear. You didn't know that."

He conferred with an assistant—the function of his assistants is to make objections—pensively he left an unconvinced man and took a taxi to the institution in which is the laboratory of Dr. Anneler.

That plump chemist bustled white-coated into the study where Reggie had been put to wait. "Good-morning, good-morning, you keep me hard at it, Fortune."

"Yes. The devil drives. Well, what about it?"

"It was heroin. Heroin again. In the banana, in the little monkey. I cannot give you the amount yet, but there were certainly two decigrams. I expect more."

"Quite likely. Yes. More than enough to kill the monkey."

"Without doubt."

"Any other results?"

"No, I do not recognize anything significant. It was probably injected into the banana in solution."

"Oh, yes. At three points. Both ends and the middle. They're thorough, these people. Very thorough." Reggie gazed at him pensively. "You're estimating in decigrams?"

"I put it so. I had in mind the tablets which killed the woman, Miss Marne. That is only the close sequence of the cases, you will say. But I am of opinion that the heroin in both was of the same quality."

"Yes. I daresay you're right. Where do you think it was made?"

Anneler shrugged. "I have no certainty. We shall not get certainty. I do not doubt that it is of German manufacture."

"You think so?" Reggie sighed. "Well, well. What did you make of the gold powder case?"

"That—that has without doubt been used to carry morphia—sulphate of morphia. I have found enough for good reactions and also some grape sugar. If the tablets in the case were of normal content for the marks they have left and not specially compressed like the heroin, I am of opinion that they were two grains of which not more than half was morphia sulphate and half grape sugar. You can draw the inference that the woman calculated her dose of morphia by single grains or less. It is enough! But if she supposed the compressed pure heroin tablets to be of the same strength, she would have killed herself without intention."

"Yes. You're very clear. Very convincing. I should say she did. Supplier of the heroin an ingenious person. However. Some other points. Tablets she was used to were compounded to English weights?"

"It is a probability. I do not put it higher. This compound of morphia and grape sugar, it is not unknown in England, it is a good marketable article. The seller charges for it as for pure morphia, and the buyer has something which, if she tastes, it tastes agreeable."

"So I've heard," Reggie murmured. "Sulphate of morphia, though. Not the usual English salt."

"That is true. Not in our pharmacopeia. But common in the United States and on the continent."

"As you say. Well, well. The probable explanation is, she was generally supplied with tablets of adulterated morphia prepared abroad for the English market; but for the purpose of killing her she was provided with tablets of the same appearance carrying a fatal dose of pure heroin, specially put up and almost certainly prepared abroad. Is that right?"

Anneler considered. "Yes, it is quite fair," he pronounced. "I should be prepared to give that as my opinion in the witness box."

"So should I." Reggie cocked an eye at him. "I always thought it was like that. Do you think a jury would believe us?"

Anneler shrugged and laughed. "My dear friend, I do not know what a jury will believe."

"I do," said Reggie. "That's why they always believe me. Well, well. Any further ideas?"

Anneler shook his head. "There is nothing else from the analysis. I have no doubt the heroin was German—"

"Yes. You said so. I wasn't going to tell the jury that. You also said the morphia came from abroad. That'll do. Better not be too definite. It may shake confidence. What about Molly Marne's scent?"

"The scent!" Anneler exclaimed. "What do you expect? The base is amyl salicylate. There are traces of aromatics for which I cannot get any reaction. It is a foul stuff to my nose, but harmless. One of the synthetic scents from coal-tar derivatives."

"Thanks very much. I knew that. Where was it made?"

"Oh, I think Germany—a stuff altogether in the German style."

"Yes, I agree. Rather got Germany on the brain though, haven't you? Other countries have chemical industries."

Anneler blinked at him. "Certainly. Let us say central Europe, then. But what is in your mind, Fortune?"

"Do you know anything about the lipstick?"

Anneler frowned. "Oh, the lipstick! That is quite innocent. It is—"

"Oh, yes. Yes. One of the aniline dyes and a blameless fat. I know."

"Very well, then!" Anneler was annoyed.

"Sorry, I do mean something. Do you mind—would you get the lipstick— and the powder case—and the scent bottle?"

Anneler departed with a manner of aggrieved dignity and had it still when he came back, but had also an enameled dish on which were the three things asked for and one more, the tube of heroin tablets.

"Thanks very much," Reggie purred. "I forgot the tablet tube. My error. We're amassin' such a lot of exhibits. Well—takin' one thing with another— what do you think?"

"Of these?" Anneler looked them over. "Of these as receptacles, you mean?" He frowned.

"That was the point," Reggie mumbled.

"Then I say that I can form no opinion. It is not within my province. I do not even know what information you want."

"Yes. Very correct. But rather modest, aren't you? Have a look at the bottle."

Anneler took it up, turned it over, held it up to the light, put it down again.

"Not only the glass," Reggie murmured. "The label."

The label had a cubist pattern in violet ink about its inscription, "Le Matin d'un Faune."

Anneler peered at it and shrugged. "What is it you are asking?" he said sharply.

"Where it was made," Reggie snapped back.

"I can only tell you the words are French and it appears that the scent was not put up in England."

Whether the heavy sarcasm of that was intentional or not, Reggie met it with meek persistence. "Thank you so much. And the other exhibits—the metalwork?"

Anneler turned them over perfunctorily. "What do I know?" He shrugged. "They look to me foreign. I am a chemist. This is not for me, Fortune. I am no better judge than the man in the street."

"Don't be unkind," Reggie smiled. "That's what I am. Well, well. This bein' thus, I'll carry on." He gathered up the articles from the dish and departed.

Chapter XVII

The Fog of War

As MR. FORTUNE came into his room Lomas sat back and produced a smile of joy, started up, moved to meet him, and took his hand in dramatic affection. "My dear Reginald, this is immensely gratifying. I have been racked with anxiety. To spend a weekend with Lady Rosnay! What reckless heroism!"

"Oh. You thought that?" Reggie was not pleased with him.

"I did, I did. When they sent me your message that you had accepted her invitation, I realized you felt the awful risk. I was prepared to hang the whole houseparty in a row if anything happened to you. Quite right of you to warn me of your peril. But you shouldn't have gone, Reginald. What use in vengeance, if we had lost you?"

"Not any to me. No," Reggie mumbled. "Get Bell in, will you? We shall want him."

"By all means." Lomas spoke to his telephone. "Sit down, my dear fellow. Let me see you safely comfortable after these harassing dangers. There,"—he pushed a cigar box across the table. "But why the deuce did you go?"

"To see her monkey, which was dead."

"Good Gad!" Lomas exclaimed. "Do you mean she asked you for that?"

"Oh, yes. Yes. That was the alleged reason. And he was dead."

Bell came in and greeted him solemnly, looked hard at him.

"What's the matter?" Reggie smiled.

"Beg your pardon, sir. You've got a hole in your coat sleeve. Left arm."

"Yes. I have, two holes. Brilliant, Bell, brilliant. I've been with Anneler for an hour. He didn't see it. Scientific mind not alert. You were dancin' round me, Lomas. You didn't see it. Higher intelligence not observant." He looked affectionately at Bell. "The natural man," he purred. "You and me, Bell. The natural man. He's the effective fellow."

Lomas came out of his chair and looked at the sleeve. "Damn, they're bullet holes," he muttered.

"I did notice it," Reggie moaned. "A little facetious, weren't you? Just a

113

little facetious. I was not amused. Here's the bullet." He laid it on the table with the cartridge case.

Lomas and Bell put their heads together in an examination. "Automatic pistol, I'd say," Bell pronounced. "German make. Most likely Mauser."

"You're pretty good, Bell. It is German," Reggie sighed. "Not Mauser, though. Luger parabellum."

"Ah! I know. There was a lot of 'em in the war. Nasty wicked gun."

"Yes. Quite efficient," Reggie purred. "Luger parabellum. I like that name. *Si vis pacem, para bellum.* If you want peace, prepare for war. Very appropriate. I do. I am. Seekin' peace and ensuin' it, by the most offensive methods. Same like the pistol."

"Who was it shot at you?" Lomas asked.

"My dear chap! Oh my dear chap, if I knew that, the case would be finished. Possibilities practically unlimited. Any one of the survivin' dramatis personae: Lady Rosnay, Alix Lynn, the man Osmond, the man Harley, the beautiful Mrs. Harley, Arthur Darett, his mamma, or Sir D. Kames, Bart., who wasn't there. Or none of 'em. Reasonably certain hypothesis, it was one of the mischief makers unlimited, or an employee of same." He smiled. "There you are. That gives you a nice, free hand."

"Well, let's hear how it happened," Lomas said and went back to his chair.

Reggie lit a cigar, wriggled down till he sat on the small of his back, and related in detail and with precision all the events of his weekend.

"There you are," he smiled. "What does the higher intelligence make of that?"

"It's queer stuff," said Lomas. "Do you trace a connection?"

"Yes, I think so," Reggie murmured. "Through these actions one increasin' purpose runs. Did I say that before? I hope I did."

"Looks to me like somebody's getting pushed," Bell said slowly.

"I didn't suppose Mr. Fortune was fired at for fun," Lomas snapped. "Obviously the attempt to kill was made because he had become inconvenient. The question is, what had he got hold of that was dangerous to anybody? I don't see it. The one definite discovery is that business of the shadows on the wall. What does it amount to? That the fellow who ran away, after Lady Rosnay was knocked down and robbed at her ball, was not Osmond and might have been either Harley or young Darett. Well, that's interesting. But suppose it was one of 'em and he believes he's been found out. That doesn't make it worth his while to murder Fortune. It doesn't really threaten him. Even if he's afraid we can prove he did the Rosnay job, what of it? He must know it's the smallest beer of a crime—assault which did no damage to speak of and stealing a paste tiara, which the owner won't admit she ever had, for fear of being laughed at. Either of these fellows knows a lot too much to think we should ever take a case like that into court. They wouldn't shoot Fortune to stop it."

"Deuced lucid, deuced convincin'," Reggie murmured. "But quite irrelevant. Not dealin' with the basic fact that somebody did try to shoot me. There was nearly an end of Reginald. That seems impressive to me, Lomas old thing. I should say Bell is right. Somebody's feeling bothered. My work, I think. Do you remember, I said to you the time had come for tactics—offensive and surprisin' tactics—when I handed out to Osmond the suggestion that Molly Marne's death was connected with Luttrell's death and his death with her doped nerves—when I told sister Sophia Minns I was interested in Molly's dressmaker and Molly's friends of high degree? Well, I seem to have been offensive. Very offensive. I thought there would be interestin' reactions. And here they are. The monkey's dead, and I only just missed it. Pardon these personal facts. There are others less affectin' but also significant."

"I agree it's the queerest stuff," said Lomas uneasily. "But you don't make out any connection that I understand."

"Look again. Shortly after those conversations, Lady Rosnay has a weekend party includin' Osmond, which is odd. She is advertised not to approve of affection between him and Alix Lynn, and there is affection all right, goin' good and strong, and I should say she don't smile on it. Not a reason for gettin' 'em together in the country, especially when he's under a nasty cloud. Her explanation—she knew Osmond hadn't bagged her tiara and she thought fair play required her to show people she had nothing against him. She may have been telling the truth. Very various female. However. She did have him. She also asked Kames, who was matey with her just before she came and lectured us on the Poyntz case. Only he cried off at the last minute. And at the same weekend Harley and Mrs. Harley came down to their adjacent place, bringing Arthur Darett and his mamma. Thus we have all the people of high degree whom sister Sophia mentioned as Molly Marne's friends getting together. Curious and suggestive! 'The more we are together, the happier we shall be.' Not to mention the baronet who didn't get together—after a kind of vague bearin' on the Poyntz case and a clear show with Mrs. Harley and Alix at the House when Osmond went off to poor Molly Marne."

"It's an odd muster to be chance," Lomas nodded. "I give you that."

"All right. The muster bein' thus mustered, the monkey is poisoned. No doubt about that. He was poisoned by a large dose of heroin, same like Molly Marne. Now you notice we haven't told anybody what killed Molly—I only hinted at drugs to the man Osmond and sister Sophia. Moreover, the heroin in the monkey was the same make as the stuff which was given to Molly. Next phase: the heroin was provided for the monkey so that Lady

Rosnay might have taken a goodish dose herself. She says she did have some. Which might be true—or not. In the ordinary way, not too likely she'd have swallowed enough to kill her, but it's one of the possibilities, quite a fair possibility. However—the monkey bein' dead in her arms, she didn't tell anybody. Thus getting on the record her suspicion of attempt to murder her. She kept the death secret and rang me up to come over quick, no reason stated. So I went—havin' in my extreme timidity let you know I was going."

"Sorry, Reginald," Lomas said.

"All right, all right. Now then. What's the explanation? Lots of possible explanations. First explanation: Lady Rosnay poisoned the monkey herself. Attractive explanation. Accountin' for her not taking enough heroin to matter. Accountin' for the monkey bein' poisoned when all these people were round about. The obvious motive bein' to put the suspicion of dealing in narcotic drugs on one of them—notably the man Osmond—and thus link him good and hard with Molly's death. So finally accountin' for her inviting him down there."

"Quite. That's very neat." Lomas frowned.

"Yes. I like it. Only objection—I should say she was fond of the monkey. I don't know whether that would bother her. However. Second explanation: Osmond poisoned the monkey—with or without cooperation of Alix. Next to Lady Rosnay herself, those two had the best opportunity of tamperin' with the banana. We have already a dubious association of Osmond with a woman who took morphia and with her death by heroin. Also he has been alleged to use drugs himself. But why should Osmond or Alix want to poison the monkey? Obvious answer, they didn't, it wasn't the monkey they were after, it was Lady Rosnay. If she had eaten a good share of the banana, as she sometimes did, that might have been the end of her—quite a fair possibility, as I was saying. Of course it would have been a gamble. Difficult to find any way of murdering Lady Rosnay without taking a chance. Moreover, somebody has taken a chance over her which would have killed her with luck—knockin' her downstairs at the ball. That might have broken her neck, might have given her a fatal shock. Quite a fair possibility again. She's acquitted Osmond of stealin' her tiara on that occasion, which may be true. I've eliminated him as the fellow who ran away afterwards. But the fellow who stole the tiara and the fellow who ran away are not necessarily the fellow who knocked her downstairs. Assumin' Osmond or Alix is tryin' to kill her, you have one obvious motive, removal of her opposition to their marriage. Alix means to marry him, Alix isn't the kind of girl to be stopped by grandma objectin', but we may take it grandmother could make things nasty financially. Eliminate grandma and Alix is the only Rosnay left. Rather a big prize. Might be other motives. Lady Rosnay has her ideas about these earlier incidents, the Poyntz case, the Luttrell case, Molly's case. Playin' a game of her own. So Osmond or Alix may have their reasons for stoppin' it. On the whole, attractive explanation also. Rather confirmed by Lady Rosnay's statement that Alix introduced her to the scent which she uses."

"What on earth has that got to do with it?" Lomas exploded.

"My dear chap! Oh my dear chap," Reggie moaned. "I pointed out the strikin' fact that Lady Rosnay uses the same uncommon scent as Molly Marne. If you believe Lady Rosnay, which may be rash, Alix and Molly have both been acquirin' a rare chemical product. And Molly acquired dope. However. Lady Rosnay, as usual, will cut both ways. If you don't believe her, she was tryin' to link Alix with Molly's drugs. So you get an objection to the Osmond–Alix explanation of the monkey murder. Some other difficulties. You remember it was put about that Osmond took drugs himself. That was the reason why you conducted me to look at him making the advertised big speech which didn't come off. However. We did look at him afterwards, in the cross-examination about his absence and Molly Marne's death while he should have been speaking. Rather quaint. Uncalculated effect. Difficult to calculate all effects. However. I suppose it didn't occur to you that he behaved like a drug addict?"

"I never thought about it." Lomas frowned.

"No. You wouldn't. I did. I also observed him at Langton. In a very different state of mind. Not carin' if it snowed. Well. He doesn't use drugs. Why should kind friends and enemies say he did? Further difficulties. He wasn't startled when Lady Rosnay came in with a monkey alive and kicking. It was other people. I don't press that. The man Osmond is a hard case—as we found. However. We must let it count. Alix was startled—but not till she had a good look at the monkey. Do you see?—not by the monkey's existence but by his appearance. Then she knew he wasn't the original and let me see she thought I was up to something. Very difficult to interpret the conduct of Alix. Might mean innocence—or far otherwise. So, takin' it altogether, the explanation that Osmond and Alix poisoned the monkey is alluring, but we'll have to do a bit of work before we can trust it. One more explanation possible: the monkey was poisoned by somebody not staying in the house—which means practically somebody staying at Harley's house. Obviously more difficult for one of them to get at the banana, but it could be done—if you believe Lady Rosnay. The banana was left alone in the cabinet in her boudoir quite a while. Harley and Co. came in and out of Langton playing golf and what not. There's the usual back door and back stairs. No risk for any one of 'em to nip in and dope the banana. If seen, well, they were friends of the house and, short of being caught in the act, they could carry on. Primary objection, none of 'em was seen by any of the servants. Don't amount to much. Which of 'em would it be? Any of 'em—

except Mrs. Darett. She's old and old for her age. I should say she's ill. That leaves Mrs. Harley, Harley, and Arthur Darett. Mrs. Harley announced herself ill after playin' golf the afternoon of the monkey's demise. She wasn't up to much on Sunday. Consider the incident of the spilt drinks. Should have been a crucial experiment. It wasn't."

"I don't follow," said Lomas.

"Oh my dear chap! Quite simple. Object in producing Lady Rosnay with live monkey to the company was to get reactions. I got 'em all right, but reactions confused and bafflin'. Osmond didn't turn a hair, nor did young Darett. Alix was only bothered when she saw it wasn't the right monkey. Of the others—Mrs. Harley was drinking a cocktail. Mrs. Darett was drinking sherry. I think Mrs. Darett dropped her glass first. But Harley mucked up the experiment. He made a dive to pick up something. And then both the women lost their glasses. Accurate observations impossible. Very annoying. After all my trouble getting another monkey."

Lomas chuckled. "Rather imaginative, weren't you?"

"My only aunt! Imaginative!" Reggie moaned. "Not me, no. Simple scientific method. One of the party planned to kill monkey—show 'em monkey alive—the murderous one ought to have displayed feeling. However. Experiment not wholly failure. Feeling was exhibited in the Harley section. All right. What motives could they have? Several motives suggested by facts. If Osmond has been innocent right through, then somebody has been very active in throwing suspicion on him. Who stands to gain by that? Our Mr. Harley. You notice if Osmond was smashed, Harley stands alone as the risin' hope of his party. Osmond's absence from that debate gave Harley a big chance, and he took it."

"Quite," Lomas agreed. "Harley's stock has gone up fifty per cent since that."

"Yes. So I'm told. And Osmond's has gone down. Quite natural, but suggestive. However. Obvious objections to suspectin' Harley. He's a superior person, he's blatantly respectable. I have no use for him myself, but he's just the sort of fellow who plays the game that politics are morals. Not at all the man to risk his little soul. Well. I may not be fair. The evidence is, he has a heart. The grouse of the fellows who hate Osmond is that Harley's blind fond of him. Luttrell told me that. Old Wilton rubbed it in down at Langton. Nevertheless Harley gains if Osmond's smashed. What about the others? Mrs. Harley might like to do her husband a bit of good. She may be jealous of Osmond's hold over him. It does happen. She may be jealous of Osmond's affair with Alix. No reason to think so. Only possibilities. I should say she wasn't the woman to do anything desperate about anything. But she's afraid of something or somebody now. There remain the Daretts. No obvious profit to Arthur Darett in smashing Osmond. The secretary of a man who's gone under don't get a good takeoff. Also Osmond and Darett and Alix, too, are thick as thieves. Darett may have an eye to Alix himself. You never know. But she uses him like a young brother. Mrs. Darett—I don't know—she was frightened by the monkey—mustn't make much of that—she's an old, sick woman, as I was saying. And she couldn't have done the poisoning herself. Moves too slow to risk it. Only by proxy. So that means somebody else anyway. Taking the two Harleys and young Darett—possible motives, to smash Osmond, because he was in their way, or to eliminate Lady Rosnay, because she might be dangerous over some of the other little incidents. Attractive explanation again. Accounts for the identification of the shadow on the wall with somebody who might be Harley or Darett. Would account for the attempt to kill me after the shadow experiment. There you are."

"Quite," Lomas smiled. "We are. You're very thorough, Reginald. Did you suppose you had explained anything? You give me a plausible theory to make any one of half a dozen people guilty of nothing definite and no evidence against any of them. We're in a blind fog."

"Oh, no. No. You didn't listen. We are workin' through a fog. But it's what military men call the fog o' war. And if you'd listened to my intelligent report on it you would have seen that the possible objectives of the enemy in this Langton campaign can be reduced to three—elimination of Lady Rosnay, elimination of Osmond, elimination of me."

"Ah! That's what I've been thinking," said Bell. He pointed to the bullet and the cartridge case. "Here's the real clue, to my mind. The whole thing was a plant to get you down there and do you in."

"Thanks very much," Reggie smiled. "Agreeable idea. I thought that at first, modest as I am. But I have my doubts now. Takin' things as they occurred, it don't fit very well. Far better chances of killing me than the last-moment effort this morning. I should say that was decided on as the result of my handling of the case. Not one of these people could be sure what I made of it. Every one of 'em knew I was experimenting on 'em. Very harassin'. Somebody was feelin' pushed, as you said, Bell."

"Quite. That's where you began," Lomas shrugged. "But you're not any nearer who it is."

"I don't know so much," said Bell stubbornly. "We've got something to work on. Find out which of these beauties had a Luger pistol and that gets us home."

"Yes. It might," Reggie murmured. "Or not. Person owning pistol not necessarily person who used it. They don't leave straight clues lying about, our mischief makers. When I see one now, I take it as left to deceive. However. Try the pistol line, by all means. Try everything."

"A nice job for you, Bell," Lomas smiled. "You'll find none of 'em has a permit for a pistol, or those who have keep another kind."

"May be," Bell grunted. "There's other ways, sir. Servants know a bit."

"Very well. Mind your step, though. You haven't a damn thing you can use against anybody, and these people all have pull enough to make themselves nasty."

"Thank you, sir. I'll watch it." Bell glowered at him and turned to Reggie. "You know, Mr. Fortune, there's another thing struck me. What about that letter that was written to Miss Minns? Seems to me it wouldn't do any harm to be asking her who wrote to her from Langton and what was in the letter."

Reggie smiled. "You don't miss much, Bell. It wouldn't do any harm. Might do a bit o' good. More offensive tactics. Surprisin' or not. That letter's very interestin'. Got a looking-glass?"

Chapter XVIII

Mr. Fortune upon Tactics

Lomas jerked open a drawer and pulled out a hand mirror. Reggie gave him with a flourish of a gesture the section of Langton blotting paper.

The writing was reflected. "There you are." Reggie lifted an eyebrow at him. "Anything occur to you?"

"Queer hand," Lomas said. It was of a marked and uncommon type, sloping to the left, the letters long and thin and regular. "Do you know any of these people's handwriting?"

"Not me. No. I must have seen Lady Rosnay's. General recollection of a Victorian flow—not reliable."

"As I understand," said Bell heavily, "this letter was written where Mr. Osmond had been writing. Well, that looks like it's him that's worrying about Miss Minns. And you said he would, Mr. Fortune."

"Yes. I did. He was bound to. Some conference with Miss Minns probably a cause of the operations at Langton. But the bearing of the letter is still obscure. Osmond may have written it. Anybody else in the whole crowd might have written it. It may have been written because it had to be. It may be a fraud to provide evidence for the inquirin' Mr. Fortune that somebody at Langton, Osmond or another, was writing to Miss Minns."

"My dear Reginald!" Lomas exclaimed. "You're getting very subtle."

"Not subtle, no. Only careful. But perhaps too careful. These people have got me into the state of mind which doubts everything that looks likely. Delusive, dangerous state. Must be controlled. Well. Have you got the anonymous letter that was sent to Mrs. Poyntz's daughter?"

"Yes, sir. I'll fetch it." Bell strode out.

"Good Gad!" Lomas groaned and jerked back in his chair. "You have the Poyntz case on the brain, Reginald. What connection can there be between that letter and this letter?"

"Both written to the bereaved," Reggie mumbled. "Shortly after dubious death. That was anonymous. This is in an odd hand. Comparison worth making."

Bell came back. The letter to Ruth Poyntz, "Ask your daddy why Mummy killed herself," and its envelope were laid on the table. They studied the writing, they studied again the looking-glass reflection of the address to Miss Sophia Minns.

And over Reggie's pensive face came slowly a benignant smile.

"Damn," Lomas muttered and frowned. "There is a likeness—and it isn't too like."

"Yes. Quite fair. Same unusual, unnatural hand. Not managed the same way. Letter to Ruth written more freely than letter to Sophia. As if the hand came easier to the writer of the Ruth letter and the writer of the Sophia letter hadn't so much practice, had to be careful."

"Imitating, eh?" said Bell. "Looks like that to me."

"Yes, I think so. Imitation of a sort. Object not clear. Might be to persuade the intelligent police that the letters came from the same person though they didn't. Might be to keep up a disguise which had been found effective. However. One thing certain—the person who wrote to Sophia knew the kind of writing somebody had sent to Ruth."

"And how useful that is!" said Lomas. "The more evidence we get, the more obscure the whole thing is."

"My dear chap!" Reggie gazed at him with large, astonished eyes. "Oh my dear chap! Not so but far otherwise. It's gettin' clearer with every little fact that arrives. You can see the strands which run through all the cases now. There's persistent effort to destroy reputations—you have to infer it in Mrs. Poyntz's death, it comes out sharp in all the business at the ball, and it's a probable factor in Molly Marne's death. There's a recurring use of men's relations with women—the Poyntzes and Lady Rosnay's talk—Molly and Alix and Osmond. There's handling of dope—and there's a thread of sheer cruelty—either to frighten, or for the love of it—the beastly letter to the child and the killing of the monkey. Put all that together—and have you never met anything like it before?"

"You suggest we're up against a drug-and-blackmail business," said Lomas slowly. "Yes, the two things do go together sometimes." He looked at Bell. "One partner in the firm supplies the dope, the other one blackmails the poor devils who use it. We've met that, what?"

"We have, sir," Bell grunted. "And it can be very awkward to handle."

"It's going to be." Lomas shrugged.

"Yes. It has been." Reggie contemplated them dreamily. "May be more so. Something bigger than the ordinary dope-and-blackmail firm. Operations on a large scale and in many departments. Don't leave things out, Lomas. We've got interference with a blameless wife, leading to suicide, murder of a decent woman after her corruption with morphia, meddling with political careers and love affairs and an old family fortune. The evidence is, we're up against people who are ready to take on any sort of dirty work which makes a big job and have a preference for cruelty—even wanton cruelty." His eyelids drooped. "That may have been the original motive. Desire to hurt. Desire to destroy. Yes, I think so. However. Now developed on a commercial basis. Organized business of crime. The mischief makers, unlimited. Ready to undertake dirty work for anybody who can pay. Speculative concern but prosperous so far. I should say the dividends have been large. Our error, Lomas old thing. Our grave error. However. They are now discoverin' the risks of the business. We'll show 'em some more."

Lomas stared at him for a moment of silence, then leaned forward and spoke in a low voice: "You mean to suggest there's a blackmail-and-dope business which is ready to work up a political scandal?"

"Oh, yes. Yes. Anything in that idea to stagger the higher intelligence?"

"It doesn't happen, that's all."

"My Lomas! You mean it doesn't come out. Do you remember any crash of a politician in which there wasn't more than met the eye?"

"Quite," said Lomas uncomfortably. "I agree. There has been generally. But that concerns the way the crash was engineered at the last. There was always something genuine to go upon."

"You think so?" Reggie murmured. "Optimist. However. Something quite genuine here. Association of Osmond and Harley with an actress who took drugs. Shockin' to public morality. However it was arranged."

"It's a deuced awkward business." Lomas frowned. "What do you want to do?"

"My dear chap!" Reggie smiled. "Onward and upward. Pursue the tactics of offense and surprise. Continuin' the open offensive—Bell should go and ask sister Sophia what about that letter—he should also continue to worry Molly Marne's dressmakers, hairdressers, and what not—especially Maison Montespan. The more we know about them, the better—and the more they're afraid of us, the sooner to sleep."

"That's all right." Lomas nodded relief. "I agree."

"But why do you put in this Maison Montespan?" Bell objected. "It's a tiptop place, the highest class by what I can make out, and Molly Marne hardly ever used it, her maid says, and that's true, I reckon. There was only one dress with the Montespan name on."

"Yes. That's the first reason for looking into it. Adequate reason. She had lots of dresses from all the other people. Connection with Maison Montespan almost obliterated. The second reason is that Alix Lynn goes there."

"Very good, sir," said Bell gloomily. "I'll put 'em through it again. But I've got to say they were very open and straight."

"They may be. However. They'll tell Alix we're being a nuisance. Now the tactics of surprise. I want to be a nuisance to Harley, Lomas."

Lomas frowned. "We shall have to go easy with him."

"That's what he'll expect. Yes. He'll be seriously annoyed if we don't. Which might produce interestin' reactions."

"He'll react officially," said Lomas.

"He might, yes. As a prominent and respectable politician. With pull. That would be interestin' in itself. But the thing can be managed. Subject of inquiry, where was Harley early and late on the day of Molly Marne's death?—who are his private associates?—and so on. Bother his servants and have him watched. It don't matter if it's bungled. Then you can disavow and regret and so on—officially. And suggest that Mr. Harley should come and have a talk. The thing is to put the wind up in the Harley circle. Can be done, what?"

"It can," Lomas admitted. "I don't much like it, Reginald."

"No. I daresay. I don't like women bein' tortured and murdered."

Lomas shifted in his chair. "Very well. We'll badger Harley. Anything else?"

"Not for you. No. I'm going abroad."

"What?" Lomas stared. "Good Gad! You don't suppose this is a foreign show?"

"No. Not in origin. But there's a foreign end to it."

"Where the dope came from, eh?" said Bell eagerly.

"There is that. Yes. Anneler thinks the heroin came from Germany. I'm going to Switzerland."

Bell's mouth came open. Lomas shrugged. "The experts differ, what?"

"No. I should say he's right. But there's another line of investigation. So I'll run over to Bern. Just wire Stein, will you, to make me official?"

"Calling it a drug case?" Lomas asked.

"Oh, yes. Yes." Reggie stood up by sections. "That gives tone. Don't look so bothered. No deception. I'm only goin' after the cosmetics." He smiled down on Lomas and sighed. "If I knew why Molly Marne used the same scent as Lady Rosnay! My only aunt! If I only knew why Mrs. Darett once used the same color lipstick as Lady Rosnay! Then we could get on. Goodbye."

Chapter XIX

Alpine Glow

MR. FORTUNE stood on the balcony of a room in Bern high above the gray river and looked out beyond steep roofs and turrets, beyond the trees and wide green spaces of the valley to the distant snow mountains. Their mass and their peaks stood resplendent in the golden light of evening, sharp against a clear blue sky.

He sighed and came back into the room and contemplated the dinner table laid there for two and read the menu with a mild, benignant eye. Then he wandered away to gaze at the mountains again, and his round face asked them bewildered, melancholy questions.

The door opened and a short, sturdy man came in briskly. The close clipping of his hair made his head look cubical, and its angles were emphasized by high cheekbones and a spade of a chin. He clicked heels and bowed formally and then was affectionate, taking both Reggie's hands and holding them. "My friend, my dear friend. This is a very great pleasure."

"Yes. And to me. Good to work with you, Stein."

Herr Stein smiled to his ears and rubbed his hands. "It is a big affair, eh?"

"Large-scale. Yes," Reggie said. "I'm feeling rather small." He looked away at the mountains.

Stein chuckled and shook his head. "Oh, no, no, my dear Fortune. I know that modesty. It means great trouble for somebody."

"Yes, I hope so," Reggie murmured. "Need to justify my existence rather pressin'." And still the mountains held his eyes.

"It is a grand prospect, eh?" Stein watched him. "Wonderfully beautiful."

"Rather awful," Reggie mumbled. "Makes you feel a speck in the universe—insignificant, futile speck. However. Let's have some dinner." He brought Stein back into the room. "What'll you drink first? Port and water?" He sighed. "Oh my dear chap. I was afraid you would. There you are. I thought we'd better dine up here. Not to advertise that Mr. Fortune has come out to meet Herr Stein."

"So. You think you are watched even here?" Stein looked at him over the glass. "It is as big as that?"

Reggie tasted the sherry of Bern without satisfaction. "Watched? No, I don't think so. I hope nobody's expecting me in Switzerland. But I might be noticed. No limit to the possibilities. Clever people in command on the other side. They were always bold. And they're fightin' back to the wall now."

"Good!" Stein's teeth gleamed. "I am happy to assist. You came straight here?"

"Oh, no. No. I came by Geneva."

"So?" Stein's eyebrows went up from his pale eyes.

"Not the straight way. No. That was one reason. Not the main reason. However. Can you eat after that stuff?" He pointed a pitiful little finger at the watered port.

"Try me, my friend." Stein finished it, and Reggie rang the bell and the waiter came.

From crayfish to carp they progressed, from the richness of tournedos Rossini to the simplicity of chicken and cold asparagus with white and red wines of Neuchâtel, and Reggie discoursed on their mild minor charms. It is a theme he loves. But when the wild strawberries came he gave Herr Stein claret, Latour of 1920.

"Ach, my friend, our little wines." Stein dismissed them with a gesture of condescension. "You are kind to them. But this, this is the grand style."

"Queenly, yes," Reggie murmured. "Don't always want to talk to queens. Cortaillod's simple, fresh, and human. I needed that. No more cream? Oh my dear fellow!" He finished it and the strawberries.

"You are forever young." Stein smiled at him affectionately.

"Want to be," Reggie mumbled. "Rather a bafflin' world." His round and amiable face had a dreamy melancholy.

The waiter left them to their coffee, and they sat by the window watching the sunset light fade. Stein lit a fat cigar at which Reggie looked with apprehension and sighed and made haste to start one of his own.

"It is a drug case, your Mr. Lomas instructs me," Stein said.

"That's what we have to work to, yes. Want you to find somebody who's been sending tablets of morphia and grape sugar and tablets of heroin to London. Any ideas?"

Stein laughed. "If I had, we should have acted. But come, you have something more than that. Why do you think your tablets were made in my poor country?"

"The evidence is, they weren't. Such as it is. On analysis they look as if they were a German product."

"So. Then my little country is only suspected to be the middle man." Stein shrugged. "That makes it still more difficult."

"Yes. I should say the materials were imported from Germany and put up here. No certainty."

"I believe you!" Stein grinned. "My dear Fortune, this is interesting, but where do I begin from?"

"Several points possible. First point, somebody who has apparatus for compressin' tablets." Reggie described the doubly compressed tablets of heroin.

"Again, it is interesting. But there are many, many firms can make up tablets. A hundred, five hundred, a thousand—what do I know?"

"No. You can't. Second point, somebody sendin' consignments of chemical products to a London house, hairdresser, dressmaker, or what not."

"Thank you very much," Stein cried. "That is very useful. If they are drugs, they go secretly, they are smuggled."

"Oh, yes. They would be. But your people might have their suspicions."

"It is possible. I will enquire very carefully. But frankly, my dear Fortune, I hope nothing. You will confess, you give me no solid matter to work on. After all, why do you suspect my Switzerland? The evidence you have, it points to Germany."

"Not all of it. No," Reggie said. He walked across the room, fetched an attaché case and unlocked it, and laid on the table Molly Marne's gold powder case, her lipstick, her tube of heroin tablets, and her bottle of scent. "What do you make of them, Stein?"

Stein gave them a prolonged examination and at the end of it came back to the powder case, screwed a jeweler's magnifying glass into his eye, and inspected the case once more, found the spring and opened the mirror.

"So." He dropped the glass from his eye and caught it and looked at Reggie, and his pale eyes flickered. "You have something here. This was made to carry drug tablets."

"I know that. Where was it made?"

"Yes, you are right. I think in Switzerland. I think in our watchmaking district. If you say around La Chaux de Fonds I do not deny it."

"I don't say," Reggie murmured. "That's for you. I thought so. However. Any opinion on the other exhibits?"

Stein looked at them again, tried the lipstick on his hand and produced a mark of raspberry hue. "What do I know?" He shrugged. "These are common. What do you find in them?"

"Nothing. Not in that color. Common form, as you say. I was thinking about the scent."

Stein smelt. "I do not know it," he said slowly. "Exciting, eh? A perfume for amours. And then?"

"What about the bottle?" Reggie mumbled.

Stein held it up to the fading light. "You suggest it is of Swiss make? I cannot tell you that."

"Have a look at the label," said Reggie.

Stein turned the bottle over and studied the cubist pattern in violet and green. "The modern art, eh? Yes, we do things like this in Switzerland. Also in Germany, my friend. There is a German touch, I think."

"And a French name," Reggie murmured. "A certain mingling of styles. You do mingle a bit in Switzerland. However. This isn't all the evidence. Where would you go to in Switzerland if you were lookin' for rare cosmetics?"

Stein made a guttural exclamation and laughed. "My dear friend, I should go nowhere. What would you have? We cater for all the world, but we do not specialize for the Jezebels. Our Switzerland has no attraction to them."

"No. As you say. Strenuous atmosphere. Respectable atmosphere. Even on the lower levels." Reggie contemplated his comely, capable hands. "I've been manicured three times today," he moaned.

"My dear friend!" Stein spluttered.

"You asked me why I came by Geneva. This is the second reason. Lookin' for rare cosmetics."

Stein slapped his large thigh. "Geneva, yes, it is the best place, it is exotic, it is not Swiss, it is not anything."

"No. In the third salon—close to the League of Nations—the fair operator sold me these things." He produced a bottle of scent and a lipstick.

Stein took the scent. It had a label of the same cubist pattern in violet and green as Molly Marne's, but the words were different.

" '*Les Yeux Folichons*,' " Stein read. "What you call wanton eyes, eh?"

"The glad eye," Reggie corrected sadly. "However."

Stein uncorked and smelt it. "Ach, so. It is the same as the other." He blinked at Reggie.

"Yes. '*Le Matin d'un Faune*' for London. '*Les Yeux Folichons*' for the cosmopolitans of Geneva. But the same coal-tar derivative—by any other name smellin' as sweet."

Stein took the lipstick. On its outer cardboard case was inscribed "*Feu de Nuit*." "Fire of the night," he said and thrust out a lip of scorn. He tried the stick on his hand and produced an orange tawny mark. "So! This is not the same, my friend."

"No. Not the same as Molly's," Reggie murmured. "But it's one I wanted. Used by others."

"Very well. And then?" said Stein eagerly.

"Well, then, it's up to you, Stein. The fair manicurist told me they came from Fora—the house of Fora of Zurich. I want to know all about Herr Fora, please. Without alarmin' him."

Stein nodded. "I understand, yes. Have no fear. He shall not be alarmed. But it is urgent, eh?"

"Yes. Quite urgent. Only four deaths yet," Reggie murmured. "I wonder." He lay back and gazed out through the twilight.

The sun was gone. The valley lay dim in shadow, and the snow mountains were insubstantial, ghostly shapes, neither of earth nor sky.

Then their silvery white was flushed with a surge of color, all the hot hues of red, scarlet, crimson, purple came over them in a mingled tide, as though the snows were ablaze with molten fire or streaming blood. And the valley beneath was black.

"My God!" Reggie muttered.

"Wonderful, is it not?" said Stein with the complacency of an owner. "You have not seen it before, my friend? It is our Alpenglühen—the Alpine glow. The setting sun has sunk low, you see, too low for the valley, but its last light strikes up to the great heights for some moments. Watch, then."

Reggie moved in his chair. "I know," he said. "Like vengeance, isn't it? Blood and fire. The last light on earth. And then—" The red glow faded and died away, and the mountains were gone into a dark void. "Then nothing." He shivered.

"My dear friend!" Stein put a hand on his shoulder. "But you are a romantic. This is the emotion of world smart. A wicked world, oh, yes. Look still." The lamps of the town shone out from the nearer twilight, and here and there in the valley house windows gleamed. "Kind life goes on."

"Yes. I believe that. Yes. But only by grace of vengeance. There's got to be vengeance. That's what we're for, Stein. A weird world."

Chapter XX

The Faithful Friend

FOR the lucidity of the history, here is put a chronicle of the labors of Superintendent Bell while Mr. Fortune was absent in Switzerland.

Against Bell it has been said crudely that he never had an idea of his own, but he does it like the devil if you tell him what to do. These are the criticisms of the official mind on the man of action and his space in the newspapers. Mr. Fortune likes to insist that the victory of justice in the case was won by Bell's work.

His first care was to organize that research into Harley's past and present desired by Mr. Fortune. He was zealous and comprehensive, and he employed upon it pushful, worrying men.

The examination of Miss Sophia Minns he allotted to himself. You may behold him in the servants' sitting room at the house where she was cook, stolid on a chair before that plump, blonde woman. She stood. Her flat face was flushed. She told him what she thought of him for coming bothering her.

"That's no way to talk, you know," said Bell. "You understand very well why I have to come. It's your own fault. You ought to have gone around to the police station some time ago."

Miss Minns tossed her head and snorted. "I never did! I never 'eard such impertinence. The police ain't got nothing against me. Nor I don't want to 'ave no dealings with them. Busies, they call you, don't they? Busybodies, I say, coming plaguing me in the middle of my dinner for nothing at all."

"Where's that letter?" said Bell.

"What letter? I don't know what you mean. I've 'ad a pack o' letters over my poor girl's death, and no business of yours, neither, mister. I'm not going to show 'em to you. Don't you think it. They're private to me. You ain't got no right to ask about 'em."

"I'm doing my duty. I'm investigating your sister's death. Do you want to hush it up? You can't do it."

"I don't want to 'ave a lot more muck about her in the papers, nor I don't mean to 'ave."

"Trying to make a mystery of it. That won't help you. Did you have a letter from Mr. Simon Osmond?"

She gave no sign of surprise or embarrassment unless it was in the moment of silence, the stubborn look before she answered. "Yes, I did. A nice kind letter. Mr. Osmond's a gentleman."

"What did he say, besides being nice and kind?"

"'E asked me for to go and see 'im. You don't need to be so tricky. You know why very well. About that there telephone message what 'e 'ad as if it was me telling 'im to go to Molly the night she died. Of course 'e wanted to clear that up."

"I see. And did you clear it up?"

"Yes, we did. We made out all right he had it and it never come from me. Someone played a dirty trick on us, that's what it was."

"Oh, you agreed on that. I see. And what about the rest of your pack of letters? Who were they from?"

"Who do you think? Our own folks and folks as knew me and Molly and her ladies and gentlemen what knew about me."

"Ah. Any letter from Mr. Malcolm Harley?"

"No, there wasn't. Mrs. 'Arley, she wrote. Very sweet, she wrote me, like a real lady."

"Did Lady Rosnay write or Miss Lynn?"

"They did not. And that's all about it. I've 'ad enough, mister."

"But I haven't," Bell grunted. He took out a photograph of the address on the blotting paper and put it into her hands. "I want that letter."

Miss Minns stared at the writing, and her red face paled.

"I know you recognize the writing," Bell said. "Come on, out with it."

"God strike me dead if I do!" Miss Minns cried. "I don't know who wrote it. I never saw the likes of that writing before. It's wicked, that's what it is."

"Where's the letter?"

"I 'aven't got it." Her voice was shaken. "I wouldn't keep the nasty thing, not a minute, I wouldn't. I burnt it."

"Oh, did you! Afraid of it, were you?"

"It made me go queer all over," she said faintly.

"Who was it from?"

"I don't know, I tell you, I don't know. There wasn't no name to it. It was only just a line or two, but a wicked thing, cruel wicked."

"What did it say?"

"I don't rightly remember, sir." She was crying. "Not to be sure now. I didn't want to. I don't want to think of it."

"Come on," Bell growled.

"Well, it was something like, 'You done well out of Molly's death, you 'ave, you be careful.' Oh, it did 'urt."

Bell waited, watching her shake and sob. "That's all you can remember, is it?" She nodded vehemently. "What it comes to, you had an anonymous letter accusing you of Molly's death." She cried out. "Ah, that's very fine. But instead of bringing that letter to the police, you burnt it quick. That means you've done your best to hide what did happen to Molly. You had better be careful, my girl. If there's any more you know, let's have it."

"There isn't, there isn't, I take my dying oath," she sobbed.

"Ah. I mean after this. That's all for now." Bell glowered at her and strode out.

When he discussed these extorted statements with Lomas they found only one conclusion upon which they could agree, that Miss Minns had made the case more difficult.

Bell thought she had mostly told the truth but not all the truth she knew. Lomas would not commit himself to believing anything except that she had been somehow frightened.

Both of them doubted her account of what was in the letter. Unless it had contained something more or something different, neither of them could see any reason for it, or who would have sent it, or fit it into the case at all.

In this Mr. Fortune finds his favorite example of what he pronounces the governing factor of the whole case and of most mysteries, the conviction of people that other people's minds work in the same way as their own. He will point out that this error produced not only all the crimes but also the long difficulties of detecting them. His own success he attributes to the simple method of believing evidence, which he sees very rarely practiced by clever creatures.

The comment of Superintendent Bell is that this is just a way of putting it; what Mr. Fortune really goes by is his wonderful way of feeling people through the things that turn up.

Mr. Fortune replies with some indignation that there is nothing wonderful about it. He only has an open mind, the uncorrupted, simple mind of the common man.

The letter to Miss Minns, he admitted pensively when Lomas defended their inability to make anything of her story, had merely this importance, that it provided evidence which linked up the whole case and a final explanation of the people who were behind it. He agreed that it gave no new light on the tactics which he had laid down for Bell. And with the way Bell managed this phase of the war, he was well satisfied. More satisfied than Lomas, who has always grumbled that the losses were heavy.

Bell went to call on the Maison Montespan. It was established in one of the quiet streets north of Piccadilly. What had been the house of a person of quality was left still maintaining, among a frank transformation into offices and showrooms, its air of genteel privacy. There was no name to be seen on it. Its double windows were all curtained. The oak door indeed stood open to a little hall of black and white tiles, but there was a glass door beyond, and anyone who came to that saw, within, a woman dressed as a parlormaid in a frock of a red so dark that it was almost black.

The maid who was on duty when Bell came had received him once before, but her pleasant smile showed no recognition. "Remember me, don't you?" He frowned at her. "Superintendent Bell. Tell your owner I want to see her."

"I beg your pardon, sir. I will see if moddam is here. This way, if you please."

He was taken to a little room, pretty in the Empire style. He was kept waiting some time before there came to him undulating a tall black-browed woman. She condescended. "I am at your service, Mr. Superintendent. But I do not know what more I can do for you."

"That's as may be, Madame Finck. I have to clear this up from the beginning. You are the proprietress of this business, are you? Sole proprietress? I mean you're responsible."

"I am the owner of Maison Montespan. I made the establishment. I told you all that before."

"And you've been here how long?"

"Seven years. I came from Paris, the atelier of Mayer. But what is this you are asking?"

"Nobody but you has any control of the business?"

She laughed. "It is plain, you do not understand. This is a matter of art, and art is of one, one only. The art, it is here,"—she tapped her brow.

"What I mean, anything that's going on here, you'd know about?"

"Ah, bah, the little details, no. The creation, yes."

"Well, now, you stand to it, you never sold much to Miss Molly Marne?"

"It is as I told you." She put up her shoulders, she spread out her hands. "I find three-four dresses in two years. Miss Marne was not for us, poor little one."

"Funny she came here, then, wasn't it?"

Madame Finck smiled indulgent contempt. "No, no. An ambition, you understand, an ambition quite natural. So many of these young people who think they have talent, they wish to make it known they are gowned by Montespan."

"Who recommended her to you?"

"Recommended!" Madame Finck sneered. "My dear sir, the Maison Montespan does not need recommendations."

"You're too important to bother about Miss Molly Marne, eh?"

"You are good enough to say so." Madame Finck gave a supercilious bow.

"She didn't count with you. She didn't matter. That's the way it was?"

Madame Finck pursed her lips with a grimace of humorous sympathy. "That is to be a little hard on her, sir. Miss Marne—it was a little talent, but genuine. One was glad to help her."

"I see. Very kind. Who got you to take notice of her?"

Madame Finck frowned. "I do not understand."

"Somebody introduced her," Bell growled.

"Oh, certainly." Madame Finck put a finger to her brow. "That would be required. We do not wish a clientele of anyone. Ah, yes, I recall. The Lady Rosnay spoke to me of her."

"Oh. Not Mrs. Harley?"

"But no. No. Mrs. Harley? I did not know there was an acquaintance."

"Who paid for Miss Marne's frocks?"

"Sir!" Madame Finck stood haughtily erect. "You will please to understand I could not tell you that. If it had been anyone but Miss Marne— which I do not say—we should be careful not to know, not to keep a record. That is a necessary condition for us. We could not concern ourselves with such matters."

"Professional discretion, eh?" Bell said. "I understand. Thank you, madame. That's all very interesting."

Madame Finck said she was pleased he found it so; she showed him to the head of the stairs with languid ceremony. As he went down he saw her reflected in the glass of the door at the bottom. She stood, not ceremoniously, but with her hands on her hips and her body thrust out, watching him.

This pose, Bell has said in subsequent discussions, seemed queer to him, though he did not exactly know why. It was somehow like a charwoman or a costermonger, that sort of person, and Madame had been so refined. He didn't really take that for meaning much—these people in fashionable businesses were often just common vulgar under the veneer—and yet in a way it got him thinking.

Mr. Fortune inclines to consider this the best effort of Bell in the whole case.

But it is a technical criticism. Bell's thinking led him to nothing definite. He went into a neighboring tavern which provided upstairs cuts from the joint and a view of the front of the Maison Montespan, and there he ate and drank, observed and ruminated. In a long stay he saw a good many cars come to the door and derived from them only a confirmation of his knowledge that Madame Finck had plenty of business with the rich. There was, however, one car, which did not come to the door, but, having stopped round the corner, emitted a woman who made haste to the Maison Montespan, and she was Mrs. Harley.

It has been much discussed between Lomas and Mr. Fortune how the case would have developed if Bell had gone in after her. But Mr. Fortune maintains that speculation is vain, and he is content with the issue as it arrived.

Bell determined to set a watch on the Maison Montespan and stimulate the inquiries into Harley. And this Mr. Fortune considers a sound decision.

The effects, however, were wholly surprising to Bell and Lomas. A day or two after, when the energies of Bell's men had failed to discover anything suspicious in Harley's past or present, Lomas was told that Mr. Osmond wanted to see him.

This time Osmond was not kept waiting, but again he came in violently.

Lomas gave him a suave and cool "Good-morning" and pointed to a chair.

Osmond flung himself at it. "You didn't expect to see me here again." His deep voice was loud and fierce.

"I had some hopes," Lomas smiled.

"And you don't know why I've come now," Osmond stormed on.

"In the matter of Miss Minns, I take it," said Lomas blandly.

Osmond flushed darker. "Nothing of the sort. I've seen Miss Minns myself. We cleared up that damned telephone message. She didn't send it. There's no doubt it was faked."

"I heard you and she had settled that between you," said Lomas.

"What are you insinuating?" Osmond growled.

"I point out to you that I'm aware of what you agreed on with her."

"Very well, we are agreed. I didn't come to waste time over that. It's for you to find out who arranged the damned thing. I take it you've failed, as usual. What I came for was to warn you to stop this vile business of plaguing Harley."

"I don't follow," Lomas drawled, put up his eyeglass, and stared. "Who is giving offense to Mr. Harley? And why does Mr. Harley send Mr. Osmond to make his complaint?"

"He hasn't sent me. Harley doesn't ask men to defend him. You'll find there are men enough who will. And see it through, whoever has to be broken. Do you follow that?"

"Not in the least. I understand that you are here as Mr. Harley's devoted friend without his knowledge. But what about?"

Osmond made a furious exclamation. "Don't shirk. You know very well you've set your fellows dogging Harley and prying into his affairs. The thing's a scandal already."

"You give me information," said Lomas blandly. "A scandal—and yet

Mr. Harley makes no complaint. Is it possible you are misjudging things? You had better think that over. There will of course be enquiries going on about everyone associated with Miss Marne. I can't conceive that any person who has nothing to be afraid of will object. You put yourself in a false position, Mr. Osmond."

"I'm not afraid of my own position. I warn you, this persecuting Harley has got to stop. It's an infamous folly. He's the best man we have, through and through. He's not going to be dragged into the muck by your damned police blundering. Stop it in time, or you're going to an almighty smash. That's all." He stamped out.

Lomas took up the telephone and asked Bell to come in. "You won't guess who's been here," he smiled.

"I shall," said Bell stolidly. "I heard him. Walks like a platoon of the Guards. I saw him. He was steaming. Mr. Simon Osmond."

"Quite. Mr. Osmond. But you will not guess what he came for. To complain that you have been worrying Mr. Harley! He says he won't have it, Bell."

"My oath!" Bell muttered.

"Yes, he was very fierce. Harley's the best of men and a pure soul and you mustn't dirty him. Very surprising. A faithful friend."

"It is a rum turn," said Bell heavily. "I did wonder what Mr. Fortune had in his mind when he said to worry Harley. I lay he never thought of this."

Chapter XXI

The Perfumer of Zurich

On a terrace above the lake of Zurich, Mr. Fortune sat contemplating a water ice. This is a subject on which he has done much work. His results are, however, not yet sufficiently established for publication. The particular ice, which was only the second of that morning, was green and had described itself as greengage, a claim which Mr. Fortune inclined to allow, though he did not think the flavor ripe. He fell into profound speculation whether the specific excellence of the greengage could be maintained in an ice. As the languid air was unfavorable to concentration of thought, this enquiry became involved with another, how to classify the pale green of the water of the lake—was it a light jade, was it willow leaves, or perhaps peridot?

A young man stopped in front of him and said, "If you please, sir."

Reggie opened wide, reproachful eyes, sighed, and left the greengage ice unfinished. A disproportionate interest in the practical has always, he is fond of confessing, impeded his work in pure science.

He was led to a room several stories up, a room with a wide view of lake and town. Its office equipment was grimly modern. Stein sat there and gave him a wide grin and a German greeting. Reggie took one of the steel chairs, moved it to a place of obscurity, and wriggled his back into its severe shape.

"So. You are the background, the unhappy, subordinate background," Stein chuckled. "Ach, you are incorrigibly an artist, my friend." He rang his bell, and Herr Fora was brought in.

Reggie found himself looking at something out of his grandmother's album. Herr Fora had the tight trousers, the half-length coat of the 'fifties, he carried a hat like a saucepan, his loose-jowled face grew whiskers.

Stein and he bowed reciprocally, and their conversation began as a duet of civilities: "I am distressed to trouble you …" "But I am delighted to assist you …" Then Stein had a solo: "This is, to give you the beginning, an enquiry about a perfume. You can certainly tell me if that is of your manufacture." He presented to Herr Fora the bottle which was labeled "*Les Yeux Folichons.*"

The perfumer took his time over looking at it and smelling it. "I give you my opinion this is mine," he said.

"That is my information," said Stein.

"I should require an analysis for certainty," said Fora.

"It is to be admitted," said Stein. "But this you confirm, the laboratories of Fora put up a perfume like this for sale in Geneva?"

"Not for Geneva in particular," Fora corrected. "For Switzerland, France, Germany—where you will."

"So. But for London you put it up like that,"—Stein set before him the bottle from Molly Marne's dressing table, identical except that it was not full, except that the violet-and-green label bore the words "*Le Matin d'un Faune*" instead of "*Les Yeux Folichons.*" "It is certainly more poetical," said Stein.

Fora gave to its examination the same prolonged, unruffled care. "In my opinion, this also is my product," he announced. "But again I must require an analysis." He looked solemnly at Stein. "It is almost unbelievable what substitutions and adulterations are made in this industry."

"Without doubt," said Stein. "And the substitution of the name? That was not made to pass off another product as yours."

"The name is perfectly in order," said Fora. "You will understand I was advised that some name less gay, less light than '*Les Yeux Folichons*' would be better for the English market. It is curious. For a perfume, and a perfume which exhilarates, a joyous name seems to me apt. But the English taste likes the sentimental flavor. So I invented '*Le Matin d'un Faune.*' " He smiled pride in the achievement. His fat whiskered jowl shook. He was not beautiful.

"An imagination," said Stein. "Then there is this, Herr Fora." He produced the lipstick of Geneva. "*Feu de Nuit.*"

While Fora inspected it, Reggie spoke for the first time. "What is it? One of the eosin derivatives and lanoline?"

Fora peered at him round Stein. "The gentleman is in the industry?" he enquired.

"But no, I only assist Herr Stein, sir," Reggie murmured.

"He is well served. You are nearly right. Forgive me if I do not say more. We have our trade secrets."

"Without doubt," said Stein. "What I ask is, is this lipstick from your establishment?"

"In my opinion, yes. You recognize always the possibility, it has been tampered with."

"I recognize what I have to recognize," Stein's voice sharpened. "Be sure of that, Fora. And this—do you send this to England, too?"

"Without enquiry I could not tell you," said Fora. "We sell some of our products in England—it is not a great market for us—we are too—let me say—exquisite. Whether this or that has an English sale I do not carry in my head."

"So. That is unfortunate," Stein sneered. "Perhaps I can find out for you. Whom do you deal with in England?"

"I shall look up the names and tell you," said Fora. "But you permit me to ask, sir, what is the object of these enquiries?"

"Without doubt I permit you to ask," Stein smiled. "And I will tell you this, Fora: I apply myself to a question how narcotic drugs go from Switzerland to England. It is whispered to me they go with cosmetics."

Fora sat up straight. "I must beg that you will be frank with me, sir," he said solemnly. "Should I understand that you suspect narcotics have been introduced into my products?"

"I do not know," said Stein. "You see, I am frank."

"Permit me then to assure you that all which leaves my laboratories is pure and harmless. For this I make myself responsible. What happens to the consignments after they go out, it is clear, I cannot say."

"I take note of that," said Stein.

"Also I beg to remind you that the establishment Fora is of the highest reputation."

"It is natural you should say so," Stein said. He stood up and bowed. "Good-morning, Fora."

Fora bowed to them both and went out.

Stein turned to Reggie, chuckled, and rubbed his hands. "That will do, eh? That should do!"

"Very neat, yes," Reggie murmured.

Stein walked to the window and, standing at the side, looked out, and Reggie joined him. "So. There he is, the worthy Fora. He is slow, he thinks of a cab, he does not take it. He goes on. That is not the way to Aussersihl, where his highest-reputation establishment is. Nor to Enge, where he lives. No. To the post office perhaps?" Stein grasped Reggie's arm. "But no. He makes for the Quai-Brücke, he is going into the Kleine Stadt. There also are post offices, but less public." Fora's saucepan hat passed out of sight. "So. Now we wait. He was slow, he is in a hurry. I think we shall not wait long, my friend. But a little cigar, eh?"

"Oh, no. No, thanks." Reggie drew back from the pungent box.

"Have no fear," Stein chuckled. "The gentleman is well provided for, whatever he does." As Reggie still recoiled, he took a cigar himself and lit it and stretched himself, thumbs in the armholes of his waistcoat, emitting oily smoke from nose and mouth.

"You're a great man, Stein," Reggie said reverently and wandered away to the window

The telephone buzzed. Stein pounced on the receiver. "So. Yes. A little moment. Then through to me." He grinned at Reggie, nodded, beckoned, and surrendered the receiver, taking a second earpiece.

There came to them the voice of Herr Fora speaking English: "Hallo! Hallo! Is that the Maison Montespan?"

In falsetto Reggie answered, "Maison Montespan speaking. Who is that?"

"Will you put me through to Madame Finck, please," said Fora. "It is a call from U."

"From 'oo?" said Reggie with a cockney twang.

"From U," Fora boomed.

Stein made small clicking sounds. Then Reggie said in a high languid voice: "Hallo, hallo, is that Fora?"

"Pst!" the telephone hissed. "Take care, Berthe."

"What's the matter with you?" said Reggie in French.

There was a moment's silence. Then Fora spoke in English again: "Take care, I say. The business is not going well. I have here questions about the consignments. Look to your stock. It must be all correct, you understand? All."

"*Bigre!*" said Reggie. "*Tu y vas un peu fort, mon vieux. Ne te monte pas le bourrichon.*" (Which may be nearly translated, "Dash it all, you're going it strong, old thing. Don't kid yourself.")

Inarticulate noises informed him that Fora was shocked. Then came a loud and threatening, "Listen, Berthe, I warn you—the consignments were correct, all correct from me. The rest is for you!"

Reggie gave a squeak of laughter, Stein banged the receiver, Reggie put up a creditable scream. Then they listened and heard Fora ring off.

"So," Stein chuckled. "You are an artist, my dear Fortune." He took the telephone again and gave brusque orders. "Come. They will bring him in presently. But come. I wish to raid the highly respectable establishment Fora before it is alarmed."

"Oh, yes. Yes. Don't want to alarm anybody," Reggie murmured. He was putting into code a telegram addressed to Lomas:

"Advise immediate search-warrant Maison Montespan. Stop. Hold Madame Berthe Finck. Stop. Evidence Montespan receives consignments drugs from Fora Zürich. Stop. Returning. Stop. Fortune."

He showed it to Stein. "Also. That should do the trick, as you say," Stein nodded.

"No. I wouldn't say that. No," Reggie murmured. "May be too late. Able minds in command of the enemy. However. We're forcing 'em into the open."

That night lights burnt late in the austere concrete block of the Fora works in Aussersihl, still later in the police headquarters.

The first airplane which rose from Zurich in the morning had Mr. Fortune on board, and an unshaven Stein waved his hat at it.

To the boom of the engines Mr. Fortune closed his mind determined, not in vain, on the sleep of simple faith in himself.

Chapter XXII

The Vanishing Lady

IF YOU have observed the chronology of this history, it is clear that the summer was now far advanced. The activities of politics had therefore waned to the lassitude of the last days before the holidays of Parliament. This is important as one of the conditions of the case, incalculable in effect because they were regular and familiar, which, Mr. Fortune has always insisted, made its worst dangers. That he was in these effects taken by surprise, he will admit with humble candor. Nevertheless he maintains that his tactics were admirable, a perfect exemplar of the art of war, attack with decisive violence on the most vulnerable point.

Pink and benign, he arrived in Lomas's room and was reproached. "Confound you! You look infernally complacent," Lomas glowered at him. "The wretched Bell has been up all night."

"So have I." Reggie smiled and settled down in a chair. "Only snatched a little sleep in the plane flying over."

"Good Gad!" said Lomas. "You're a wonderful animal, Reginald."

"No. Well organized. Well trained. You might be quite capable physically, too, if you lived with care. However. What are your results?"

"Nothing. Nothing definite."

"Oh my hat!" Reggie moaned. "Did you act on my wire?"

"Yes, we carried out your kind instructions," said Lomas with a prim ferocity. "I regret to report that we have obtained no evidence to connect the Maison Montespan with the murder, if any, of Molly Marne—or with any other part of the case, if there is a case."

Reggie snuggled down in his chair. "Then you haven't been very clever, Lomas," he murmured.

"No, we are only able to deal with facts," said Lomas acidly. "We're not competent to use fancies. Pardon my official curiosity, Reginald, but what were your results? What were you relying on to start this stunt?"

"My dear old thing! Facts. Molly Marne's scent, which is also Lady Rosnay's scent, and Lady Rosnay's lipstick were found to come from a perfumer of Zurich, Herr Fora. Fora, being put through it, and told there was a suspicion of dope coming from Switzerland, said he didn't know whom he sold his stuff to in England. After which he went off and telephoned to Madame Berthe Finck at Maison Montespan. But they take pains in Switzerland, Lomas. They can carry out a plan. In accordance with instructions Herr Fora's call was switched on to Stein and me. And the substance of his message was that Madame Finck must look to her stock. So Stein arrested him and raided the Fora factory. There he found a tablet-making plant and stocks of morphia and heroin. Also correspondence with Madame Finck. Well? Was that enough to justify a search warrant?"

"Quite. Prima-facie evidence of drug-running. I agree. But what then?"

"My only aunt!" Reggie moaned. "What did you do in the great war? After all the trouble I've had making a nice soft job for you, do you mean to say you haven't got anything out of it?"

"We've got Madame Finck," said Lomas. "We found a cache of morphia in the place—packed in lipstick tubes. I agree we can get her convicted on the drug charge. Quite a useful little bit of work, Reginald. But it hasn't brought us an inch nearer how Molly Marne died."

"You think not?" Reggie murmured. "Well, well. Not a hopeful spirit. Have you asked Madame Finck?"

Lomas laughed weary contempt. "Bell gave her a grilling. She wouldn't utter. Not a word. Only to say she must see her solicitor. And he's that little devil Josh Clunk. We shan't get anything out of her."

"Not unless Clunk thinks it's her best chance. No."

"Well, he doesn't, so far. He's demanding to bail her out."

"Oh, yes. Little man Clunk bluffs well," Reggie said dreamily. "No one better. Except me. Tiresome little man. Well, well. What about the papers of Maison Montespan?"

Lomas made a grimace. "A cartload. Bell and his minions are working at 'em like beavers. When last heard of, they hadn't found anything to signify except traces of your friend Fora. You can worry 'em again if you like." He called up Bell.

That solid man came in heavily. His square face was of a mottled pale color, his eyes swollen and red. He gave Reggie a tired smile. "Glad to see you back, sir."

"Damn, don't be civil," Lomas cried. "He don't deserve it."

"We haven't made much of it this end, that's a fact," said Bell gloomily, watching Reggie. "I don't know what you hoped for, Mr. Fortune."

"Oh my Bell!" Reggie smiled. "That sad, paternal manner! I've seen it before, thank you. What's up the paternal sleeve?"

"There isn't much so far, I give you my word. Not that I see any use in. I wish you had the job of these books and papers. I never was quick at book work. We've got this woman Finck for the drugs all right. There's a good lump of fishy correspondence with her and that Swiss, Fora. But we can't find anything to take the dope business behind her, we don't get anyone else in. And she seems to have been the boss of the dressmaking concern, done very handsome out of it, too. The only thing we've come on that looks queer is in the beginnings—that's years ago. Finck had a bit of money then from Lady Rosnay and Mrs. Harley."

"Good Gad!" Lomas exclaimed.

"You think so?" Reggie smiled.

"We've just worked back to that this morning—found it in the oldest books. Each of those two put up five hundred pound for Finck, and she credits herself with a thousand of her own. You can't make much of it, to my thinking. Nothing new for society ladies to do a bit of financing for a smart dressmaker. Them giving Finck a pushoff four or five years ago don't mean they knew anything about her handling dope now. I don't trace dealings with Fora more than two years back, and there's no sign Lady Rosnay or Mrs. Harley ever had a penny out of the business—not even their capital. So all you could do with them is to bring their names into the case and make a nice society scandal of it."

Lomas grinned at Reggie. "Give Harley a nasty jar, wouldn't it?"

"Yes. There is that," Reggie murmured. "Might be useful."

"Damn,"—Lomas's amusement faded into a stare—"I suppose that's what you've been after all along. That's why you wanted us to watch Harley and get him rattled."

"No. No. Wasn't after that," Reggie mumbled. "Don't mind it. There's going to be scandal, however it works out. Big scandal. May be used as requisite. May be merely inevitable by-product. I want justice. That's all." His eyes were almost closed, his round face passionless as a drowsy child's. "I'm going to get it, Lomas," he purred.

"Do you pretend to see your way?" Lomas exclaimed.

"Not all the way. No. They're fighting hard, they've got to fight now. They're on the edge of hell. They're very close on the edge. They'll be rather desperate. That will do."

Lomas made a noise of impatience. "We're no nearer any evidence of anything in all the infernal case—unless the Finck woman talks."

"You think not? Well, well. The Finck woman may be useful too. That's one of the things that's worrying them."

An inspector came in with a manner of apologetic importance. "I thought the superintendent should see this at once, sir," he explained to Lomas.

"All right. Stand by." Lomas nodded. "What is it, Bell?"

Bell read the typed report given him. "My oath!" he muttered and looked up. "Mrs. Harley is missing."

"The devil she is!" Lomas jerked back in his chair.

Reggie did not move. "Who says so?" he murmured.

"Mr. Harley," Bell answered. "Mr. Harley came into the Mayfair police station this morning. His object being, as he told the inspector on duty, to give information that Mrs. Harley did not return home last night—"

"Absent without leave." Lomas made a grimace.

Bell's solemn eyes rebuked him. "—and to request police enquiries, sir. Mr. Harley was then asked to make a statement, and he said he last saw Mrs. Harley at lunch yesterday, when they had lunch together at home. She was then just as usual. She has not been in good health lately, but he noticed nothing particular. In the afternoon he went down to the House of Commons and was there till after eleven o'clock, when he came home and went to bed, not knowing whether Mrs. Harley was in the house or not. He says there was nothing out of the way in that. They have separate rooms, and it's not their habit to see one another last thing unless they happen to meet. This morning he was told that Mrs. Harley's bed had not been slept in and none of the servants had seen her in the house since she went out yesterday after tea. That was something like six o'clock, when she drove off in her own car. The car has not been brought back to the garage. It's a dark green Longman saloon, ABCD.0001. As far as Mr. Harley can say, she took nothing with her. He has no idea where she went to. She had an engagement last night to dine and dance with Lady Fosham, but he is informed she didn't go. She wasn't in evening dress when she went away— that's likely, at six o'clock. Mr. Harley thinks she must have met with an accident. That's the whole of it."

"Does he!" said Lomas. "Any report of an accident that fits?"

"Nothing come in, sir."

Lomas laughed disagreeably. "There wouldn't be."

"Well, well," Reggie murmured. "She went out at six. What time did you raid the Maison Montespan, Bell?"

"We got in just before five, sir. As near five as no matter."

"Oh, yes. Time enough for the news to get round before Mrs. Harley went out."

"It might have been managed," said Bell reluctantly.

"You never know who is standing in with a drug business. But we didn't let anybody off the premises till after seven."

"You can bet it was managed," Lomas smiled. "This is going well, Reginald. They're playing into your hands."

"No. I wouldn't say that. No. They're playing as I make 'em play. It is going all right. But it's going to be nasty yet. Quite nasty."

"Playing as you make them?" Lomas repeated. "You mean you wanted Mrs. Harley to bolt. That was what you were after in getting men put on to worry Harley. You're very ingenious—"

"Oh, no. No. Didn't want anything definite. Didn't know enough," Reggie mumbled. "General principle, 'He only does it to annoy because he knows it teases.' General expectation, somebody would get strained to breakin' point. If Mrs. Harley has broken first, that's all right. We can get through over her."

"—and rather diabolical, Reginald," said Lomas.

"Me?" Reggie's eyes opened wide. "Not me. I'm on the other side. I'm for the people that suffered. That wife and her husband who were tortured to suicide—and their little girl left with that to remember—Molly Marne with her life poisoned before she was killed. Do you think they are the only ones Maison Montespan has played with? I don't. And I know there'll be more till we've smashed the pleasant folks who organized the Montespan business. Anyone in the way must go down. That's all."

"Quite." Lomas looked down and shifted his papers. "I agree. Your idea is, the Harleys are behind the whole thing. I own it looks like that now. Or Mrs. Harley at least."

"Yes. It could be. Or was in it. Or he was. Or both. However." Reggie sat up. "When Harley reported his wife missing, did he say anything about your men having been after him?"

"Not a word, sir."

"He must have known? They've been making themselves obvious, as instructed?"

"They have. He knows all right. Don't know if Mr. Lomas told you, it's a rum thing, we did have a complaint about the police annoying him, but not from him, from his friend, Osmond."

"Oh, yes. David on behalf of Jonathan," Reggie smiled. "David as the protector. Reversin' the parts. And was the man Osmond very explosive?"

"Detonating violently." Lomas shrugged.

"Well, well. And what about the letter from Langton to our Sophia?"

"Ah, of course, you haven't heard that either," Bell said. "Miss Minns was very sticky. She owned up she got the letter and then said she burnt it. Her tale is, it was just a line, something like 'You did well out of Molly's death. You be careful.'"

Reggie's mouth twisted in a sideways smile of pain. "I see. Yes," he muttered.

"I got to own I don't," said Bell heavily. "She may have been telling the truth. But there's a bit more to it. I had out of her she's seen Mr. Osmond and fixed up friendly with him."

"Which was being careful, wasn't it?" Lomas sneered.

"I wonder," Reggie murmured. His face was without expression. "Clever work. Damn clever." He turned to Bell. "You haven't had any of your fellows watching Mrs. Harley? No. You wouldn't. I didn't suggest that. I didn't mean to. Best way to work through the man. However. How we've got to find her. And the sooner it's over the sooner to sleep. You're doing all the routine things, what?"

"They seem to have got things going all right." Bell looked over the report again. "Sent out a general warning for the car, raking over the Harley servants, making enquiries of Mrs. Harley's friends. But she may be out of the country by now. Might have got across the Channel last night—there's two or three services after six o'clock. We'll have to try and check that—had she got a passport?—is it gone?—and so on."

"Yes. There's that," Reggie nodded. "Mustn't leave anything out. And you won't lose sight of the deserted husband, will you?"

"Mr. Harley? I will not," Bell said grimly.

"All right. Then you might come along with me and call on his dear friend Osmond. I should like to hear his opinion of the vanishing of Mrs. Harley." Reggie turned dreamy eyes on Lomas. "Might be more explosive than ever, what?"

Lomas chuckled. "I shouldn't wonder. Take cover behind Bell."

"Yes. I will. Yes. But do you notice a little contrast? When Harley was being worried by the nasty police, it's friend Osmond who comes along and protests. When poor Harley is deserted by his wife, he comes to the police himself and the faithful friend don't appear. Quite correct. Quite natural—if Osmond hadn't pushed in before. But by contrast odd. Hasn't he told the devoted Osmond of his bereavement? Or does Osmond feel it's not a thing for him to take an interest in? I think we'd better ask him, Bell."

"Very good, sir," Bell nodded.

"Mind your step," said Lomas. "We've nothing definite on Osmond."

"I had thought of that," Reggie moaned and looked at him without respect. "The mind is not wholly futile. Come on, Bell."

They walked across to the House of Commons. From the whips' room they learned that Osmond was not in the House. He had been there the day before and left early in the evening. That morning the chief whip had received a note from him which said that he would not be able to attend again before the adjournment. The whip thought it quite like Osmond to leave out any explanation—always a casual fellow—but after all, of no importance. The House was only sitting a few days more, and they all knew nothing could turn up to matter.

"All the same, it's a bit funny, sir," said Bell as they came out into Palace Yard. "Looks like he hopped it about the same time as Mrs. Harley did."

"Yes. That is implied. Striking coincidence. However. Better verify it. Let's call on him."

Chapter XXIII

The Artery Forceps

THE block of flats which provided Osmond with his habitation stood in one of the byways of Westminster. It had never been luxurious, it was not modern when it was built a generation ago, it showed a front of dreary respectability.

They climbed—there was no lift—to the second floor. Three doors were upon that landing as on those below. Reggie arrived first and rang at Osmond's and looked curiously about him. "Yes, modest sort of place, isn't it?" said Bell. "These other people here, one's a solicitor's managing clerk and the other a young chap just got into the civil service. About what you'd expect. But you wouldn't expect a politician that's making a big noise to be satisfied with it."

"No. Marked frugality in the man Osmond," Reggie murmured. " 'We ain't got much money but we do see life.' That may be one of the factors. As conjectured before." He rang at Osmond's door again and waited, staring at it, and rang a third time and still got no answer. "Well, well. Mr. Osmond's statement that he wouldn't be able to do any more politics is thus confirmed. So I think we'd better have a look at his humble home." He smiled at Bell, he gazed dreamily at the keyhole of the door. "Can do, what?"

Bell rubbed his chin. "I don't know, sir. We haven't got anything to act on—not what you'd call anything."

"The vanishin' lady—and the vanishin' gentleman," Reggie murmured. "The humble home might contain information where they've gone to."

"I don't much like it, sir." Bell frowned at the shut door. "We've got to be careful with these people."

Reggie laughed. "The golden rule of the police force. Be careful with the big folks. We've kept to it, haven't we? They've relied on that. They're too important for the police to touch them. So they can always get away with anything."

"You're a bit hard, sir," Bell protested.

"Oh, no. No. Very soft. Very feeble. Hitherto. But I've had enough, Bell.

Look at that." He pointed to a dark smear on the grimy paint of the door-post. "That's fresh. And I should say it was blood."

"My oath!" Bell muttered. "Yes, it does look a bit gummy. Like as if somebody put his hand there while he was opening the door—or shutting it. All right. You stand by, Mr. Fortune. I'll have a try."

Reggie was left gazing pensively at the smear.

Bell made haste downstairs and sought the porter at the central entrance—one porter only, the flats provided. He was told that Mr. Osmond had given notice the night before of going away for some time—that would be about six or seven o'clock—didn't give any address—said he didn't want any letters forwarded.

Mr. Osmond's servants? Well, he had a man who didn't live in and a woman who came in daily to do for him. The man was gone off on holiday, the porter knew that and did not know where, only it wouldn't be with Mr. Osmond, it was a proper holiday. The woman had notice she wouldn't be wanted again till she was told.

Bell went on to the office of the manager of the flats and declared himself a superintendent of the Criminal Investigation Department. The manager was duly impressed, nervous, and anxious to oblige. Bell assured him there was nothing to worry about. It was a matter of getting into touch with Mr. Simon Osmond over a case he had brought to the police, and most unfortunately he had gone away without giving his friends his address.

The manager was very sorry—he had no information—Mr. Osmond did go away from time to time—as usual, letters were to be kept till his return. No doubt he wouldn't be away long. He seldom was.

Bell shook his head. The manager must understand it was very urgent. Probably Osmond's servants could help. Again the manager regretted. He had no idea where they could be found. In point of fact, he knew that Mr. Osmond had given them an indefinite holiday. They had left their keys at the office.

Bell was portentously disappointed—it was most unfortunate—he didn't mind saying it was a serious matter. He implied doubts and suspicions of the manager. He could not leave it like this. Perhaps there might be something in the flat which would throw light on what had become of Mr. Osmond. He must have one of those keys.

He got it.

Triumphant and a little short of breath, he returned to Reggie on the gloomy landing. "Well, I wangled that nicely, Mr. Fortune. Here we are. Nobody been about, eh?"

"Oh, no. No. Nice quiet place for anything to happen."

"We'll see," said Bell grimly and opened the door.

Osmond's flat was composed of a tiny hall, a living room of some size, bedroom, bathroom, and a dark hutch of a kitchen. There was no one in the place alive or dead.

When they had made sure of that, Reggie turned to the bedroom and opened wardrobe and drawers. "He has gone away, or somebody's stolen his clothes. And if he has gone, he don't mean to be social. The only things left are evening dress with et ceteras and morning coat and toppers. The rest was packed in a hurry."

"Sudden flit, eh?" Bell grunted. "He slept here, though, or we were meant to think he did. The bed's all pulled about." He turned into the bathroom. "No sign of any mess here. If there was a cleaning up it was cleaned up careful and thorough."

"Yes. It would be," said Reggie.

"But there has been some washing not so long ago. The towel's damp and this bathmat."

"Oh, yes. Corroboratin' the evidence of the bed, that somebody slept here last night. Provisional inference, our Mr. Osmond didn't depart till this morning. Very interesting, if true: but far from certain. We want more facts. One source not yet tried, the man Osmond's secretary, young Darett." Reggie wandered into the living room and used the telephone directory and the telephone. "Is that Mrs. Darett's house? Could I speak to Mr. Arthur Darett? ... Oh ... Is Mrs. Darett in? Oh. Thank you. Goodbye." He turned to Bell. "Arthur is away on a motoring tour. Present position unknown. Mrs. Darett is staying with Lady Rosnay in the country. They both went away last weekend." He gazed at Bell sorrowfully. "Which was before you raided the Maison Montespan, before the vanishing of the vanishin' Mrs. Harley. Days before."

"Ah. Lets them out of the business, don't it?" Bell grunted.

"Yes, that is indicated. Leavin' us to rely on the work of our own simple brains. Very distressing." He looked pensively round the room. It was furnished comfortably to the standard of a man who had no interest in his furniture. It was tidy but did not suggest that it had been tidied up. There were papers in a basket on the writing table; a report on the cotton trade lay open, with slips of paper in it. "Well, well. Political to the last," Reggie murmured.

Bell tried the drawers of the table, found them all locked, and stood surveying them hungrily. "I don't hardly like to meddle with 'em," he decided. "Not yet." He stared round the room. "You couldn't say there's a look of anything having happened here," he said slowly. "See what we can find, though." He went about, prying everywhere, methodical and minute in his labors.

Reggie picked up, from beside the most ample and shabbiest easy chair, a thin book which lay on the floor open face downwards and read, and his pensive face became benign.

"Here, sir," Bell cried out and rose from his knees at the far side of the writing table. "What do you make of this thing?" He gave Reggie an article of bright metal. "Seems like some sort of tweezers. Do you know what it's for?"

"Oh, yes. Yes." Reggie handled it delicately with affectionate recognition. "Surgical instrument. It's a pair of artery forceps."

"My oath!" Bell muttered. "That looks ugly, don't it? Blood on the doorpost and a surgeon's tool inside."

"Yes. Curious conjunction. Very curious," Reggie mumbled. "Connection not obvious. If you were going to kill anybody, you wouldn't be wise to use artery forceps. No offensive value. Function of forceps to repair wounds, not make 'em."

Bell rubbed his chin. "You've got to own it's queer, though," he protested. "Taking them with the blood."

"I do. Yes. Takin' them with the blood, I don't know what they mean. Takin' the blood with them, I haven't the slightest idea what it means."

"Well, now, what I was thinking," Bell said slowly, "could there have been some sort of surgical operation done—somebody damaged, perhaps, or somebody cut about in a queer way—might be to mess up a body to hide identity or something like that?"

"My Bell! What imagination!" Reggie purred. "Yes. Somebody might have operated. It could be. Almost anything could happen in this case."

"You're laughing at me, sir!" Bell complained.

"Oh, no. No. Something queer did happen. And I haven't the remotest idea what it was. But I don't believe there was a major operation here. Very difficult to clear up afterwards. And there's no sign of any cleanin' up. No need of artery forceps to disfigure a body. Quite superfluous. I don't account for the blood on the doorpost. I can't. Bafflin' problem. But I think I know why the forceps are here. There is other evidence on that." He handed Bell the book which he had picked up. "New Collected Rhymes, by Andrew Lang. Bless him. That's where our Mr. Osmond left it open. Read that page."

And Bell read "The Contented Angler" and frowned at him.

"Yes. Don't be so superior. I'm not an angler myself, but I can respect all decent vices. Go on."

Bell read:

> " 'The Angler hath a jolly life
>   Who by the rail runs down
> And leaves his business and his wife
>   And all the din of town.

The wind downstream is blowing straight
    And nowhere cast can he:
Then lo, he doth but sit and wait
    In kindly company.' ' "

Bell glowered at Reggie. "Well, what about it? What's this got to do with anything?"

"Oh my dear chap! Relevant and interestin' evidence. Evidence of what the man Osmond was thinking about just before departure. Evidence of the purpose of the artery forceps."

"I don't know what you mean, sir," said Bell heavily. "I don't see it at all. The angler 'leaves his business and his wife and all the din of town'—well, that might signify he was thinking of bolting, and he has bolted. But what about the wife—my oath, do you think Mrs. Harley had been mixed up with him? Not married to him, eh?"

"I wouldn't say that. No."

"On what we've got, it might be he's bolted with her. 'Sit and wait in kindly company,' you know—that'd fit, too."

"Yes. One of the possibilities," Reggie murmured. "I wonder."

"The pair of 'em run away together," said Bell with grim relish. "That would do all right. But there—" he rebuked himself—"it's all fancy. Just a bit o' poetry. And where do you get these forceps into it? What's artery forceps to do with running off with Mrs. Harley—or going fishing, either? It don't make sense anyhow."

"Not all of it. No. You're so comprehensive. I didn't say the forceps had anything to do with Mrs. Harley. But as regards fishing—further evidence available. Look in the wastepaper basket."

Bell pounced on it and turned it upside down on the bare mahogany of the larger table. It made only a small heap of papers, and he dealt with them quickly. "Last post last night—circulars—circulars—a bill: unpaid—his wine merchant—another unpaid bill—tobacconist—he wasn't a good payer—another unpaid bill, garage at Southbury, Berkshire, forty gallons of petrol." Bell looked up and whistled. "Forty gallons delivered. Don't say where. And you wouldn't think a chap living cheap like Osmond would keep a stock of petrol at all. Why should he? If he has one car, it's the limit. But that's the lot, Mr. Fortune. And if you can tell me what it has to do with artery forceps and poetry about fishing, I'll be surprised."

"I can't. No," Reggie murmured. "Nothing definite. And introducing a further complication." He took the garage bill.

"Ah. That's right. Looks more like he was bolting from his creditors."

"No. I didn't mean that. No. The complication is, why did he have forty gallons of petrol delivered? Bafflin' question. However. Southbury, Berkshire. There's trout-fishing in those parts. But the conclusive evidence you missed."

"Did I?" Bell bristled. "P'r'aps you'll tell me what it was, sir."

"Oh my Bell," Reggie purred. He extracted from the sides of the basket some fragments which clung there, scraps of cock's feathers, strands of orange silk. "See?"

"I see. I don't know what you make of it."

"My dear chap! Quite obvious. Debris of material for flies. Our Mr. Osmond was tying trout flies before departure. Hence the artery forceps. Instrument often used for that purpose by the amateur expert."

Bell gaped and shook and grinned. "That's got me beat all right. That's a wonderful bit o' work."

"Oh, no. No. Only joinin' up the facts. Not all joined. However. Next action clearly indicated. We drive down to the garage at Southbury, Berkshire, and ask where Mr. Osmond goes fishing with forty gallons of petrol. Come on. My car will do it and get us back tonight for your beauty sleep."

But in that prediction he was wrong.

As they went out, he stayed by the door and cut from the doorpost the slip of wood which bore the blood smear. "The other fact that isn't joined up," he mumbled, looked at it with dislike, and put it carefully away. He stood gazing about the murky landing and the stairs. "Yes. Better go on. Must go on," he said with a sort of sharp defiance of doubt unspoken. He ran down to the waiting car.

Chapter XXIV

Champagne for Dinner

IT WAS already past six o'clock when the big car slid out of the delays of London traffic onto the western road.

"My only aunt! We passed a car then," Reggie said for his chauffeur to hear. "Marvelous. Perhaps we'll catch up another before dark." The neck of the chauffeur reddened, the big car shot forward.

"Well, I thank heaven you're not driving, sir," Bell said with braced apprehension. "That's the only comfort."

"Me? Oh my dear chap! I'm safety itself. The danger is timidity. Sam isn't very brave. However. We must take some risk. I want to sleep. Possibly safer driven by Sam awake than by me dozing. I hope so." He closed his eyes and slept, and Sam made an average of fifty an hour.

The car was running along a valley with glimpses of still water flashing through willow and poplar. Low sand hills on either side sloped up to fir woods, and behind these to southward rose a high, bluff mass of down.

Reggie opened his eyes and blinked at it: "Getting somewhere, what? That's Inkpen. Well, well. Very good, Sam. We might be in Southbury some time tonight."

Sam drove on furiously into the level glare of the setting sun. The great ridge of chalk closed upon them, and on the other side blunt waves of chalk broke out.

A little busy town of timbered red-brick houses checked them. "I make it seven-thirty, sir," said Sam haughtily. "Did you 'appen to know where this 'ere garage is?"

"No. No. Probably gone to bed," Reggie mumbled.

Sam slowed into the marketplace, conferred with an ancient inhabitant and swung the car round an acute angle into a narrow byway, and came to the pumps and sheds which declared themselves the Southbury garage. "Very retirin'." Reggie blinked at them. "Now you distinguish yourself, Bell."

It took some time, but Bell came back cheerfully brisk. "You turn round again into the marketplace, my lad," he instructed Sam, "and take the Oldbourne road, matter of ten miles. Village called Lower Upham is your point."

With the expression of a genius set to amuse spoilt children, Sam proceeded to turn the car in a space which gave him only inches to spare from impossibility.

"He couldn't reverse and back out, you know," Reggie moaned. "Too easy. The expert must be an expert. That's how I made my name. However. We do sometimes get somewhere."

"You're getting somewhere now, sir," Bell said. "These people know Osmond quite well. He has an old cottage made over new, like people do, out beyond this village. Snap Close, Lower Upham, is the address. He comes down there for fishing, same as you said. Sometimes with another man. Mostly by himself. It's quite a small place. He don't keep any servants there. A woman comes in from the village to do for him."

"What about the petrol?"

"That works out all right. He had electric light put in, little petrol-electric plant, you know, and so he has a stock of petrol sent out every once in a while. They don't know if he's down at the cottage now, and it's not on the telephone, he wouldn't ever have it, said he wanted to be quiet. But it's quite likely he is there—they had the order for this batch of petrol only last week. That looks as if he meant coming."

"Yes, I think so," Reggie murmured.

"I'd say you've got right onto him," said Bell. "But what it all means— search me." He looked curiously at Reggie.

"I wonder," Reggie murmured.

They had come into a narrow valley of the chalk hills, fields golden with charlock climbing to the gray-green turf of the rounded ridges. Close by the road a little river ran sparkling clear, a silvery line strung with pools that gleamed and dimpled.

In the white village of Lower Upham, Bell asked the way to Snap Close and was told to take a lane on the right, not the first lane, nor the second, neither, but a little bit of a lane up to the down beyond.

By this time the sun was behind violet clouds, and the line of the hills was vague, and a faint haze of mist dimmed the valley. As they passed the second lane, Reggie turned in his seat, looked back and settled down again, and stared a question at Bell: "Did you see that?"

"I saw a car waiting in the lane."

"Yes. A car. Empty car. Dark closed car. Bonnet looked like a Longman. Registration might have been ABCD something."

"My oath! You mean it was Mrs. Harley's car?"

"Not certain. No. Interestin' question."

"What about having a look?"

"No, I don't think so. Secondary question. First question, who is at Snap

Close? We'll go on."

That decision, Mr. Fortune likes to point out, the decision of a moment, was the action which determined the result of the war. He is very pleased with it. He considers it the supreme example of the practical common sense and confidence therein which are the only qualities of mind that distinguish him, making him merely the most ordinary of ordinary men and therefore successful among them.

The criticism of Lomas that it was anything but common sense to omit investigation of the car, he dismisses curtly as a delusion characteristic of the ambition of the higher intelligence to be clever.

They came to the third lane, a chalk track, untarred, unmetalled.

"All right. Don't go up," Reggie said. "Stop so that nothing can get out. That'll do. Come on, Bell."

The car was drawn up across the end of the lane. Bell and he strode on between unkempt hedges draped in masses of old man's beard.

"That'll be the place," Bell said, pointing to a thatched cottage of white cob walls which stood close beneath the steep of the down.

"Yes. Lonely habitation," Reggie murmured. "Lonely fellow. I wonder."

The lane climbed in curves, and the banks on either side rose higher.

"Well, he won't see us coming," Bell grunted.

"No. Even if expectin' visitors. Which I don't think."

In the depths of the lane it was dark twilight. Through the misty air above, color and form grew dim. Two of the cottage windows flashed out.

"Ah. There's his electric light," Bell grunted. "He is there."

"Yes. Go easy."

They went on cautiously, keeping under the nearer hedge. A white gate opened on a drive of cinders which led to sheds at the back of the cottage.

They stopped and unseen could see the front. An unkempt patch of grass had starved disorderly flower beds about it, all rawly new.

"Oh my hat!" Reggie moaned. "Graceless place. The noble savage tryin' to be civilized." His hand closed on Bell's arm.

Bell breathed hard.

Across the garden they could see into the room of the lit windows. A table was spread there, and two people sat at dinner, a man and a woman. The man faced them, and they saw Osmond's heavy dark face and bull neck.

"But that's never Mrs. Harley," Bell muttered.

"Oh, no. No. The other one," Reggie smiled.

The woman had the red head of Alix Lynn.

Her arms were bare; her neck, which had some jewels round it, and some part of her back showed white: but Osmond wore gray flannel.

"She's in evening dress and he isn't," Bell said. "That's funny."

"The sexes are different," Reggie mumbled. "In some ways."

"They're doing themselves handsome," said Bell.

It appeared that they had lost interest in eating, but between them the gold foil of two bottles of champagne gleamed. Osmond filled her glass, though her hand protested; filled his own, too. They touched glasses, making a slow business of it, and drank. Osmond leaned across the table, smiling at her. Her arm went out towards him, and hands met.

Osmond stood up and came to sit beside her and kissed her with possessive authority but not much ardor. She swayed to him, lay against him. After a little while of that, they rose together awkwardly, in some trouble to get clear of chairs and table.

They moved to one of the windows and stood looking out at the misty night, their faces hidden by their own shadows, their shapes silhouetted against the light of the room.

Alix was held in his arm, leaned upon him, her head drooping and falling to his shoulder. There was a murmur of talk which seemed to be in Osmond's deep voice. He picked her up and carried her out of the room and put out the lights as he vanished.

"Ah. That's it, is it?" Bell growled angry disapproval. "What about it, sir?"

"Yes. I think we must interrupt," said Reggie. "Come on."

As they made for the cottage, a light shone from the upper windows.

Reggie rapped on the door—it had neither bell-push nor knocker. They waited some moments without an answer, but seemed to hear movement. Bell walked away to look round the cottage. Reggie knocked again. Still there was no answer.

Bell returned. "This is queer, sir. No sign of them getting out at the back. But the light's gone upstairs. Let me have a go—Oh my Lord!"

From the back of the cottage came a burst of flame which shot up to the thatch. "That petrol!" Bell gasped.

The fire was roaring in one of the sheds, and out of the flames came explosions which drove them surging over the cottage. "There's the cans bursting. Now it's got the thatch. The whole place'll go up."

"Stand by," Reggie said, ran to the open ground-floor windows, scrambled through into the room, blundered his way to the outer door and opened it. In the flickering firelight he stumbled upstairs with Bell at his heels, shouting, "Osmond! Where are you? Alix Lynn!"

There was no answer. The air about them was hot and smoky. They heard crackling of fire and falling timbers overhead. They broke into a room, fumbled round it, could find nobody, and went on, sweating, panting, and choking, to the next.

Something held the door against them. They flung themselves at it together and came down in a heap on a mass of plaster. Through a gap in the ceiling came the glare of blazing thatch and beams. Osmond was on his knees trying to lift Alix from the floor, feeble and falling upon her, and she lay still.

Bell pulled him away. "Get up and get out with you." But Osmond rolled over and made no effort to rise. "The dog's drunk," Bell snorted.

"Can you manage him?" said Reggie.

"Give me a hoist of him," Bell grunted. "There. That'll do. You go on with her, sir."

Reggie gathered up Alix and made off, and Bell lumbered after with Osmond on his back like a sack of coals.

As they came downstairs the roof was crashing in. Showers of sparks and tufts of blazing straw floated in the smoke. Red-hot wood fell about them, and the timber in the walls smouldered and broke into flame.

Breathless, choking, blind with smoke and sweat, they came out to the air and laid their burdens on the grass. Neither Alix nor Osmond stirred.

"My God! That was touch and go," Bell said thickly. "Drunken swine!" He poked his foot into Osmond's ribs. "Dead to the world. Where would they be now if we hadn't been here?"

"I wonder." Reggie wiped his streaming, smarting eyes and stooped over the unconscious bodies. "Interesting question. However. Better keep 'em in this world if we can. Go and get the car."

"Right." Bell went off at a jog trot.

Reggie stood up and contemplated the blazing cottage for a moment, then made his way through the smoke and falling embers to the ground-floor window and once more scrambled in. He came out with one of the champagne bottles, stumbled through the smoke, and reached clean air again to sit down and fight for breath.

The car slid up to the gate. "Come on, young fellow," Bell exhorted Sam. "This is where you do a job o' work."

"'Struth, you 'aven't 'alf made a bonfire of it," Sam chuckled. "Please to remember the fifth of November. And don't forget the guy. Look at the guv'nor, a real old, smutty old, jolly old Guy Fawkes, all of an 'eap."

"Shut your mouth," Bell growled and called to Reggie: "You all right, sir?"

"Oh, yes. Yes." Reggie scrambled to his feet. "Carry on."

"Now, my lad, give me a hand with this lump," Bell commanded, and Sam and he carried Osmond down to the car and came back for Alix. Reggie followed them with his champagne, and, while they arranged the two unconscious bodies on the floor of the car, put it away with an improvised paper stopper.

He turned to look back at the blazing cottage. "Ah! All gone to glory, isn't it?" said Bell. "Won't be nothing but a heap of ashes in no time."

"No. Burns very well. It would. It's only plaster and timber and thatch."

"Nice place to keep petrol in bulk," Bell grunted.

"Yes. Livin' dangerously. He has, our Osmond."

"I believe you. Well, we've done him proud, we have. What is it now, sir? Police or hospital?"

"Hospital first," Reggie said. "Back to Southbury, Sam. Get on, get on."

Bell inserted himself into the back seat over Osmond and Alix, and the big car slid away down the curves of the lane.

As it turned to the main road Reggie looked over his shoulder. "Watch out, Bell."

"What for, sir?" Bell leaned forward.

Reggie was watching the side of the road. It slid by fast in the gathering dark as the car shot into its best speed.

"Well, well. Didn't you notice?" Reggie sank back in his seat. "The car that was stopped in that other lane?"

"What, the car like Mrs. Harley's? What about it?"

"It's gone," Reggie murmured. "That's all."

Chapter XXV

The Lady in the Flat

A POLICEMAN on a bicycle came into sight. He stooped, he labored hard. Behind him were some other cyclists, and behind them a small hurrying crowd. "Village turnin' out to see the fun," Reggie murmured.

"Half a minute, if you don't mind, sir," said Bell.

"Rather. Stop and block the road, Sam. Sorry to interfere with their simple pleasures, but you're quite right. Here's your purple constable."

Bell leaned out of the window, revealed his authority to the policeman, and gave orders that no one must be allowed near the ruins of the cottage, while the car across the road delayed the inquisitive but docile villagers.

"Go ahead." Bell relapsed to his seat. "That'll do them all right, sir. I must have the ground kept clear. I want to know how that fire started."

"Yes. Quite useful," Reggie murmured. "If possible. However. Apply the appropriate experts. We must try everything. You'll be anxious to get the local police gods in action, what? There'll be a telephone in this village. Drop you at it. Before you wrestle with the constabulary, warn Southbury Hospital to get ready for me and my two patients. Might have a policeman sent up there to ward off kind enquiries."

So Bell was left in the cottage post office at Lower Upham, and through little clusters of people who stood gazing at the glare which lit the dark northern sky the big car drove on.

The hospital of Southbury is a low block of red brick, in the style of seventeenth-century almshouses. It stands outside the town on a green knoll which slopes to the river in a garden of old trees and banks of shrubs.

As the car stopped in the bar of light from the open door, a brisk young man came out. "Mr. Fortune? I'm the resident medical officer, Hammond. We've just had the police message. Two drunks pulled out of a fire, I understand."

"I wouldn't say that. No. Police diagnosis. Hasty diagnosis. Narcotic poisoning. Probably morphia or heroin. Taken by the mouth. Stomach pump and then atropin injections. But nobody must know anything. You see? Criminal case."

160

"Right," said the young doctor with relish.

Some seven hours afterwards, Reggie came into the hospital waiting room. Lowered blinds kept it dark. He drew them up, and the cold, pale light of a hazy morning showed his face yellowish for want of shaving, something flat of cheek and small of eye.

It showed also Bell and Sam, each in an easy chair, each with a chair to hold up his legs, comfortably asleep.

Bell's solid body stirred, resenting the noise of the blinds. He sat up and looked for the cause.

"Had a good night?" said Reggie.

Bell rubbed his eyes and stretched and came to his feet. "Not too bad," he decided and contemplated Reggie with sympathy. "Eh, you've had a doing. You're about all in, sir."

"Oh, no. Still effective. However. A little sleep between the acts is indicated. Wake up, Samuel." He shook the chauffeur into action. "Home, my child, home. Are you coming up, Bell?"

"I don't know. I've got a fire-brigade man coming down this morning." Bell looked at his watch. "But I'd like to have a talk to Mr. Lomas. I can fit it in. I'll go along with you, sir."

"That's all right. You've fixed up with the local police to keep people off the cottage and this place?"

"I have. And there's a general warning out for Mrs. Harley's car. But what are you doing about these two?"

"They ought to come through now. Quite a good staff here. It's been touch and go with Alix. But I think we've saved her. Osmond's all right. Won't be able to tell us anything yet awhile. Give him twelve hours or so. Come on."

The car carried them away.

"But look here, sir," Bell objected. "Why are they so bad—just over a bottle or two of fizz and a little smoke?"

"My dear chap! Oh my dear chap. They had more than that. Another case of dope. Morphia or one of the derivatives. Probably heroin again."

"Both of 'em?"

"Oh, yes. Yes. Osmond had more than she did. But he's the tougher subject."

"Well, what's the idea, then?" Bell frowned. "Both doped—but that looks like they doped themselves, or one of 'em fixed it—do you mean they came down for a night of dope, like Molly Marne?"

"Ingenious idea. Yes. It could be. On present facts. Except the fire."

"One of 'em might have been trying to do the other in."

"Yes. That is so. You mean Osmond meant to eliminate Alix. Some miscalculation, then. However. There has been miscalculation. Several miscalculations. Think it over. I'm going to sleep." ...

Against those who accuse him of living too luxuriously Mr. Fortune is wont to quote his physical history during these days of climax. From the first exchanges of the conversation with Fora in Zurich to the end of the main battle, some sixty hours passed. Through all that time the issue was uncertain, and any blunder or negligence might have brought defeat. It was at every moment possible that a new fact would arrive requiring study or a change in tactics. Several such facts did, as you are observing, arrive. The only periods in which he could be sure that no call would be made on him were while he was traveling by 'plane and car. Through those he slept and, which he considers a greater achievement, on his return to London from Southbury, with the crisis plainly imminent, he rolled into bed and was instantly asleep and stayed sleeping four hours more. Such control of the faculties, he will point out, is only possible to a mind and body wisely managed in a beautiful harmony of efficiency.

He made a large and hungry breakfast of grilled salmon and raspberries and clotted cream. Then he went to his laboratory and set his assistant Jenks to work on the champagne. A glass rod let fall a drop or two of fluid to a speck of fluid on white porcelain, and a blue color came. Another test was tried, and the color was purple which changed to blue and then to green.

"Yes. Morphia or derivative. As expected. That'll do. Take it round to Anneler and ask him to work it all out. Then come back." Reggie retired from the disappointed Jenks to his own room.

Then he took out the slip of wood cut from the doorpost of Osmond's flat. He considered it long, he examined it with a magnifying glass, and on the return of Jenks called him into consultation.

"What do you think about this, young man?"

Jenks inspected it and meditated. "I should say it's a bloodstain, rather a thick deposit."

"Yes. Good and not so good," Reggie murmured. "Probably blood. Other terms confused. If a thick deposit, then not a stain." He applied a steel point to it. "And it is thick." He looked plaintively at Jenks. "The right word seems to be 'smear,' " he moaned. "Provisionally a thick smear of blood."

"It is smeared," Jenks agreed. "As if somebody had wiped off blood on the wood."

"That is indicated. Yes. Which is without meaning. The wood came from the doorpost of an empty flat. No obvious reason why anybody should wipe blood off there. However. Photograph it: showing up the smear and the thickness of the blood. Might be wanted as evidence, with luck. Then we'll do a serological test. Better know what group it belongs to." He gazed at Jenks. "No present use. May never be. But we won't miss anything."

That test was never made by him. He called up Lomas while Jenks prepared it. "Fortune speaking. Any news of Mrs. Harley's car?"

"My dear Reginald, how zealous! I wasn't disturbing you because Bell said you were done up after your night in the country."

"Like his cheek." Reggie was shrill.

"All in kindness. You have been going it. And he's probably rather scared of you. Nice little dinner party you arranged for him."

"Yes. May be some more while you're making conversation. Have you found that woman's car?"

"We have. Abandoned in a by-street of Reading."

"Reading. Not many hours from Southbury," Reggie murmured. "Big station. Lots of trains to anywhere."

"Quite. Come round, will you, when you're up?"

"When I'm up!" Reggie moaned. "Been in the lab for hours." A taxi took him to Scotland Yard.

He came into Lomas's room with a brusqueness uncommon to him. "Anything to notice about her car?"

"You are on the jump, Reginald," Lomas smiled. "No, nothing of any use. The car has run about two hundred miles since Mrs. Harley took it out—if you believe her chauffeur. It must have filled up somewhere. But no evidence where yet. Car all in order. Harley declares he can't imagine why she should go to Reading. We haven't told him about the affair at Osmond's cottage."

"That's right. And it wasn't in the morning papers. One function of the police in which they're quite efficient, keeping things out of the papers. Has Harley shown any curiosity what's become of Osmond?"

Lomas smiled. "No. He hasn't. I thought that rather odd, Reginald. When we started shadowing Harley, it was Osmond who came and protested, like a loyal, devoted friend. But now that Harley's wife is missing, Harley doesn't try to get in touch with friend Osmond. He may have telephoned Osmond's flat, of course. He hasn't done anything more. We've made sure of that. Quite odd. He tells us his wife has vanished. He don't mention that Osmond has."

"Yes. Interestin' point," Reggie murmured. "Obvious inference, Harley knew Osmond was going."

"Quite. I inferred that," Lomas smiled. "How much more did he know, Reginald? That Osmond was taking Alix Lynn with him?"

"One of the possibilities. Yes. Probable possibility."

"I should say so. Would you like to give a straight answer to a straight question—just for a change?"

"My dear chap! Oh my dear chap. This insinuation is distressin'. I always answer straight—when the subject permits."

"With a smile that is childlike and bland. Come now, did you expect that the woman you found with Osmond would be Mrs. Harley?"

"Oh my Lomas! Not me, no. Recognized it as one possibility. Only remote possibility. Never believed in it."

"Really? Yet it was hunting for Mrs. Harley that took you there."

"No. No." Reggie's round face was distressed as a child's whose elders will not understand. "Mrs. Harley was always a side issue. I was hunting for Osmond because all the case converges now on him. My dear old thing, haven't you seen that? And it was essential I should hunt for him—and find him—or there wouldn't have been any Osmond this morning."

"You're sure Osmond was drugged?"

"Yes, thank you. I do know narcotic poisoning when I see it. Simple as I am. No deception. Both of 'em doped. Quite a big dose. In the champagne. Details from Anneler later. I only just managed to pull the girl through."

"Well, I take that," said Lomas slowly.

"How kind of you," Reggie purred.

"What have we got, then? Osmond and Alix go off secretly to his cottage and drink themselves silly on doped champagne. That might be an intentional orgy—"

"Oh, yes. Like poor Molly Marne's, as Bell said. A morphia debauch. One of the possibilities. By the way, Alix was wearin' a wedding ring. Might be for that occasion only. But the fact has interest."

"We've met occasional wedding rings before." Lomas put out his lip. "She was there to spend the night with him. We can pass the ring. But you remember that we had rumors long ago of Osmond using drugs."

"We did. And found he showed no drug symptoms. Well?"

"Tough fellow, isn't he?" said Lomas. "Still, I agree, there's no good evidence. And further, if he did drug himself, it's not likely he meant to burn himself to death."

"You think not?" Reggie murmured. "Well, well. You may be right."

"Though he did get in forty gallons of petrol," said Lomas. "And the place was like a stack of firewood. How did the fire start?"

"I haven't the slightest idea," Reggie mumbled. "Matter for the specialist—if any evidence remains. I can tell you where it started. In the petrol-electric plant. Flames came from that shed."

"So Bell thought. He's gone down again with a fire-brigade man to turn over the ashes. I don't expect much myself. But supposing there was foul play—who arranged it?"

"My dear chap! Oh my dear chap. The old firm. The mischief makers, unlimited. Their crowning effort. Probably not last effort. They'll fight on while they can. But this was the great big gamble. And it's failed, Lomas."

Reggie contemplated him with a slow benign smile. "Rather good work by Reginald."

"Modest fellow." Lomas made a grimace. "I'll hand the bouquets later. Your theory is, this is one more of the operations of the Maison Montespan crowd. Which means that behind it are Lady Rosnay and Mrs. Harley. Either or both. Well, I don't say no. I don't mind owning I thought Osmond had gone off with Mrs. Harley. It seems to me there's something in that still. Suppose she hoped he would—and found Alix Lynn was the woman he wanted. There's the motive—a motive that will serve for everything that has happened."

"Yes. Twisting it a bit here and there. Passion of Mrs. Harley for Osmond—the various attempts to make scandal of his affair with Alix—the elimination of the other rival, Molly Marne. Yes. Possible motive." Reggie's eyelids drooped. "Yes. Might be complicated with Lady Rosnay's objection to Alix marryin' the man. Another motive, what?"

"It wouldn't make the old lady murder her granddaughter," Lomas frowned.

"It shouldn't. No. Assumin' the natural affections."

"Everything points to Mrs. Harley, doesn't it?" said Lomas sharply.

"Actions of Mrs. Harley one of main factors, yes," Reggie mumbled.

"Then the crux of the case is to find her. Well, I rather think we have found her, Reginald."

Reggie sat up. "Well, well. You, too, have not been idle. What have you done with her?"

"I'm not quite sure," said Lomas. "It's like this: One of the flats on Osmond's staircase—"

"My only aunt!" Reggie groaned.

"It's a flat below his on the first floor that's been empty for some time. People came to look at it this morning. When the manager opened the door for 'em they found a dead woman inside. I've not long had the news. I've sent round a fellow who knew Mrs. Harley by sight from shadowing her husband. We ought to hear—"

"We'll go and see." Reggie started up. "Come on."

When they were in a taxi, "You haven't much doubt, what?" Lomas asked.

Reggie squirmed. "It's been in the back of my mind," he said jerkily.

"You mean to say you thought she'd be found in Osmond's place?"

"Didn't think," Reggie mumbled. "Didn't work at it. Concentratin' on Osmond. Mind registered something queer about those flats. Reserved for consideration. Quite right." He turned to Lomas a cold, defiant stare. "I was right. Osmond's the decisive point. We had to win there or lose. And we're going to win."

Lomas raised skeptical eyebrows. "Rather flamboyant, Reginald. Not your usual method when confident. Talking to keep your spirits up? Or is it merely nerves?"

Reggie gave a sudden, short, and mirthless laugh.

The taxi stopped. Two policemen saluted Lomas and passed them up the gloomy stairs.

The door of the empty flat was opened on a tiny hall, the counterpart of Osmond's, but this was blazing light and populous. A photograph was being taken of the dead woman on the floor.

The flare faded out, and they were left in the twilight of an electric bulb.

"It is Mrs. Harley, sir," said a detective. "I'd know her anywhere." Lomas waved him and all his forces away to the rooms within. Reggie knelt down by the body.

The woman lay on her back. She wore coat and skirt of blue silk. The blue hat was dragged awry from her yellow hair. Her face showed livid white above a purple smear, a dark red hole in her neck and a mess of dried blood on the floor.

Reggie stood up slowly and gave a long sigh of relief. "Yes. Been dead some time. More than twenty-four hours. Thank God. Yes. I was quite right. Cause of death, that big wound in her throat. Cut everything that mattered. Some sign of violence about the lips. Probably hand over her mouth while she was stabbed. She wouldn't make much noise afterwards. Stab apparently made by that trench knife lying beside her. Adequate weapon."

"Would she die quickly?"

"Oh, yes. Yes. Matter of minutes."

"She wouldn't suffer?" Lomas frowned.

"Not much. No."

"She looks as if she had. Her face is rather horrible."

"Yes. Much distress. Face not easy to read: rather gaunt: she'd been worried, we know: there's a sort of horror: probably not physical pain: call it ghastly surprise. I should say she was surprised. She didn't expect this end to things."

"That means she was surprised at being attacked or at the person who attacked her."

"Yes. I think so," Reggie murmured. "Both."

"You said the time of death was more than twenty-four hours ago. Will you be able to get it nearer than that?"

"On the medical evidence alone—question of the state of the blood. Provisionally I should say thirty-six hours—might be thirty-six hours plus. However. I'll set my man Jenks to work on it. He does quite well when he knows what he's doing."

"Thirty-six hours," Lomas repeated. "That fixes the murder on the same night that she vanished. So she couldn't have had anything to do with the fire at Osmond's cottage."

"She couldn't have made the fire. No."

"And when she was murdered, Osmond was still here. He spent the night in his flat. He didn't go away till the morning after."

"That is the evidence, yes," Reggie murmured. "And she was killed by a trench knife. And Osmond went through the war and likely enough kept one by him. Fellows do. His sort of fellow. And you can add that yesterday Bell and I found a smear of blood on Osmond's doorpost. It was fairly fresh then. And the young Jenks will be able to tell you whether it's blood of the same group as Mrs. Harley's. There's your case, Lomas."

"So you think Osmond murdered her?"

"One of the possibilities," Reggie mumbled.

"Oh, damn your possibilities!" Lomas exploded. "That's all you ever give me. A tangle of conjectures. You won't commit yourself to anything."

"My only aunt!" Reggie was plaintive. "Won't I! Don't I! Haven't I! I told you the causes of things long and long ago. And I'm going to be right."

"Your stuff about shadows on the wall and the people who show them to us," Lomas sneered. "Very edifying, Reginald. But no practical use in the world."

"Think again," said Reggie sharply. "My stuff about trading on vice, envy, hatred, and malice. There's the effective force through all the case. We have to go for that. Not argue from the shadows."

"Oh, most impressive. But without any meaning."

"My dear old thing! Meaning here practical and urgent. Look at these shadows. The place and the time throw suspicion on Osmond. So does the blood on his doorpost. You can work out an adequate motive. Mrs. Harley came here to threaten him, make an appeal to him, give him some sort of trouble about Alix Lynn. He'd settled to go off with Alix. Mrs. Harley was in the way. So he killed her. And you have one of the commonest kinds of murder known to science."

"Quite. Why aren't you satisfied?"

"I say it's one of the possible theories. But not complete. Doesn't account for all the facts. Take one fact: if Osmond murdered her the night before last, how did her car come to be in a lane near his cottage last night?"

"You're making your own difficulties," said Lomas impatiently. "The woman came here in her car. After she was killed it had to be removed. So it was removed—to be hidden near Osmond's cottage. Does that clear your mind?"

"No. Not wholly. No. Quite a good explanation. That may be how the car got there and why it got there. One of the possibilities. But it doesn't explain how it went away and why it went away after the cottage was on fire, after Osmond was unconscious."

"Confound you," said Lomas. "Do you expect me to explain everything? There are half a dozen ways that might have happened. The car may have been stolen. There may be other people concerned. Damn, you're not even certain it was her car in the lane. Bell wasn't sure."

"No. Couldn't swear to it," Reggie said wearily. "However. As you say, several ways it might have happened. Several possibilities—which is what I was pointin' out. Take another little fact: Look at the blood on her neck—there, above the wound."

Lomas stooped and looked and swallowed and said thickly, "What about it?"

"How did it get there? Blood above the wound, smeared up her neck, round the jaw to her cheek. Blood don't run up. And that's a smear."

"I agree," Lomas nodded. "What do you make of it?"

"Somebody wiped the blood up that way. Only possible purpose, to get hold of a good deal of her blood."

"But that's mad," Lomas muttered and stared at him. "You mean there is madness at work?"

"Oh, no. No. Only cleverness. The blood was wanted to smear on Osmond's doorpost. Where we found it." He gazed at Lomas with large eyes of plaintive indignation. "I couldn't understand that," he moaned. "Well, well. They've always misjudged me. I never was clever. A simple mind. Their error. Limits my interest in their shadow play." He looked sadly round the little hall. "You saw that, of course,"—he pointed to the mark of a hand on the dusty wall. "Gloved, I fear. No fingerprints. But you'd better photograph it and get the size and the height from the ground. It's rather high up for Osmond. Like the shadow on Lady Rosnay's wall. I'll telephone the lad Jenks to work on the blood. Goodbye."

"Where are you off to?" Lomas cried.

Reggie gazed reproach. "My dear old thing! Goin' to see my patients. The daily round, the simple task will furnish all we ought to ask." Having departed, he put his head round the door. "By the way—if you feel you ought to do some work—have a heart-to-heart talk with Sir D. Kames, Bart."

"Kames?" Lomas gasped. "Why? What about?"

"Oh, things. Things at large. Kames was in with Lady Rosnay when the case first emerged, and Lady Rosnay was in with Maison Montespan at the start. Send for Kames. Goodbye."

Chapter XXVI

Account of a Honeymoon

WHEN Reggie's car slowed into the narrow streets of Southbury he woke up to see that it was three o'clock. This implies some resolute driving by Sam. It is of importance as a fixed point in the events of the day.

Southbury gave no sign that anything had happened or could happen there. The normal quiescence of a country town's afternoon prevailed.

They drove through it to the hospital. The gate of the grounds was shut, but the precaution seemed superfluous. The road was empty. A constable in uniform sauntered out of the shade as they stopped, recognized the car and Reggie and saluted, and opened the gate and shut it after them. "That's all right. Managin' very well," Reggie purred. "When you've dropped me, you'd better obliterate self and car, Sam."

"Very good, sir," Sam approved.

Deposited at the hospital door, Reggie stood contemplating wistfully the grounds, slopes of green sunlit turf, dark shade of copper beech and chestnut, thickets of rhododendron and lilac and thorn, the flowery banks of the river below.

From a seat in the dappled, fragrant shadows of a row of limes Dr. Hammond rose and came briskly to meet him. "Well, how's the lady?" Reggie asked.

"Not too good. I should be glad for you to see her, Mr. Fortune. She doesn't seem to be getting clear of the stuff."

"You think not? Well, well. What about the man?"

"Oh, he's all right. Coming through splendidly. He must be as strong as a bull."

"Tough stuff, yes. All right. I'll have a look at the lady first. Anybody been enquiring after her?"

"No enquiries at all, I'm told."

"Sad lack of interest. Well, well. Ring up Lady Rosnay at Langton." Reggie gave the number. "Tell her her granddaughter Alix is in Southbury Hospital and the authorities thought she should be informed. That's all. You can't say anything more. Not a case to be definite about, you know."

"Right." Hammond marched off, and Reggie followed him in and went up with the matron to Alix's room. The nurse met them, looking anxiety.

Alix lay still, her face of a milky pallor in the midst of her red hair. Her eyes were open but dull and very dark, and she seemed neither to see nor hear Reggie as he came to the bedside.

He felt her pulse, and nurse and matron questioned him with troubled eyes. He listened to her breathing. As his hands moved about her breast she seemed to wake, she frowned, she raised her head and peered at him. Then she said drowsily: "You—is it—Mr. Fortune?" She looked down at the hands on her body, she stared at him again and began to laugh. "It's you! Why should you?" There was a queer, bitter sound in her laughter.

"Now, now." The matron was shocked. "You mustn't be like this, my dear. Mr. Fortune saved your life."

She laughed louder, she dropped her head back on the pillow and grasped feebly at Reggie's hands. "What are you doing?"

"Just seeing you're all right. Don't worry," Reggie smiled. "You are." He took his hands away. "Having any gastric pain?"

She did not answer. She was busy fumbling at herself and arranging the clothes. The nurse took over that work, and Alix submitted to the ministrations and looked up at Reggie resentful, unhappy, puzzled. "Where is Peter?" she said. "Tell me. What happened to Peter?"

"Simon called Peter? Yes, I knew you were thinking about him. He's here. He's doing nicely."

"Was he hurt?"

"Not as much as you. Now you rest and be thankful."

Her dull eyes watched him go.

In the hall below he met Dr. Hammond. "Well, what about it?"

"I got through to Langton House, but they say Lady Rosnay is out, gone motoring, they'll inform her as soon as she's back, but they don't know when that'll be."

"Well, well," Reggie smiled. "Time will show."

Hammond made a gesture towards Alix's room. "Were you satisfied with her, Mr. Fortune?"

"Oh, yes. Yes. Pulse rather quick and feeble, respiration shallow and irregular. That's what's botherin' you, what?" Hammond nodded. "Don't worry. She's better than I expected. Vigorous girl. Leave her to nature now. She wants to come through. Trouble with these cases is when they don't. That's all I was afraid of. Now I'll call on our Mr. Osmond."

Osmond was sitting up in bed propped by pillows which he did not seem to need. He had a newspaper in his hands peering at it and turning the pages petulantly.

"No, there's nothing about you in it," said Reggie.

"What?" Osmond crushed the paper down and stared at him. "Fortune, is it? Damn it, I can't see anything clear."

"Not yet. No. That's the atropin we gave you. Antidote to the morphia, you know. It'll pass off presently. Well, feeling comfortable otherwise?" Reggie took hold of his wrist.

"Feeling like the morning after the night before," Osmond grunted.

"Yes. Natural sequence. You did make a night of it. However. That also will pass."

"I'm all right," said Osmond. "The hell of a head and the hell of a throat. How's Alix?"

"A stage behind you. Physically. She's anxious about you."

Osmond made an impatient movement and winced. "Oh, damn it all. Tell her there's nothing the matter with me."

"I have. Speakin' physically."

"Is she coming round?"

"Oh, yes. Yes. She is round the corner. We'll have her story soon, Osmond."

"Thank God," Osmond said and blinked his big-pupiled eyes and stared.

"Yes, I think so," Reggie murmured.

"Look here, Fortune, how do you come in?" Osmond muttered. Reggie sat down and watched him. "They say it was you got us out."

"Strictly speakin' Bell got you out and I got the lady."

"I suppose we should have been burnt alive if it hadn't been for you."

"Some form of death by fire, yes," Reggie mumbled. "That was indicated. Hence our action."

Osmond glowered at him. "No use saying thank you for that sort of thing."

"Not required. Part of our job. Quite easy, quite interestin'."

"Was it!" Osmond's heavy sallow face flushed and broke into a smile. "Take it I see how big it was, will you? You might have been caught in the fire for your pains. And God knows you had no reason to help me."

"You think not?" Reggie murmured. "Well, well."

Osmond took time to consider what he should say to that. "I'm not thinking so much about your coming into the fire. That was for Alix, I suppose. You'd feel you had to. It's your being there, your getting there. You took some trouble to look after us, didn't you?"

"Yes. You have made trouble. Hasn't paid you very well. Time you tried another line."

Osmond frowned. "Damn it, that isn't fair, Fortune. I daresay you don't believe me, but it isn't. I know I didn't help you over Molly, poor kid— over all the other damned mess—but I've been straight with you. Take it or leave it. I tell you I kept nothing back. I never had a guess in my head how Molly's business was managed or that rat Luttrell's or Lady Rosnay's knock-out or what was behind it all. Do you believe me?"

"Believe?" Reggie's eyelids drooped. "Wants faith, doesn't it? However. It could be. What about the dope in the champagne last night and the subsequent fire with forty gallons of petrol handy—and the presence of the lady when these arrangements had been made and no one was told where you'd gone to? Any guess in your head how all that happened?"

"My God, do you think I meant to murder Alix?" Osmond groaned.

"Somebody did," Reggie mumbled.

"You say the champagne was doped?"

"Oh, yes. Yes. Morphia or derivative. As with Molly Marne."

"You've proved that? You've got some of the champagne?"

"Yes, thanks. That's all right. You didn't finish the second bottle. I went back for it."

"God! I can't believe—" Osmond muttered.

"Faculty of faith sufferin' from strain. Yes. Now begin at the beginnin'. Why were you there with Alix and in secret?"

"Damn it, you know we were married," Osmond said loudly.

"I inferred that, yes. Takin' one thing with another. Custom of announcin' marriages may be coarse but has practical advantages. However. You were married and this was the honeymoon. My original question is still unanswered. Why so secret?"

"I couldn't wait any longer," said Osmond.

"Good reason for marryin' a girl. No reason for not tellin' her friends of your intention."

"You're devilish suspicious." Osmond's temper blazed out and was suppressed. "Well, I admit you have the right. Alix hasn't any people to matter but her grandmother. She was told. Alix left a letter for her."

"Oh. Lady Rosnay knew all about it," Reggie murmured. "That is rather relevant."

Osmond's eyes tried to see into him. "What do you mean? You think Lady Rosnay—No, damn it, I won't have that. Look here, Fortune, take things from the start."

"Yes. It would be better. As I was sayin'. If possible."

"The start is, I found out I wanted Alix. That was about a year ago. And after a bit she—well, we fixed it up." Osmond had become quaintly bashful. "There wasn't an open engagement because of Lady Rosnay. We never knew where we stood with her. She told Alix to wait. And that seemed fair enough to me. Wait till I had made good, you know. I was a nobody to her, and I'd rather take my wife as an equal. The old lady was sometimes as kind as I could want and sometimes blasting. So we carried on till all the mess this summer—"

"One moment. Any other objections to your engagement besides Lady Rosnay's?"

"How the devil could there be?"

"Any other woman in the case?"

"No woman has any hold on me." Osmond flushed. "You're hinting at Molly, are you? I never thought of her that way nor she of me, I'll swear."

"Well, well. To resume—after the mess of this summer, Lady Rosnay was still blowing hot and cold, what?"

"That's about true. You saw us at Langton. She didn't mind my meeting Alix. I believe she amused herself bringing us together. But she was devilish hard on Alix—hinting the deuce and all about me—playing a sort of cat-and-mouse game. Well, that couldn't go on. Alix agreed to marry. We kept it dark, because the old lady might have made a foul scandal of it with all this mess of mystery about. So I fixed it up at the registry office down here—that was the likeliest way nobody would get wind of it, and they didn't. I drove down yesterday morning, picked up Alix near Langton, and we were married in Southbury and came out to the cottage."

"For the honeymoon. Yes. Nice place. Any champagne at the wedding breakfast?"

"No." Osmond gave him a sullen look. "There wasn't a wedding breakfast. We only just got the marriage in the legal hours. We had lunch before. At the inn at Whitbourne."

"The two of you alone?" Osmond nodded. "None of your friends asked to the marriage?" Osmond shook his head. "You didn't tell any of 'em about it?"

"I didn't want anyone but ourselves. Nor did Alix."

"Feelin' like that," Reggie murmured. "Yes. Yourselves against the world, what? Well, well. And the champagne for the dinner of the marriage night. Where did that come from?" Osmond lay silent. "Why won't you tell me?"

"Oh, well," said Osmond miserably, "I shall have to. Harley sent me down a case of champagne."

"Did he? Very kind."

Osmond raised himself. "If you think Harley had anything to do with doping it, you're wrong, you're damned wrong. I'd trust him before myself."

" 'What is it ends with friends?' " Reggie murmured. "That's why you took so long to say anything about the origin of the champagne. Well, well. You didn't notice anything queer about its condition?"

"Do you think I should have let Alix drink it if I had?"

"No. You shouldn't. However. Awkward wine to tamper with. And it was doped. When did it arrive at the cottage?"

"I don't know. The woman who looks after the place ought to remember."

"Very appropriate of Harley to chip in with champagne for the dinner of the marriage night. You're not tellin' me everything, are you?"

Osmond's face was wretched. "You mean Harley knew we were going to be married. Yes, he did. I told him. We don't have secrets. But damn it, Fortune, you shan't put it on to Harley."

"I haven't put it on to anyone yet." Reggie watched him with closing eyes. "Have you any proof the champagne did come from Harley?"

"He telephoned that he was sending it," Osmond muttered.

"To your flat in London?"

Osmond nodded.

"And you took the message?"

"No, it was my man there."

"I see. Anything else you haven't told me? You didn't mention the marriage to anybody else?"

"No, I didn't," said Osmond with a sullen stare.

"Well, well. Pity. However. You've survived and she's survived. She has. She will. Goodbye."

He went downstairs and found Bell waiting for him. "My dear chap! Splendid. Are we yet alive and see each other's faces? Yes. We are. And will try to remain so. Well, what about love among the ruins? Investigations by the conflagration expert concluded? What's he say?"

"He's pretty sure the fire started with a short circuit in the petrol-electric shed. He can't swear to it, but he thinks there was dirty work with the wires."

"Yes. So did I. Why are experts, if they can't swear?" Reggie moaned. "However. We will carry on with the common mind of the common man. Found anything in the ruins?"

"I reckon there was pretty well a whole case of champagne, sir. All gone to glory, of course. I picked up half a dozen corks."

"My dear chap," Reggie crooned affectionately. "Got 'em?"

Bell showed him the charred remains, and he turned them over delicately. "Oh my hat," he smiled up at Bell's stolid face. "Anything occur to you?"

"They're so burnt," Bell complained.

"Yes, that is so. Yes. But here's one that isn't the right cork. Brand obliterated. But it was a mature wine. 1921. This cork's new stuff. Soft stuff. Indicatin' that one or more bottles had been recorked lately. Probably the top range in the case. That's very interestin'."

"Can you recork champagne?" Bell objected.

"Done regularly in the process of maturin' it. Dégorgement, they call it. No special skill required. Easier to put in a new cork than the old stiff one. So that was done. And we infer that the dope was put into the champagne before it was opened by the happy couple at their weddin' feast. Thanks very much, Bell. Splendid fellow. This is just what I wanted." He caressed the cork with a finger. "Hallo!" His head was lifted, he stood very still, listening. "A car, I think."

Chapter XXVII

Kind Enquiries

TOGETHER Reggie and Bell moved to the window. A car had stopped at the gate of the hospital grounds, and the policeman on guard there was parleying with someone in it.

"Woman, eh?" Bell grunted.

"Yes, I think so," Reggie smiled. "As expected. Kind enquiries. I'll go and talk to her. You stay in reserve, Bell. You're useful but formidable. My gentle ways command confidence."

He wandered away through the grounds. He saw at the window of the car the bright painted face of Lady Rosnay, ogling the stolid constable, chattering hard. He approached, and she gave a scream of excitement and tumbled herself through the car door.

"Mr. Fortune! You dear creature! Are you here? How wonderful of you!" She seized his hands.

"Oh, no. No. Simple rational process," Reggie murmured. "I thought you might be comin' over."

"My dear! I'm frightened out of my wits. They say that Alix has been brought to this horrible hospital. The officer here says I mustn't come in, he can't tell me how she is, he can't tell me what's happened. It's distracting."

"Very distressin' to the natural affections. Yes. However. Policeman's quite right. He can't."

She made a squeak of dismay. "Lord! Don't torture me. You know all about it."

"You think so? Yes. You may be right. We had better have a little talk." He moved past her to the car and glanced at the chauffeur and up and down the road before he looked inside. Mrs. Darett sat there.

"Amy!" Lady Rosnay cried. "Come along, my dear. I can't bear it alone."

"If you please." Mrs. Darett looked at Reggie.

"Oh, yes. Yes. No secrets to keep," Reggie murmured and gave her his hand.

She leaned on it heavily as she came out of the car, she thanked him with a bow. Her measured movements, her calm made the excitement of Lady Rosnay more feverish.

Reggie held open the gate of the grounds for them. "We can go in?" Lady Rosnay panted. "Oh you angel." She snatched at Mrs. Darett's arm and drew her on.

With a monitory finger Reggie directed the policeman to continue on guard. "You can't go to your granddaughter." He came to Lady Rosnay's side. "She's not fit for any more shocks yet. But I'll tell you all about it. Oh, no. No. Don't thank me. I should like to."

"My dear! How is she?" Lady Rosnay squeaked.

"Yes. That is the first question. You're right. Crucial question. She's quite alive. She's goin' to remain alive. See that square fellow in the doorway? That's Superintendent Bell. Watchin' over her. One of the little cherubs that sit up aloft lookin' after the lives of people. The little cherubs have been rather underrated. Perseverin' species of mammal. However. You'd like to hear how everything happened. This is a nice place. We shan't be disturbed."

He shepherded the two old women to a seat in the shade of a copper beech. A bank of shrubs stood between it and the offices of the hospital. It looked over a green slope to the ripples of the river gleaming between sedges and purple loosestrife and swaying feathers of meadowsweet. The almond scent of that was in the warm air.

Reggie moved the seat to his satisfaction, end on to the shrubs.

Mrs. Darett sat down and Lady Rosnay beside her, and Reggie stood looking at them. He remembered how on the night of the ball he had thought them somehow alike. Except that they were both old and women, the likeness was gone. Neither of them had put on the orange lipstick of Herr Fora. Yet Lady Rosnay was amply decorated. Her lips were a purple red, her sunken cheeks made pink and white, the brown eyes brighter by artificial shadows, the wrinkles filled up.

Beside such art Mrs. Darett seemed clean. She had no wrinkles to hide, not many lines, her thin lips were so pale, the close mouth made little show in a face of yellow, waxen surface stretched tight upon the bones. She had given it neither paint nor powder. She sat stiffly, looking straight before her, an old woman older than her age and content she should be so.

A car came fast along the road and vanished.

"Oh my dear boy," Lady Rosnay giggled, "don't be such an owl. Do sit down."

They both moved to make room for him with some confusion of purpose. Which first decided to draw away from the other that he should sit between them, he was not sure, but there he sat.

"Thanks very much. Yes. Alix is recoverin'. But not seein' visitors yet.

So is our Mr. Osmond."

"The wretch!" said Lady Rosnay.

"You think so?"

"Of course I do. The fellow's a cannibal. My poor Alix! But what was he doing? How ever did it happen, Mr. Fortune?"

"Yes. You would naturally ask that," Reggie murmured. "Rather a long story. Begins quite a while ago. Not to go further into the past, begins with the establishment of Maison Montespan under the management of Madame Berthe Finck."

They both stared at him and, as he sat back and settled deeper into the seat, found themselves staring at each other. "What's the man talking about?" said Lady Rosnay in a high voice. Her bird's claw of a hand gripped his leg. "My good creature, I want to know what happened to my Alix!"

"And that is what I am goin' to tell you," Reggie drawled, removing her hand. "Activities of Maison Montespan primary factor in what happened to Alix. Which is their conclusion. In addition to the resources of Madame Finck, workin' capital for Maison Montespan was provided by Lady Rosnay and Mrs. Harley. Mrs. Harley is not able to be present. Pity. However. Lady Rosnay is. Soon after it began to work, Maison Montespan made contact with Fora, a perfumer of Zurich who supplied it with scents, cosmetics, and other chemicals. A fashionable dressmaker had opportunities for doin' a profitable business in these articles. Some of 'em rather assertive. I never liked Fora's orange lipstick myself, and that '*Matin d'un Faune*' scent—no, not nice."

"You quaint person," Lady Rosnay gave a crow of laughter.

"Yes. Old-fashioned taste. Simple mind. Yes. The other chemicals were more dangerous to morality. I quite agree."

"What ever do you mean?"

"The morphia supply service," Reggie murmured. "Destructive to the individual. Also gettin' people into the power of Maison Montespan. Not in the public interest."

The lines about Lady Rosnay's mouth appeared. "I never heard of such a thing," she said faintly and felt in her bag and used a smelling bottle.

"Hadn't you? Your error. People who provide the money for a business ought to know how it's run." Reggie turned to Mrs. Darett. "Don't you think so?"

"They should, shouldn't they?" she said.

"Amy! But how horrid of you," Lady Rosnay squeaked and leaned round Reggie to look at her.

Mrs. Darett's close mouth curved a moment. Her thin shoulders made a little movement.

"Thus prosperin', the Maison Montespan opened other departments,"

Reggie murmured. "If a man wanted a woman, it was happy to assist. Natural development—if somebody wanted somebody ruined, it would arrange the matter. Very profitable work when the clients were wisely chosen. But pure artistic pleasure in destroyin' people—delight in cruelty for its own sake—a great inducement, what?" He turned a placid gaze from one old woman to the other.

"Ugh! You're hateful! You make my flesh creep!" Lady Rosnay stared at him in the fascination of fear and quivering.

"If I were you, I should say nothing," Mrs. Darett advised her coldly.

"But I like to hear her comments," Reggie drawled. "Resumin' the history—these activities of the Maison Montespan first attracted my attention in the Poyntz case. Lady Rosnay was very helpful there. Result of nervous alarm. On investigation it became clear that failure to obtain the favors of Mrs. Poyntz for a gentleman of means—don't worry, he's bein' attended to—was followed by informin' the husband that his wife had been unfaithful. Primary intention no doubt to punish the woman, secondary hope that she might be separated from her husband and pushed into the lover's arms. Miscalculations, however. Actual result, suicide of wife and husband in despair at broken lives. Not unsatisfactory to the amiable directors of Maison Montespan. But they made a second miscalculation. Grave miscalculation. They sent an anonymous letter to the orphan daughter which had no purpose in the world but cruelty. Thus underratin' my simple mind. That letter showed the sort of people who were at work, you know. You talked about a cannibal, Lady Rosnay. These people are worse. They haven't been killing to eat, but to torture. They're not content with the body, they want to have souls in agony."

"O my God." Lady Rosnay shrank upon herself.

Reggie turned to Mrs. Darett. "You hurt her," the thin lips said. "She calls on God now."

"Yes. A little late. Second phase: contract to ruin Osmond. Mrs. Harley, one of the Maison Montespan capitalists, wanted him out of the way to give her husband a clear field in politics—"

"Mrs. Harley?" Lady Rosnay gurgled and rolled her eyes.

"Unavoidably absent. However. Lady Rosnay is not. Lady Rosnay, the other capitalist, didn't want him to marry her granddaughter."

"I—I didn't do anything against the man," Lady Rosnay wailed. "You know I didn't. I told you it wasn't Osmond stole my tiara. I showed everybody I didn't believe it. Didn't I ask him to Langton after all the scandals, Molly Marne and everything? I stood by him."

"You did. Yes. But you let yourself be used. If anyone suspected the scandal about him was invented, you left them to think the motive was to break his affair with Alix. You wouldn't agree to their marriage. You amused yourself playing with him like a cat. You didn't tell me you were one of the people behind the Maison Montespan."

"Why should I? I never thought that it could matter. I never knew all this you're telling me. Amy!" she screamed at Mrs. Darett. "You know I didn't?"

"Didn't you!" Mrs. Darett laughed. "You say so now."

"Yes. Didn't you, Lady Rosnay?" Reggie asked. "Didn't you think it mattered who was behind Maison Montespan when you knew that Molly Marne was killed by their drugs?"

"I didn't know," she gasped. "Molly—I didn't know she got them from Montespan. And then—my monkey and me—oh Amy—you wretch—" She started up, shaking with fear and rage, her painted face distorted, she screamed at Mrs. Darett and struck at her.

Reggie put out his arm to keep them apart.

Lady Rosnay reeled away from it and fell and lay on her face.

Reggie stood up, called out "Bell," and beckoned. Then he bent over her. "It's only a faint. Nervous excitement. Carry her in, will you, and tell the doctor. That's it." As Bell picked her up their eyes met in a glance of understanding.

Reggie sat down again by Mrs. Darett. She had not moved. She was still between him and the shrubs.

Chapter XXVIII

"—Wherewith the Soul of Man

is Blackened"

Mrs. DARETT smiled. "That was well managed, Mr. Fortune."

"You think so? Well, well. Resumin' the history—"

"Oh, you had not finished?"

"No. No. A good deal more. I suppose we shall never get it clear whether Mrs. Harley thought of hating Osmond spontaneously or had the idea suggested to her. Very difficult to distinguish. Probably she couldn't tell us herself. Probably she never quite knew, what?"

"You had better ask her," said Mrs. Darett.

"She bein' dead yet speaketh," Reggie murmured. "Yes, so she does. But not on that point. However. Psychological points like that don't interest the law."

"Dear me, is she dead?" said Mrs. Darett. "Poor thing. When was that? How did she die?"

"Without physical pain," Reggie drawled. "You can't have everything. You must have noticed that. She died the night before last. About seven or eight o'clock."

"How precise you are!"

"Yes. I am careful. That hasn't been sufficiently recognized. But we're takin' things out of order. The point was the motive of Mrs. Harley in desirin' to ruin Osmond."

"Oh, a devoted wife," said Mrs. Darett. "Of course she would have done anything for her husband's career. And Simon Osmond was on the way to eclipse his useful friend. But the good woman had another motive, Mr. Fortune. She was so fond of her husband's dear friend she couldn't bear him to neglect her and fall in love with Alix. Too ungrateful of him."

"Thank you," Reggie murmured. "I thought you'd tell me that."

"You asked me." Mrs. Darett jerked her thin shoulders.

"Not asked, no. Offered opportunity. We'll take it she was worked on and worked up. For there was another factor makin' for attack on Osmond.

Decisive factor. Another man wanted Alix and her fortunes. You don't mention him. However. The whole energies of Maison Montespan were thus directed to the destruction of Osmond. First attack: the ball. Unfortunate that I was there. You may call my presence the product of the Poyntz case. As I was there, Luttrell was directed to prime my innocent mind against Osmond, and the attack developed accordin' to plan. I take it Luttrell was commonly used as a mud slinger by the Montespan firm. Good choice for the purpose, but a dangerous employee, what? General plan was ingenious. Lady Rosnay knocked down in the dark, tiara stolen, at the moment when Osmond was somewhere upstairs. Result ought to have been big scandal over stealing of tiara, Lady Rosnay furious, snapping at the chance to accuse Osmond, general suspicion of the impecunious political adventurer. With any luck, he would never have been able to live that down. But there wasn't any luck at all. The inconvenient Luttrell was active. He found out who did the stealing. He threatened to be troublesome. There was a row and a fight. And as he had the impudence to carry a rotten heart, he got killed. Not accordin' to plan. Another hitch—the fellow who stole the tiara let me see his shadow on the wall, and I knew one thing about him, how tall he was. And finally the plan fell down altogether by sheer ignorance. The directors didn't know that the tiara Lady Rosnay wore was paste, didn't know Alix knew it and Osmond would have known, too. So Lady Rosnay couldn't start a scandal, and the whole thing was futile, and the Maison Montespan had to write it off as a damagin' failure. That must have been disheartening."

"I don't know," said Mrs. Darett.

"You think not?" Reggie purred. "Well, well. 'The reason firm, the temperate will, endurance, foresight, strength and skill.' Yes, all those qualities present. 'The perfect woman nobly planned to guide, to comfort, to command.' " He contemplated Mrs. Darett with eyes half closed. Her lean face was yellow in the sunlight, and of a metallic sheen. "I have never underrated the directors of the Maison Montespan," Reggie said in a soft, respectful tone. "That's why we're sittin' here together in the beauty of the summer evening." He turned, looking about the hospital garden from the dark shrubs behind Mrs. Darett to the river, to the policeman standing at the gate and Bell sitting by the door. "Charmin' scene of peace, isn't it?"

Mrs. Darett did not answer.

"Well, well. Next phase of the war: the grand offensive. The masterpiece. The attack on Osmond through Molly Marne. One of the ablest crimes that have been tried on me. And it had its success. Poor Molly. I don't forgive that, you know."

Mrs. Darett's thin lips smiled.

"Brilliant work both in strategy and tactics. Foresight and preparation of high merit. Dashin' execution. You don't mind my usin' that word? And the whole thing showing masterful use of all the resources of the Maison Montespan. When introducing Molly Marne to morphia, possibly the firm had only the usual purpose of corruptin' a woman whose corruption might be profitable. But considerin' her cultivated friendship with Osmond, Mrs. Harley, Lady Rosnay, and all, we can say that purpose soon developed. The directors of Maison Montespan took long views. And their foresight was rewarded. Molly offered a way to get at Osmond when they needed it. First operation, spreading of rumors that the erratic Osmond was a drug addict. Very damagin', very plausible—unless expert observation was applied— even then the kind of mud that sticks. Second operation, to refuse Molly her usual morphia till she was starvin' for it. In that crazy condition she ought to have lent herself easily to compromise Osmond, she ought to have done anything at the orders of the people who could get her the drug. Another miscalculation. You notice the brilliant minds of the Maison Montespan were continually baffled by ignorin' the fundamental decency of people."

"Were they?" Mrs. Darett laughed.

"Oh, yes. Yes. You should recognize that. Better to get things clear now. That was one force misjudged. The other was my simple mind. Molly wouldn't be used against Osmond, and as the proposal had been made to her she was an urgent danger to the Maison Montespan. She could give the whole thing away if her poor muddled soul went straight. Operations to prevent that of skill and force. The original plan to compromise Osmond was still used but amended. Osmond was got down to her country place on a night when his absence from the House would be conspicuous. It was further arranged that she should die that night and he should have no good story to explain himself. Tactics brilliantly carried out. Fora provided heroin tablets of strength to kill, lookin' like Molly's usual dose, and she went off for a happy night of the drug she was starvin' for. I always admired the manipulation of Molly and Osmond. The Maison Montespan knew 'em both very well—up to a point. Puncturin' Osmond's tires to delay his gettin' back was probably an error. Made the thing rather too neat. Usual tendency of clever people. However. That might have passed. The fatal error was underratin' the simple mind of the investigator. Which wasn't able to believe that if the vehement Osmond wanted to kill a girl he would do it by faking tablets of drugs to be double the right weight. Not in his style at all. The directors of the Maison Montespan should have realized the natural man might notice that before they committed themselves. Afterwards—it was too late. Effort to link up Osmond with heroin poisoning by arrangin' an attempt to poison Lady Rosnay and monkey, which he had the chance to make, very ingenious but rather wild. Writin' an anonymous letter, indicatin' guilty knowledge of Molly's murder, so that he could be suspected of writin' it, quite unsound. Minds were gettin' hectic, what?"

"No doubt Mrs. Harley had become nervous," said Mrs. Darett.

"Yes. I noticed that. The handwritin' of the letter had the defect of linkin' up Molly's case with the wanton cruelty of the Poyntz case, which wasn't in Osmond's line at all. But I always appreciated the subtle point that it threw suspicion on Mrs. Harley and Lady Rosnay as possible authors. For a piece of ingenuity, I admired that very much."

"You are so quick," said Mrs. Darett. "I can't keep up with you. Do you mean there was another anonymous letter sent from Langton—and in the same writing as that which the poor little Poyntz child had?"

"Not the same, no. Imitation of it. So we had evidence of two operators. Two minds with but a single thought, two hearts that beat as one. Useful information. Well, you remember my modest proceedings at Langton. Those produced some more evidence. Introduction to the dinner party of Lady Rosnay with monkey still alive caused an interesting exhibition of surprise. You must have noticed that, Mrs. Darett. And it wasn't Osmond who was surprised."

"Mrs. Harley did make a scene, didn't she?" Mrs. Darett said slowly.

"There were reactions, yes. Further operations of mine informed the company that I was lookin' for somebody who could cast a shadow such as seen at Lady Rosnay's ball. Strong reaction followed. Somebody tried to shoot me in the park next morning."

"Really?" Mrs. Darett looked at him. "How dreadful, Mr. Fortune. You should take more care of yourself."

"You think so? Protection quite adequate, thank you. Moreover, the time is past. Murderin' me might have muddled the case then. Thrown fatal suspicion on Osmond. Now that's impossible. The whole thing is clear and everybody's in our hands."

"Dear me, how clever you have been," she smiled.

"Oh, no. No. Only graspin' the essentials and takin' the necessary action. The simple mind. After Langton, it was quite clear what had to be done, trace the origin of the drugs, takin' meanwhile a vigorous offensive against the weak point in the Maison Montespan position—which was Mrs. Harley. Well, we did trace the drugs, and Fora's in jail in Zurich, and we have the invaluable Madame Finck and all her papers. We acted against Mrs. Harley by puttin' police on her husband. You know how she took that."

"How should I?" said Mrs. Darett. "She was always an excitable woman."

"Yes. I suppose you did find her impressionable," Reggie purred. "Yes. Expert in human weakness, aren't you? Not so good on virtues. Final miscalculation—you didn't allow for some fundamental decency in the woman."

Mrs. Darett laughed. "In Rose Harley? Oh, are we to be sentimental now? After all she had planned and done, you talk of her decency!"

"At the last, yes. When she saw the police working against her husband, she couldn't bear that. She had to find a way out. I suppose she tried you first, and you wouldn't be helpful, what? Anyhow, she went to Osmond. She meant to tell him everything, didn't she? I don't know what would have happened if he'd heard. Probably he would have done something crazy to save her and Harley. That kind of man, isn't he? But the final arrangements had been already made by Maison Montespan. The directors knew all about the plans for the secret marriage and the quiet honeymoon. The petrol was ordered, the champagne was doped—"

"Champagne?" said Mrs. Darett. "The Harleys sent him his champagne. They always did."

"Well, well!" Reggie stared at her with round eyes. "That isn't worthy of you."

She bit her lip. "Oh, go on," she said.

"We've finished, haven't we? Mrs. Harley went to Osmond's flat. She never saw him. Somebody killed her just before she got there. But leavin' a handprint high on the wall. And the last futile, rather foolish effort to fix a crime upon him was smearing her blood by his door. Then somebody drove off in her car to set the fire going in Osmond's cottage and burn up Osmond and his wife as they lay doped. Only other people were there too soon. So they didn't die. They're not goin' to die. And the night Mrs. Harley was murdered, police raided the Maison Montespan and took the useful Madame Finck and her useful papers. That's the end of it all. Defeat. Absolute and fatal defeat." Reggie slid down into the corner of the seat and looked dreamily into the shadows of the shrubs behind her and across the sunlight to the square shape of Bell smoking a pipe by the door and the policeman at the gate. He lifted a finger. Bell stood up and began to stroll across the turf.

Mrs. Darett sat still and erect. "You must be very pleased with yourself, Mr. Fortune," she said.

"Not pleased, no. Too many casualties. I should like to have saved Molly. Content. I did quite well in the conditions. The Maison Montespan is smashed. And there'll be a vengeance. I've enjoyed this little conversation."

"You like vengeance?" Mrs. Darett smiled. "How human of you. When you're so shocked by cruelty." She laughed. "How cruel nice people can be, can't they? Well, you have had Mrs. Harley killed and you've caught Lady Rosnay. The two directors of the Maison Montespan."

"Oh, no. No," Reggie was plaintive. "Not worthy of you again. I know Lady Rosnay never directed anything. And Mrs. Harley was murdered by the directors. I said this was the end, Mrs. Darett." His eyes directed hers to

Bell strolling to and fro but always nearer.

"I see. This was to amuse yourself," she said.

"I did want to hear what you would say," Reggie purred. "I like to be just."

"Just!" Her quiet voice rose a tone. "Very well. You are sure you can prove that I arranged it all. You have been very clever." She made him a little bow. "Quite clever—with everything on your side. I wonder what you would have done if you had been like me?"

Reggie made a little gesture towards her. "There, but for the grace of God, sit I?" he murmured. "I don't know. Not a question for me, Mrs. Darett. I do my job. Which is to stop yours."

"So comfortable for you," she said. "Well, I have nothing to deny now. I did do everything, everything. It was I. Why shouldn't I? I lost all my money. I had to make money. What are you to judge me? I suppose you never lacked anything in your life?"

"Not much, no," Reggie nodded.

"And you're well, you're strong. I am dying, and dying in pain. You've been sentimental about what I made others suffer. Do you know how I've suffered?"

"I can guess." Reggie bent his head.

"Can you?" she laughed. "How easy to say that. What do you know? I can hardly drag myself along now. There is a cancer in my lungs. You're a doctor. You know what that means. You know you fools of doctors can't do anything. You don't know what the pain is."

"Yes, I thought it was something like that," Reggie murmured.

"Why shouldn't I make others suffer as I suffer? What justice is there it should be I and not others, all the others? You won't bring me to trial. I shan't live long enough. But I've had my day. You like vengeance, do you? So do I, and I've had mine."

"On the innocent," Reggie said.

"Who is innocent?" she cried. "Not anyone, while I have my pain."

Reggie beckoned to Bell, and Bell with no great way to go came quickly towards them.

"Oh, don't think I shall live to amuse you any more," she said. She fumbled in her bag and was putting something to her lips.

Reggie grasped the closed fingers. "Not that way," he said, and she gave a hoarse cry.

Through the shrubs behind her came Arthur Darett. "Look out, sir," Bell shouted and ran on, calling the policeman from the gate.

A pistol glinted in Darett's hand. He lifted it and fired, and as Mrs. Darett turned to look, a small wound opened in her sallow face and with a sigh of laughter she fell on the turf.

Bell flung himself at Darett, brought him down, and they lay together struggling for the pistol. Darett had it near his own head when Reggie arrived and dragged it away. "Oh, no. No. That's another thing," he murmured.

The policeman arrived panting.

"Come along." Reggie gave place to his weighty strength. "Here you are. Your job. Name, Arthur Darett. And the charge is, murdering his mother."

Darett ceased to struggle and looked up at him and grinned and gasped: "You devil."

"Not me. No," said Reggie. "I'm on the other side."

"The devil's own luck," Darett spat at him.

"Oh, no. Only careful," said Reggie. He took the pistol from Bell. "Yes. Luger parabellum. I thought so." He looked down at Darett. "Thanks very much."

Chapter XXIX

The End of the Day

ON THE next afternoon Mr. Fortune arrived in Scotland Yard. As he made his way to Lomas's room he was met by a little man who had gray whiskers and a flat white tie with a ruby pin and hummed a jerky tune.

This complacent anachronism took off his hat, showed two rows of teeth resplendently false, and said in a smooth and caressing tone: "Mr. Fortune! My dear sir, pray let me give you the warmest congratulations."

"Thanks very much," Reggie murmured. "Why?"

The little man tittered. "Really now! That is too modest. But so like you." Stroking at it, he took and shook Reggie's hand. "An admirable, a brilliant piece of work, sir." He tripped away chirruping.

Reggie found Lomas at work with the telephone, took a cigar, wandered to the biggest chair, sank into it and smoked and let his eyes close.

Lomas put down the receiver. "Well, Reginald, you have made a case of it now," he said. "My congratulations."

"Thanks. That's what little man Clunk said."

"Oh, you ran into him, did you?" Lomas put up his eyeglass.

"Yes. Chirpin' hymns and handin' out butter. Very flatterin'. Little man Clunk bluffs well. No one better. Except me. As I may have remarked before. I infer that he has decided the time for bluffin' is gone by, what?"

"I'm not sure. He's been talking round and round with me. The meaning seemed to be that his client Madame Finck might put in a general confession if we give an undertaking to let her down gently. Deuced useful, now we don't need her. Very like Josh Clunk, isn't it?"

"Yes. Quite in his best style. He wasn't bluffing. Worse men in the trade than Mr. Clunk. We do need her, Lomas."

"Now? What for? The whole case has wound itself up. Mrs. Harley murdered—Mrs. Darett murdered—and that young devil Arthur Darett taken in the act of killing her. We can hang him without any evidence from Berthe Finck."

"Oh, yes. Yes. He's provided for." Reggie blew smoke rings.

"Very well. Those three were the principals, weren't they?"

188

"Yes, I think so," Reggie murmured.

"Damn, what more do you want?"

"I told you to talk to Sir D. Kames, Bart.," said Reggie. "I want him."

Lomas frowned. "The deuce you do! That's what Clunk was hinting at, I suppose, with his talk about our natural desire for a complete case against the principals."

"Yes, he would put it like that," Reggie smiled. "However. Fair-minded man, little man Clunk. You remember, I said he wouldn't let us get anything out of Madame Finck unless it was his best chance."

"I believe you," said Lomas with an unpleasant laugh. "So now he hopes to save her neck by turning her on to swear crimes against Tom, Dick, and Harry."

"Oh, no. No. He's much too clever. We can't hang Madame Finck, you know. She may deserve it. But not by law. You can be sure she wasn't let into the Daretts' little murder plans. They wouldn't put their sweet lives in anybody's hand. She was only used to run the drug-and-scandal and woman-hunting business. We may as well take what we can get out of her. I want D. Kames. I like to finish a case."

"I don't see my way," Lomas objected. "All there is against Kames in the Montespan papers is that they had some money out of him. So they did out of Lady Rosnay. And others. I can't have a general mudslinging and let the Finck woman slide out."

"Oh, no. No. Nothing like that," Reggie purred. "A lighter sentence for the wretched Finck and evidence to ruin D. Kames. That's all."

"You're a ruthless animal, Reginald. What's your grudge against Kames?"

"I think he was the man who coveted Mrs. Poyntz. I want to make him pay. That's why I want the woman Finck to talk."

"Good Gad!" said Lomas. "Well, if you're right—"

"Yes, I think so," Reggie smiled. "Little man Clunk knew he had somebody to give us, and it must be Kames. Some nasty evidence to link him with the Maison Montespan will blast his glorious career, what? I should say he has a thick hide, but that will hurt."

"I agree," Lomas said slowly. He looked at Reggie with a twist of a smile. "I shouldn't like to be on your black list, Reginald. Persevering and resourceful hater, aren't you?"

"My dear chap! Oh my dear chap!" Reggie moaned. "Not me. No. A simple, gentle nature. I like seein' fair. That's all. I don't like people bein' hurt."

"Do you think Kames was a leader in the business?"

"Oh, no. Merely the rich man payin' for his vices. One leader only. The late, lamented Mrs. Darett. Very able mind. I should say that her son was inferior. You notice the wilder strokes were his. Man of action. With the weaknesses of the type. Still, a clever fellow. And he kept his loyalty to her. Curious and interestin'. He's quite evil, except for affection for her—"

"But he killed her," Lomas objected.

"Oh, yes. Yes. Which was affection. The last duty of love. Didn't you see that? He killed her so that she shouldn't go to trial and be hanged. No notion of saving himself first. I wonder if she was like that. Not quite sure. She took all the crimes on herself. She must have known I shouldn't believe her. Nobody was going to believe she stabbed Mrs. Harley or fired the cottage. She hadn't the strength. But she kept me talking there in the garden while her son was coming up behind. She was hoping to use him for something even at the last. Probably to kill me. Not a self-sacrificing affection. I don't think she was a very good mother."

"You surprise me." Lomas made a grimace. "Well, you always said there were some fiendish creatures behind the case. You were right. The real parallel is with the wholesale murderers for profit—Landru and Smith and that tribe."

"I wouldn't say that. No." Reggie blew a smoke ring. "Some resemblance. But more refined. Chief motive of Mrs. Darett not gain but desire to hurt. Better parallel, the bullies of the world. Husband who beats his wife, physically or otherwise. Wife who nags her husband. Children who harry their parents. That's her class. Only she had a brain. Dangerous quality in a fiend."

"What did you think of her story that she was revenging herself for the pain of her disease?"

"I should say she believed it. Probably some truth in it. Not the whole truth. Queer force, pain. Sometimes makes saints, sometimes devils. However. It didn't make her. She hadn't known pain very long. Her disease is swift. She started the Maison Montespan years ago. She made it a business of drugs and vice and scandal before she began to suffer. Her excuse— she'd lost her money and had to make some. No doubt she believed that, too. She would. Weakness of the egoist. Nobody had any rights but her."

"It's all a lie, you know," said Lomas. "She never was poor. She had a life income under her husband's will."

"Had she? Yes. If she'd been a millionaire, she'd have done the same sort of things. She was what she was—which isn't an explanation. Made to be a force of evil—like the plague flea—like the malarial mosquito—like the carcinoma that was torturing her—and to bring forth more power for evil. Producin' her wretch of a son. Queer world. All these cruel things, they play with us, they show us shadows that cheat us, and we can't get to what they really are and kill it till they've made a flood of misery." He gazed at Lomas with dreamy, plaintive eyes. "I wonder," he murmured.

"My dear fellow!" Lomas laughed uncomfortably. "I don't know how the world's made."

"No. Devilish element in it very puzzlin'. Why is the insect, why is the malignant bacillus? Mrs. Darett thought it was very unfair. Well, well. I wonder if she knows now. However. We've done our job this time. About as efficient as the surgeon who saves one case and knows he don't know how to save the next. Not quite true. We are rather more effective than the surgeon. We do frighten our malignants. Extirpate a Darett or so and other Daretts observe that the game isn't always worth the candle. Such is human progress."

He raised himself a bit at a time and stood contemplating Lomas pensively.

"Are we downhearted?" Lomas smiled. "No. My dear Reginald, you've made a brilliant thing of it. There's no occasion for this philosophic melancholy. You want your tea."

"My only aunt!" Reggie moaned. "I do. I do. Come on. I want to have tea with Joan. She's nice. She's awfully nice."

"Quite," Lomas agreed. "Sometimes I think you deserve her."

"No. But study to improve." He linked arms with Lomas, and they went out. "I have been rather potent. But it wasn't really me that did it. And I'm not melancholy. Decisive factor was the fundamental decency of people. That's why I'm not melancholy. Look at 'em. Something ultimately decent in 'em, however far they'd gone wrong. There's the force that broke the Daretts. The Rosnay, an old feline imp of a woman, worked on to hate Osmond—but she wouldn't stand for him bein' accused of what she knew he didn't do. Poor little Molly Marne, debauched with morphia, cravin' mad for it—but she wouldn't buy it by compromisin' Osmond. Even Mrs. Harley, led on to ruin Osmond, whether it was jealousy of him and Alix or ambition for her husband that the Daretts set ablaze—when she found her husband threatened, she wanted to throw up everything and run to Osmond and confess. They gave you your case. Not me, Lomas."

Lomas laughed. "A pretty modesty, Reginald. But I would rather rely on a police force than some elements of virtue in the tools of rogues. Where would Osmond and Alix be now if you hadn't been active?"

"Yes. Fightin' force is required. This war has been very well fought—since we discovered we had to fight. Osmond and Alix"—he laughed—"they seemed rather hard, didn't they? Not gentle spirits. Will you guess how I left 'em this morning? You will not. They were wanting to get out of hospital quick—"

"Naturally. They're on their honeymoon."

"Yes. That wasn't the idea. They want to go to Harley and stand by him."

"Good Gad," said Lomas.

"As you say. People aren't so bad."

They came into the street. The offices of Whitehall were already pouring forth men and women bound for home, a complacent, bustling crowd.

Lomas checked. "Let's dodge this, what?" He looked for a cab.

"Oh, no. No. Walk across the park. Grateful and comfortin'."

"Just as crowded," Lomas complained.

"I know. I like it."

"You?" Lomas smiled. "You dodge every crush you can."

"Social orgies. Yes. Very depressin'. This is different. All sorts and conditions of people. Makes you feel human. I like that."

They turned into the park and made their way through a stream of humanity which flowed in all directions.

"Devilish alike, aren't they?" said Lomas. "Do you feel proud of being human, Reginald? About as individual as a flock of sheep."

"You're so superior. Delusion of the higher intelligence. All brothers one of another. That's good enough for me. Look at 'em, all glad they're alive and lettin' live and goin' home to enjoy it. Same like me. The common people of whom I am the chief." He sighed happily. "In the simple joy of bein' decent. And so man is an advancer and the centuries evolve. Yes, that's the real force of progress, old thing. The common man's common virtues. Not the eminent expert."

THE END